**Praise for New Yor...
Vicki L...**

"Count on Vic...
sharp, sassy, sexy read...
—*New York Times* bestselling author Jayne Ann Krentz

"Devour…Vicki Lewis Thompson's books immediately."
—*Fresh Fiction*

**Praise for *New York Times* bestselling author
Rhonda Nelson**

"Well plotted and wickedly sexy, this one's got it all—
including a completely scrumptious hero. A keeper."
—*RT Book Reviews* on *The Ranger*

"I loved *The Keeper*. Jack and Mariette strike sparks off
one another from their very first meeting and there is
an emotional intensity to the mystery that will
bring a few tears to your eyes."
—*Fresh Fiction*

Praise for Kira Sinclair

"A satisfying balance of light kink, heart a...
—*RT Book Reviews* on *Captivate M...*

"With a dense plot and ample tension on all fr...
book lives up to the imprint's monik...
—*RT Book Reviews* on *Testing the...*

Praise for Andrea Lau...

"Laurence's latest is ...well-written hit
from start ...finish!"
—*RT Bo... Reviews*

"A sweet, sexy story…"
—*Romanc... Reviews Today*

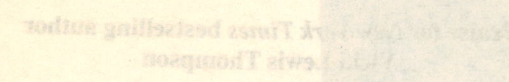

JINGLE SPELLS

VICKI LEWIS THOMPSON
RHONDA NELSON
KIRA SINCLAIR
ANDREA LAURENCE

MILLS & BOON

All rights reserved including the right of reproduction in whole or in part in any form. This edition is published by arrangement with Harlequin Books S.A.

This is a work of fiction. Names, characters, places, locations and incidents are purely fictional and bear no relationship to any real life individuals, living or dead, or to any actual places, business establishments, locations, events or incidents. Any resemblance is entirely coincidental.

This book is sold subject to the condition that it shall not, by way of trade or otherwise, be lent, resold, hired out or otherwise circulated without the prior consent of the publisher in any form of binding or cover other than that in which it is published and without a similar condition including this condition being imposed on the subsequent purchaser.

® and ™ are trademarks owned and used by the trademark owner and/or its licensee. Trademarks marked with ® are registered with the United Kingdom Patent Office and/or the Office for Harmonisation in the Internal Market and in other countries.

Published in Great Britain 2014
by Mills & Boon, an imprint of Harlequin (UK) Limited,
Eton House, 18-24 Paradise Road, Richmond, Surrey, TW9 1SR

Jingle Spells © 2014 Harlequin Books S.A.

The publisher acknowledges the copyright holders of the individual works as follows:

Naughty or Nice? © 2014 by Vicki Lewis Thompson
She's a Mean One © 2014 by Rhonda Nelson
His First Noelle © 2014 by Kira Bazzel
Silver Belle © 2014 by Andrea Laurence

ISBN: 978-0-263-91411-5

89-1114

Harlequin (UK) Limited's policy is to use papers that are natural, renewable and recyclable products and made from wood grown in sustainable forests. The logging and manufacturing processes conform to the legal environmental regulations of the country of origin.

Printed and bound in Spain
by CPI, Barcelona

CONTENTS

NAUGHTY OR NICE? 11
Vicki Lewis Thompson

SHE'S A MEAN ONE 85
Rhonda Nelson

HIS FIRST NOELLE 167
Kira Sinclair

SILVER BELLE 241
Andrea Laurence

NAUGHTY OR NICE?

VICKI LEWIS THOMPSON

Because *NYT* bestselling author **Vicki Lewis Thompson** lives in the Arizona desert, she hardly ever has a white Christmas, but she always celebrates an enchanted one. Elves and flying reindeer make perfect sense to someone who's lucky enough to write love stories all day. Vicki's writing career has gifted her with several awards and a magickal connection to readers around the world. With the life she has, how can she doubt the existence of Santa Claus? Connect with her at www.vickilewisthompson.com, www.facebook.com/vickilewisthompson and www.twitter.com/vickilthompson.161

To the Sisterhood of the Traveling Pens—Andrea Laurence, Rhonda Nelson and Kira Sinclair. We've been to Dublin, London and Paris together, but I'm still partial to Gingerbread, Colorado!

Chapter 1

INTERNAL MEMO: Christmas countdown, minus 20 days
FROM: Cole Evergreen, CEO, Evergreen Industries
TO: All staff
Thanks to centuries of intel monitoring, the North Pole is widely accepted as the home of Santa Claus. That misinformation has allowed the Winter Clan, under the guise of Evergreen Industries, to operate undetected in Gingerbread, Colorado, as we employ our magick in the service of Christmas.

But magick has its limits, and computer technology is more efficient for information storage and retrieval. Because of the sensitive nature of our database, specifically the "Naughty or Nice" list, our security system is constantly being updated.

However, I regret to inform you that despite our best efforts, we've been hacked. While I investigate the source of this breach, be advised that your current usernames and passwords are invalid. When you create new ones, use the strongest possible codes. Failure to maintain secrecy is not an option.

The memo, as Cole had expected it would, brought his three siblings to his office on the fifteenth floor of the Evergreen Industries building within minutes. It was the tallest structure in Gingerbread, and also the deepest. Besides having fifteen floors aboveground to house Evergreen's Christmas ornament business, it had five subterranean floors dedicated to the secret task of Christmas toy production.

Ethan, Cole's next oldest brother, arrived first with a typically optimistic attitude. There was a reason Ethan had been put in charge of Christmas cheer. Ethan was the sort of wizard who, if he found a box of horse manure under the Christmas tree, would look around for the pony.

"It was a fluke." Ethan commandeered one of the two leather swivel chairs in front of Cole's desk. "I'll bet it was a total accident and they won't be back."

"They knew exactly what they were doing. They left me a message." A message that had made his pulse leap when he realized who had been prowling through his database.

"What message?" Belle, the youngest Evergreen, walked in carrying a mug of coffee, because she had to be different. Everyone else in the company drank cocoa.

It must have been an emergency ration she'd brewed herself, because it clearly hadn't come from Cup of Cheer, her favorite coffee shop in Gingerbread. She claimed that the stress of her job as head of human (and elf) resources, especially her work with Santa, Mrs. Claus and the elves, required large quantities of caffeine, specifically double-shot peppermint lattes.

Belle grabbed the other swivel chair and glanced at her brothers, eyebrows raised. "What's the deal?"

"Whoever hacked into the database left a message," Ethan said. "Can you trace where it came from, Cole?"

"Don't have to. I know who it is." A memory of Taryn from ten years before, her slender body naked and willing beneath his, scorched a path through his brain. He ignored it.

"That's great!" Ethan looked even more encouraged. "So you can nip this in the bud, right?"

Oh, yeah. Even after ten years, Cole remembered nipping, and tasting, and... He banished that memory, too, and propped his hips on the edge of the desk. "Sort of. I'm planning to—"

"I see we're all here." Dash, two years younger than Ethan, sauntered into the office, followed closely by Noelle Frost, who'd recently come back to Gingerbread to head up company security while her father recovered from a health scare.

Dash and Noelle were exes, which made her return problematic and their working relationship tricky. Dash was in charge of elf transportation and Christmas magick, including Santa's sleigh and flying reindeer. Noelle had to make sure the sleigh was properly cloaked to avoid detection by military radar and civilian air traffic controllers. Dash and Noelle had no choice but to cooperate on sleigh duty, whether they wanted to or not.

Cole couldn't worry about their issues today. But he noted with some amusement that a love seat positioned against the wall was the only place left to sit. Noelle eventually took it and Dash chose to stand, leaning against the opposite wall, arms crossed.

Ethan turned his chair to face them. "Cole just said he knows who hacked into the database. That means we're halfway to solving the problem."

"Not exactly." Cole looked at each of his siblings in turn. Their generation was in charge now. Their parents, following a time-honored Winter Clan tradition, had turned over the operation to their adult children. The senior Evergreens were currently in Ethiopia helping create clean water sources for impoverished villages.

No one would doubt those four were Evergreens. They'd all inherited the fabled green eyes from their wizard father, and the brothers had their mother's dark, slightly wavy hair and their father's height. Belle was blonde, like their father, and petite, like their mother.

Anyone entering the room would identify Noelle, with the straight, dark hair and the clear blue eyes of the Summer Clan, as the unrelated participant. But despite not being an Evergreen, Noelle was an important component of any strategy meeting. Her experience as a CIA operative would be very helpful.

She sat forward, her gaze intent, her tablet at the ready. "So, who's the hacker, Cole?"

"An old girlfriend from college."

Dash grinned. "Ah. So it's Taryn."

"How do you know that?" Noelle was in full interrogation mode.

"Because Cole only has one old girlfriend from college who counts," Dash said. "That makes this easy, bro. Pay her a visit and find a way to offer her some of Noelle's memory-erasing cocoa. Problem solved."

"Negative on that, Dash." Noelle's tone was brisk, even a little defensive. "Our current formula isn't sophisticated enough to create selective memory loss, which is what's needed here."

Cole turned his attention to her. He hated to put her on the spot, but he needed to know his options, just in case. "How fast can you beef up the formula?"

"It shouldn't take long." She said it quickly, as if forestalling any discussion. "I'll have a more versatile batch soon."

"How soon?"

A hint of panic flashed in her expression, and was quickly replaced by a confident smile. "Not today, but very soon. I'm just saying that if you give Taryn the cocoa we have on hand, she'd forget hacking into Evergreen, but if she's trying to get a rise out of you, she'll hack in again."

"Get a rise out of him?" Dash chuckled. "Under the circumstances, you might want to rephrase that."

Noelle rolled her eyes. "Oh, grow up, Dash."

"Not planning on it, Noelle."

Their banter hit too close to home. Cole ducked his head and studied the wreath pattern in the thick green carpeting as he fought the heat climbing his cheeks. This was hell. His brothers and sister knew too much about Taryn, which was his own damned fault.

He'd left MIT in the middle of his senior year, right before Christmas break. All his fanciful dreams about Taryn had died that Christmas when he'd realized he wasn't ever going back to college. He'd abandoned her without an explanation. But what could he have said? That he was a wizard going home to help his family straighten out the "Naughty or Nice" list and make sure Christmas went off without a hitch?

Lying hadn't been an option. He'd learned early in life that his brain didn't work that way, and everything that came out of his mouth was true, no matter how embarrassing or unwise the statement. Over the years, he'd trained himself to hold his tongue in delicate situations.

But leaving Taryn so abruptly when she'd done nothing to deserve that treatment had gnawed at him. On New Year's Eve at the clan's ancestral lodge on Mistletoe Mountain, he'd mainlined champagne and spilled his guts to his brothers. Belle had found out the whole story eventually, as sisters usually do. He could feel them all waiting with bated breath for his next move.

He prayed it wasn't a stupid one. "I need to find out how she got in." He lifted his head and glanced around the room. Everyone seemed to be with him so far. "It's not surprising that she could do it. I've done some digging, and discovered she freelances as a computer security tester. Multinational corporations hire her to see if she can hack into their systems. If she can hack in, she takes care of whatever weakness she finds."

"And she's a certified genius like Cole," Ethan added helpfully. "I remember you telling us she's very smart."

Cole let out a breath. "Actually, she's smarter than I am."

"Whoa!" Dash pushed away from the wall. "They must

be ice-skating in hell. Did you just admit someone was smarter than you, big brother?"

"Yep." He'd fallen in love with her brain first and her body second. He still remembered that first glance into her eyes, framed with enormous tortoiseshell glasses. The intelligence shining in those hazel depths had stolen his breath. "That's why she was able to hack in. But if I hire her to strengthen the system, then we shouldn't have to—"

"Wait a minute." Noelle glanced up from her tablet, where she'd been typing notes. "Hire her? How can you do that without creating an even bigger security risk?"

"My question, exactly." Belle polished off her coffee and set the mug on Cole's desk.

"I've given it a lot of thought," Cole said. That was the understatement of the year. He'd discovered Taryn's handiwork at midnight and hadn't slept since. "The good people of Gingerbread are convinced we operate a Christmas ornament factory in this building, and that's all Taryn has to know. I'll code her access card so she's restricted to the IT floor."

"What about the categories in the database?" Ethan asked. "Won't she wonder about those?"

Cole shrugged. "I'll say it's appropriate to our Christmas-themed business, which it is. It's not her job to worry about what's in the database, anyway. I'm hiring her to correct a flaw in our system. I'm sure she's worked with other corporations that maintain a high level of secrecy about their products."

"Yes, if you're talking about military applications and technical innovation." Noelle frowned. "But why be secretive about Christmas ornaments? It makes no sense."

"Doesn't matter." Ethan glanced up at Cole. "I see where you're going with this. The fact is we *do* make Christmas ornaments that are prized the world over. If Taryn suspects that's a cover for something else, so what? It's not her job to speculate. If she made a habit of prying into things that don't concern her, she'd be out of business in no time."

Belle swiveled her chair back and forth. "Even so, I don't like it. I can keep the elves off the IT floor while she's here, but what if she runs into Santa? He could show up anywhere, including the lobby, and he's something of a loose cannon these days."

Noelle groaned. "Tell me about it. Did you know he's started jogging?"

"Jogging? Well, *sugarplums*!" Belle let her head fall back against the chair. "No, I didn't know that." Raising her head, she looked at Noelle. "Merry told me he's acting weird and is on some crazy diet, but I hadn't heard about the jogging. I don't know how that's supposed to help matters."

"What in St. Nicholas's name are you talking about?" Cole stared at them. "And why don't I know about it?"

"I hated to bother you unless it was urgent," Belle said. "We all hoped it would blow over."

"It still could." Ethan sounded determinedly cheerful. "Okay, so Kris forgot their twenty-fifth wedding anniversary and Merry's pissed, but I'm sure after all these years together she'll come around."

"Don't count on it," Dash said. "Women are complicated creatures."

"We have to be," Noelle said, "in order to compensate for men being so—"

"That's enough of that." Cole scrubbed a hand over his face. "We need to focus. So Kris and Merry are having marital problems. What's that got to do with the diet and jogging?"

"My best guess?" Noelle glanced up from her tablet. "He's intimidated because Merry's signed up for skiing lessons with Guido, who is, admittedly, a fine specimen of Italian manhood. I think Kris is trying to recapture his inner stud so he can compete with Guido."

"His *inner stud*." Cole sighed. "But he's still on track to drive the sleigh, right?"

"As far as I know," Belle said. "If he trims down, the suit will automatically adjust, but I doubt he'll lose much weight in three weeks."

"Thanks for that hopeful thought, Belle. I want you to send a memo to Kris and Merry about Taryn's visit, though. They should avoid her if possible, but if she happens to meet Kris and notices his resemblance to Santa Claus, he can say he was hired as a mascot."

"A mascot?" Dash laughed. "Oh, he'll just love that description. Not."

"Then he needs to stay out of sight." Lack of sleep was sapping Cole's patience. "I'm leaving in a couple of hours for Seattle. I'm taking the corporate jet. I'll be back tonight with Taryn."

"Too bad you can't apparate and bring her back the magickal way," Dash said. "Speaking as your transportation coordinator, it would be faster and cheaper."

"I realize that, but I'm hoping to engineer this operation without the use of anything magickal, cocoa included. But Noelle, please get that more complex batch up and running, in case I need it for Taryn."

"I'll make it a top priority. But when you say you're bringing her back, I hope you don't intend to take her to the lodge. There's no way I can keep security tight if you do that."

"No, not the lodge. Too much magick going on there, too many witches and wizards randomly casting spells. Even meals are...well, anyway. The lodge is out. I'll get her a reservation at the Nutcracker Inn. Dash, I'll need a car and driver for her. The less she wanders around on her own, the better."

"I suggest you be that driver," Noelle said.

"I'd rather not."

"Then who?" Noelle met his gaze. "This is our busiest time of year. Everyone's schedule is packed."

"That's for sure," Ethan said. "I'm booking talk show appearances as fast as I can to counteract the effect of Lark DeWynter's new bestseller. *The Christmas Lie* was just reviewed in the *New York Times* and it's playing havoc with Christmas cheer. I can fix that. I always do. But I have no spare time."

"Elf personnel issues tend to peak about now," Belle said. "It's the stress of the season, and with Kris potentially going off the rails, I—"

"I know." Cole hadn't considered how this part of his plan would work, but he could see the trap closing on him.

"I have to agree with Noelle," Dash said. "The driver should be someone with maximum clearance, which means it has to be one of us in this room, and we're all working on last-minute Christmas preparations. You, not so much. You're the logical candidate, big brother."

"Okay." Cole rubbed the back of his neck. "I'll take the driving duties."

"In fact, you probably should shadow her while she's here," Dash continued. "You know, keep close track of her and make sure she sticks to the program, literally."

Cole met his brother's gaze. Mischief danced in those green eyes. "She's a professional, Dash."

"If she's so professional, why did she hack into your database?"

That was an excellent question, one he'd been struggling with. "Maybe for old times' sake, to prove she could. I don't know, but I'll find that out, too. I can assure you, excessive monitoring of her activities won't be necessary."

"Maybe not." Dash winked at him. "But I'll bet it would be fun."

Cole glanced away before Dash could read his reaction. Oh, yeah. Monitoring Taryn would be more fun than he'd had in ten years. But indulging in that kind of fun would land both of them in an untenable position. He wouldn't do that to himself, and he certainly wouldn't do that to her.

Chapter 2

Taryn Harper powered down her computer, picked up her glass of red wine, and walked over to the floor-to-ceiling windows to admire the view. Her high-rise luxury apartment faced the Seattle harbor, and this time of year it sparkled with festive lights. Christmas was a big deal for a girl born on December 25, and she always made sure to party hearty.

This year she had more elaborate plans than usual, because she was about to hit the big three-oh. She was the highest wage earner among her family and friends, so she'd decided to foot the bill for a Christmas Day cruise through the San Juan Islands. Yes, it might be a tad chilly on deck, but the music and dancing and food inside would keep people warm and happy.

And she would be happy, too, damn it. So what if she didn't have a yummy guy to invite as her date on the cruise? So what if all her friends had either a serious boyfriend or a husband, and a few had kids, too? She wasn't in some relationship competition with them, and besides, being unattached allowed her to concentrate on a job that she loved, a job that allowed her to live very well.

But a girl about to turn thirty might logically take stock of her situation and look for loose ends to tie up before launching into her third decade. In Taryn's case, that meant settling the Cole Evergreen question.

She'd never found out why he had dumped her ten years before, and a lack of resolution made forgetting him near impossible. Well, that, and the memory or how perfect they'd been for each other, mentally and sexually. She needed to talk to the guy, and she knew exactly how to get his attention.

Last night she'd hacked into the Evergreen Industries database and left a clear message—*You're vulnerable. Call me. I can fix it.* If he was still the Cole she'd known and loved, she figured he would respond to that. But he hadn't called, and waiting was no fun.

Maybe he hadn't found it yet. Maybe he'd found it and was discussing it with his staff. Maybe he was discussing it with whatever woman was currently in his life. He wasn't married. She'd researched that.

But she was prepared to discover that he was involved with someone. At twenty-two he'd been so beautiful—brilliant green eyes, luxurious dark hair and an amazingly taut body for someone who didn't put much effort into keeping in shape. And he could make love like no one she'd found since. Add to that his intelligence and his adorable tendency to blurt out the truth, no matter what, and he'd been all she'd ever wanted in a man.

There was the rub. She'd compared every guy who'd come along after to Cole. No one else had stood a chance. And that was why she lived alone in this elegant apartment overlooking the harbor, and why she would be dateless for her birthday party.

Draining her glass, she turned away from the view.

Her intercom buzzed before she'd made it to the kitchen to start dinner. Setting down her wineglass, she walked to the front door and pressed the button connected to the lobby's video camera. She wasn't expecting anyone. And then she spotted the man standing in the lobby talking to Tom, the security guard, and nearly had a heart attack. Never in her wildest dreams had she thought Cole would appear in person, and unannounced, at that. She pushed the intercom button. "Hi, Tom."

"Hello, Miss Harper. You have a visitor. Shall I send him up?"

She gulped. "Yes." The elevator was fast. He'd be here in no time. Running into the bathroom, she finger-combed her short curls, but she couldn't change clothes or put on makeup, or—damn it! Her doorbell was already chiming.

Heart pounding, she made herself walk back to the front door, but she was shaking. She fumbled with the lock and finally managed to open it, but her head buzzed from a massive adrenaline rush. "Cole?"

Those emerald green eyes hadn't lost a fraction of their intensity. His gaze swept over her in typical Cole fashion, as if he were taking inventory. "Hello, Taryn. May I come in?"

"Sure." Doing her best to breathe normally, she stepped back from the door.

He strode through it confidently. His long wool coat, black as his hair, carried with it the cool tang of December in Seattle. There was another scent, too. Apparently he still wore his distinctive peppermint aftershave.

In college he'd shaved twice a day, especially if they were spending the night together. Judging from the smoothness of his square jaw, he'd used a razor sometime in the past hour. One whiff of his freshly applied aftershave rocketed her back to long winter nights spent in his bed.

Dear God, her physical reaction to him hadn't changed. He showed up and instantly her body became welcoming, yielding and decidedly moist. How inconvenient, especially because he didn't look particularly happy to see her. No smile, no warmth, only a strong sense of purpose, which she recognized from the old days.

He'd identified a problem and he'd come up with a solution. Once Cole Evergreen saw his way through an issue, he proceeded with single-minded intent. But she couldn't figure out why he had come *here* instead of contacting her by phone or even by email. That didn't seem particularly efficient.

He pulled off his black leather gloves and turned to her. "It's about the database."

"I figured." She noticed he wasn't wearing a wedding ring, confirming her intel about him not being married. The coat underscored the drama that had always lurked beneath the surface of this complicated, beautiful man. As he unbuttoned it, her quick survey confirmed that he hadn't let himself get soft in the middle. "Can I take your coat?" she asked.

"I'm not here to chat, Taryn. Obviously I need your services. Knowing your talent, the job shouldn't take long. Two or three days, at most. Can you leave tonight?"

She stared at him. "I beg your pardon?"

"I want to hire you, exactly as you suggested. You're the only person who's ever hacked into my database, so I want you to fix whatever weaknesses are there. The situation is critical. I'd like you to start tomorrow. Can you do that?"

"No, I can't do that!" She'd expected a response, a conversation, maybe even a request that she correct the problem, but not with this kind of urgency. "Look, Cole, I—" She'd thought bringing up the past would be relatively easy, and maybe it would have been on the phone. But face-to-face, her courage failed her. "Just because I did it, don't get paranoid and think you have a huge security problem. You don't. I was able to get in because I know your design habits, which made it easier for me."

"What prevents you from coming with me tonight?"

"That's none of your business."

"You hacked into my database. That makes it my business."

She wished that his forceful pursuit of a goal didn't turn her on so much. But she remembered he'd been that way in bed, too. Her pleasure had been his goal at all times, and wow, had he delivered on that promise.

He sighed and glanced away. "I'm sorry. I'm going about this all wrong."

Oh. Her heart gave a familiar lurch, as it used to do anytime he revealed the vulnerability beneath his determined exterior. With a flash of insight, she understood the motivation behind his steamrolling behavior. She'd embarrassed him by hacking into a system he'd designed.

Chances were he hadn't kept the situation to himself, either. "Who knows I hacked in?" she asked gently. "Besides you, I mean."

His attention returned to her, his expression resigned. "Everyone at the administration level of the business, which includes both my brothers, my sister and our new head of security. I had to tell them."

No, he didn't *have* to tell them, but she should have guessed that he would. His unflinching honesty and sense of responsibility would have forced him to admit that his database wasn't a hundred percent secure, no matter how painful that admission had been for him to make.

She hadn't thought of that possibility. She'd somehow imagined this would be a little game between the two of them, but instead his whole family was now involved. That was unfortunate.

"I regret pulling such a stupid stunt, then," she said. "I have no defense, really. I was curious about what you were up to, so I poked around until I found your company, and then I couldn't resist trying to crack your code."

For the first time, a spark of humor lit his eyes. "Well, that's typical."

"I know. And I have to say, it was fun figuring out how to unlock the database."

The corner of his mouth curved in something that resembled a smile. "You always did relish the idea of outsmarting me."

"I did. It gave me a challenge." She'd missed their intellectual sparring more than their sex, and that was saying something. "But I'm sorry you're on the hook because of my prank."

"Then get me off the hook, Taryn. Come to Colorado and strengthen my security so even you can't get in."

It was a gold-plated opportunity to have her personal

question answered. But if she was still attracted to him, and he was over her, spending a few days working together could be hard on her ego.

He cleared his throat. "You do realize I'll compensate you for your time, right?"

"Well, yeah. You said in the beginning you wanted to hire me, so that usually involves money." She wished she could figure out what was going on in that excellent brain of his. "Unless you had some other type of compensation in mind?"

Heat flared in his eyes for just a moment. "No."

Interesting. That bit of heat had indicated he wasn't totally immune to her. But he might not be available. "Forgive me if that was inappropriate. You probably have a steady girlfriend. Maybe even a fiancée." She could at least satisfy her curiosity on that score.

"I don't."

"Really?"

"Really."

She waited to see if he'd ask about her love life. He did not. So if she'd cherished a tiny hope that he had something besides business on his mind, she should kill that hope right now. Once she'd thought he was in love with her, but then he'd abandoned her without a word. She'd been hurt and confused, but she hadn't been able to convince herself that his feelings had been bogus.

Perhaps she should finally face the possibility that he'd grown tired of her and hadn't wanted to say so. Honest as he was, he would have blurted the truth if she'd asked him. She wanted to ask now, but she hesitated. Sad to say, he still had the power to hurt her.

He focused his green eyes with laser precision. "Are you in the middle of a project you can't leave for a few days? Is that the stumbling block?"

"As it happens, no. I only take small local jobs in December, so I have time to celebrate Christmas and my birthday." It was the truth, but she didn't mind that it also served as a little dig. Ten years ago she'd invited him home for Christmas and her birthday, and he'd accepted. Then he'd bailed without an explanation.

"Right. Your birthday." His expression once again became difficult to decipher. "I promise you'll be back here long before then. I remember how much you looked forward to Christmas."

"I do."

He glanced at her tree. "But if it's Christmas cheer you're after, you'll find plenty of it in Gingerbread. It's Christmas year-round there, but winter snow adds a lot to the ambiance."

"I saw the pictures online when I was looking up Evergreen Industries. Cute little town." The landscape had reminded her of the long walks in the snow at MIT when she and Cole had been lovers. They'd often debated the merits of some new computer technology, and whenever they'd disagreed on some obscure point, the argument usually had turned into a snowball fight, which led to kissing, which led to racing back to his apartment to have sex.

"I've booked you a room at the Nutcracker Inn."

His comment detoured her trip down memory lane. "You've already booked me a room?"

"It seemed like a good idea. They're extra busy in December. The place is loaded with Old World charm. All the rooms have feather beds, and yours is one of the few with a woodburning fireplace."

"I admit that's tempting."

"There's more. The proprietor, Mrs. Gustafson, bakes apple strudel every morning. She brings a tray to your door with warm strudel, fresh-squeezed orange juice and hot coffee."

"Sounds pretty cozy." Too bad when she pictured staying at the Nutcracker Inn, she automatically put Cole in the picture, too. He wouldn't be there, and she needed to remember that.

"It is cozy. Or so I'm told by anyone who's stayed there."

"You mentioned hot coffee as if that's a selling point. Don't tell me you're a coffee drinker at last."

"Nope."

"Wuss." She used to tease him about that all the time.

He smiled. "Addict." His gaze held hers, and his voice softened. "Whatever happened to those big glasses you used to wear?"

"Got contacts." As she looked into his eyes, she remembered another very important thing. Before they'd been lovers, they'd been good friends. Sex had been an enhancement of that friendship, at least in her mind. But sex had raised the stakes, too. At the time he'd left, they'd been so deeply enmeshed that they couldn't have dialed back the relationship to a friendship level.

After ten years, though, they ought to be able to do that. She'd like to stay in touch. Not many people communicated on the intellectual level that she and Cole had.

"Okay," she said. "I'll take the job."

His shoulders sagged with relief. "Thank you. That means a lot to me."

"I'm doing it as a friend, though. I'll be insulted if you try to pay me."

"That's not right. You should be paid your going rate. In fact, because I'm hauling you away during the holidays, you should get more than your going rate."

She folded her arms. "Then you're willing to insult me?"

"No! But let me pay you. Please."

"Nope. Either I do it because I'm your friend or I don't do it at all."

He opened his mouth as if to offer another objection. Then he closed it again. "All right. I'll take you any way I can get you."

Her traitorous pulse leaped at that comment, damn it.

She'd have to ride herd on her emotions and not allow them to get the best of her. Agreeing to this might have been a mistake, after all.

Chapter 3

Cole had what he'd come for, and now he wondered how in hell he'd survive the next few days in close contact with Taryn without doing something stupid. Like kissing her. She'd been dynamite at twenty. At almost thirty, her sexuality had gone nuclear. The men in Seattle must have been blind. They should have been lined up outside her door.

She was still tall, still slender, but her curves had a lushness that hadn't been there before. How he longed to pull her into his arms and explore those curves. She moved with more grace and assurance than she had when they'd been in college. He knew, just *knew* that she'd be an even better lover now, and she'd been terrific back then.

They had to get out of her apartment and on that plane, where they'd be properly chaperoned. He glanced around her living space. Her computer was turned off and he didn't smell dinner cooking. "How soon can you be ready to leave?"

"What time is the flight?"

"Whenever I tell them."

She blinked. "Oh. You came in your own plane. I didn't realize that. Is it tiny?"

"It's the Evergreen corporate jet, which is a decent size."

"Evergreen has a corporate jet? The Christmas ornament business must be booming."

"We do okay. Can you be packed in about fifteen minutes?"

"Uh, I guess so. But aren't you hungry? It's dinnertime, and I could make us something."

That wasn't going to happen. Even if he didn't have the jet waiting at SeaTac, he wouldn't dare sit through an intimate dinner in this apartment. He'd noticed the wineglass she'd left on an end table. Wine, a little candlelight, the glow from the Christmas tree, and he'd be done for. They'd be stretched out on her pricey rug in no time.

The thought of that scene had a predictable effect. He walked toward the window and pretended to take in the view so she wouldn't notice the state of his crotch. He had a spell for controlling an inconvenient arousal, but it involved muttering an incantation, which would make him sound crazy as a loon.

He was feeling sort of crazy, but he didn't want her to know that. "The galley's stocked and we can eat on the way," he said. "It's getting late. By the time we fly into Denver and make the drive to Gingerbread, it'll be after midnight. We should get going."

"I suppose you're right." She turned and started down a hallway. "Give me ten minutes to throw some things into a suitcase," she said over her shoulder.

He watched her walk away and swallowed a moan of frustration. A pair of old jeans and a faded sweatshirt shouldn't be the sexiest outfit in the world, but on Taryn, it was. Her cap of milk-chocolate curls made her look sassy and down-to-earth.

You could mess around with a woman like Taryn, because she wasn't coifed and tailored. He'd always loved that about her. She could roll in the snow, run home to have sex, and never give a thought to how she looked. In those days, all he'd had to worry about had been her precious glasses.

Once she'd left the room, he called the car service he'd employed and told them to be waiting in front of the apartment building in fifteen minutes. Then he prowled around the living room and recorded impressions of who Taryn was, now. The fireplace mantle was crowded with framed pictures. These would be the family and friends he'd been destined to meet during that Christmas vacation when he'd abandoned her.

Knowing she was surrounded by loving people cheered him. Knowing she hadn't found the right guy gave him an unholy amount of satisfaction. That was wrong of him, and he knew it. He should want her to find Mr. Wonderful, settle down with him and be blissfully happy.

For years he'd assumed that had happened, but after finding her cheeky message on his database, he'd investigated to the full extent of the internet's capabilities. The evidence had been conclusive. Taryn didn't have a man in her life.

Although she didn't realize it, she currently had a wizard in her life. And if that wizard really cared for her, he'd keep his hands to himself and deliver her back to this apartment without ever once giving in to the urges that plagued him whenever they were together. Even if she wanted him to. And he could tell that she did.

After replacing each picture frame exactly as he'd found it, he wandered over to her Christmas tree. And there, nestled in the branches, was an Evergreen Industries ornament. He'd forgotten that he'd given her one right after Thanksgiving ten years ago, when they'd reunited after the long weekend.

He'd chosen it with care out of the hundreds manufactured that year. The round ball was green, but through a trick of the light and a sprinkling of wizard magick, it seemed to glow from within, as if it held sunlight inside. That theme was echoed in a gold filigree border circling the sphere with repeating sun symbols.

Cole loved the green ornaments most of all, because they symbolized the Evergreen family name, which in turn harkened back to the trees that stayed green all winter. The sun represented light, both physical and intellectual. He thought of Taryn as the embodiment of light, and he'd told her so when he'd presented her with the ornament.

"Yes, I still have it."

He turned to find her standing in the living room wearing a tan parka with the hood thrown back, a khaki messenger bag over her shoulder. A small black suitcase sat upright beside her.

"I wouldn't have blamed you if you'd gotten rid of it," he said. He didn't want to talk about their breakup, but he wasn't sure how to avoid talking about it.

"I considered giving the ornament away, but quite honestly, it's the prettiest one I have, and I couldn't part with it. I don't know how your company manages to make something glow like that when there's no solar chip involved. Is the entire covering solar? Is that how it works?"

"Can't tell you. Company secret."

She cocked her head. "Do other ornament companies try to steal those secrets? I wouldn't expect that, because it's so contrary to the spirit of Christmas, but I suppose anything's possible."

"I doubt they could steal that particular secret." The incantation involved was known only to the Winter Clan, and no other wizard would be able to make it work right. In the wizard world, this incantation had the equivalent of a failsafe component attached to it.

"But maybe they'd try, and that's why you're so intent on shoring up your security system."

"Something like that. Ready?"

She nodded. "Just need to put out the cat."

"The *cat*?"

"Gotcha! There's no cat, and even if there were, I couldn't very well put out a cat on the eighteenth floor, now could I?"

"Guess not." He'd forgotten how much she enjoyed teasing him. It was easy to do, because he didn't expect anyone to say things that weren't true.

"I'd love to have a cat, preferably a black one, but that wouldn't be fair. I travel too much."

"I didn't know you liked cats." Cole thought of the lodge

on Mistletoe Mountain, which was chockablock with cats, especially black ones.

"In our life at MIT, it didn't come up. Both of us lived in places that didn't allow pets."

"Guess so." He was impressed with how she referred to that time so casually, as if the memories didn't affect her at all. Maybe they didn't. He might be the only one who had vivid color images of those days rolling through his brain. And right now that video was playing in a continuous loop.

He gestured to the tree. "What about the lights?"

"They're on a timer. The apartment is as maintenance-free as I can make it. I'm gone so much." She reached for the handle of her rolling bag.

He started toward her. "Let me get that."

"Why? It's my suitcase." She released the handle, though, as if sensing he wouldn't take no for an answer.

"But you're my guest." He came up beside her and grasped the handle.

"Your guest?" Her eyebrows lifted. "I thought I was your independent contractor."

"You would have been if you'd allowed me to pay you." Instead of kissing her, which was what he wanted to do, he rolled the suitcase across the thick carpeting to the door. "But now that you've insisted on doing the job for free, that makes you my guest."

She followed him to the door. "I think you're bossier than you used to be, Cole."

"No, I'm not. I've always been this bossy." Or so he'd been told by his siblings.

"Maybe you're right." Once they were out the door, she locked up and dropped the keys in her messenger bag. "I might not have noticed it because we spent so much time in bed, and I kind of like a man to be bossy in bed."

His sharp intake of breath was pure reflex. He couldn't have stopped himself from doing it if someone had put a gun to his head.

"Whoops. Did I say that out loud?"

He turned to her, his heart racing. "Yes, ma'am, you did." He couldn't tell from her expression if she'd truly slipped up or if the comment had been deliberate, like her line about the cat. She seemed unapologetic as she met his gaze, so he suspected the latter.

She quickly confirmed his suspicions. "I'm trying to figure you out, Cole, and I'm having a very tough time doing it. Sometimes, when you look at me, it's like the old days, as if you're ready to gobble me up. But then you turn all logical and businesslike, and claim that the only thing you care about is shoring up the database. Which is the real you?"

He gave the only answer he could come up with. "Both."

"What the heck does that mean?"

"It's complicated."

"Apparently. And you seem really stressed about it."

"That's because I am." How he hated to admit that.

She took a deep breath. "Okay. Can you explain what the issues are? Because I didn't get that explanation ten years ago, and I'd appreciate hearing it now, before we hop on that plane."

He wondered how he'd ever expected to get involved with her on a business level and keep it from morphing into something more personal. Of course it would. They'd been together less than an hour and it already had.

Facing her, he realized he'd missed a blindingly obvious fact. "That's why you hacked in, isn't it? To get that explanation."

"Yes, it is. So if you'll tell me, then I'll go fix your computer system. All will be well."

If only it were that easy. "Do you trust me?"

"In some things, yes. In other things, no."

"Fair enough. I deserve that. Let me put it this way. Do you trust me to want the best for you?"

Her answer was a long time coming, but at last she nodded. "Of course you want the best for me. You're a nice guy.

But the problem with that is you can't always know what's best for me. I'm a far better judge of that than you are."

"I'm sure that's true in general. But in this particular situation I'm confident I know what's best. You and I aren't meant to be together." Even though he knew that with a white-hot certainty, saying it cut like a knife.

She didn't seem to like hearing it, either. "Why not?"

"I can't tell you that. You have to trust me to know what I'm talking about."

"Okay, look, before we walk down the hallway and get on the elevator, I need to know at least this much. Are you involved in criminal activity?"

That made him smile.

"It's not funny! I care about you, but I'm not willing to be an accomplice!"

"You care about me?" The words warmed him more than he could say.

"Of course I do." Her voice softened. "I'll never forget our time together. Which is why, now that I'm about to turn thirty, I wanted closure on that relationship. I hacked in to get your attention and an explanation. You probably wish I hadn't."

"I'm not sorry you hacked in." That popped out before he'd known he was going to say it, but once he had, he knew it to be true. This episode promised to be a challenge, but having a chance to see her again and talk with her was worth any inconvenience. He never tired of looking into her hazel eyes and imagining the wheels turning in that amazing brain.

"I'm glad you're not sorry. Neither am I." Without warning, she stepped forward and pressed her lips to his.

He'd been hanging tough until that moment, but as her velvet mouth made that achingly familiar connection, he came unglued. Her suitcase toppled to the floor when he let go of the handle, but the resulting clatter barely registered because he had Taryn in his arms again. A herd of reindeer could have stampeded through the hallway and he wouldn't have noticed.

With a groan, he pulled her close, enveloping the whole package, including her bulky parka and her messenger bag. She could have been wearing a space suit for all he cared, as long as he had access to her sweet lips. This kiss, this Taryn kiss, had been ten years in the making, and he was desperate for it.

As he reveled in the remembered pleasures of her mouth, his world clicked into focus for the first time in ages. He hadn't realized how blurred his view had been, but holding her made one thing crystal clear. She was the only woman he'd ever loved.

He was still cruising in the land of infinite joy when she grasped the back of his head in both hands.

Holding on tight, she drew back, depriving him of that amazing connection. "Open your eyes."

He obeyed. In his current state of mind, he would have jumped from the eighteenth floor if she'd commanded him to.

"Tell me the truth, Cole. Are you a crook?"

He had to clear his throat before he could talk. "No."

"Then what's the problem?"

With his arms around her and his mouth inches from hers, he couldn't think straight. She was the only person he'd ever known who could short-circuit his brain. "I can't tell you."

She tightened her grip on his scalp. "Yes, you *can*. You just *won't*. I've thought of every possibility. I know you're not gay, not by the way you kiss me. And you said there's no other woman in your life. Are you dying?"

"No. Well, technically we're all dying, but—"

"Don't give me some existential bull. Are you terminally ill?"

"No. Taryn, don't quiz me, okay? It's getting us nowhere."

"It could get me somewhere, because if I guess the right thing, you won't be able to lie about it. I know that about you."

"You won't guess it."

"That's what you think." The light of battle gleamed in her eyes. "I've solved tougher puzzles than this, buster."

"Then I'm asking you, for both our sakes, to stop trying. Please let it go."

"But that means I have to let *you* go."

"And vice versa."

"And that's what you want?"

"No." His brain continued to fizz with sexual frustration. "Well, yes, for your sake."

"Damn, you're stubborn."

"Says the pot to the kettle."

She looked into his eyes for a moment longer. Then she sighed. "Okay, then, let's head to Colorado and get this over with." She loosened her grip on his head and backed out of his arms.

"Right." He leaned down and picked up the handle of her suitcase. He couldn't remember feeling more lost and alone.

They walked in silence to the elevator. As the doors opened and she stepped inside, she glanced at him. "Nice kiss, by the way."

"Thanks." He was afraid his longing was being reflected in his eyes, but he couldn't summon a poker face right now. "You, too."

She leaned against the brass railing as the elevator started its descent. "So let me get this straight. You want me, and I want you, but we can never be together for reasons you can't tell me, and it's all for my own good. Is that what you're saying?"

"Yes." He stayed on the opposite side of the elevator.

"But, because I hacked into your database, you need me to correct the weaknesses in your system, which means we'll be in the same general area for a few days."

"True. In fact, I'll be the one driving you back and forth from the inn to the office."

"Hmm." Speculation shone in her hazel eyes.

He'd always enjoyed watching her think about technical issues, but now she was thinking about *him,* and he wasn't entirely comfortable with that. "I'm the logical one to do it."

"Makes sense. You hired me, and we already know each other. I also assume you want to know about what I find, so we'll have to work together during the day."

"Some."

"Won't that be...frustrating?"

He couldn't pretend to misunderstand. "Probably."

"Won't you want to kiss me again?"

"Yes."

"And take me to bed?"

He swallowed. "Yes, but—"

"Then why not enjoy each other before we go our separate ways?"

His heart hammered. Earlier today he'd been very clear in his mind about why that was a bad idea. But he wasn't the one who'd suggested it, which made all the difference. "You'd be okay with that?"

She smiled. "I'll take you any way I can get you."

Chapter 4

Taryn loved having the last word, and handing Cole's earlier comment back to him had been a triumphant moment. The elevator opened immediately after she delivered that line, which worked out well, because they were no longer alone, and wouldn't be for some time. He'd have hours to contemplate her suggestion with absolutely no way of acting on it.

At the end of that time, he should be a testosterone-driven, heat-seeking missile. That was the Cole Evergreen she wanted in her feather bed at the Nutcracker Inn tonight. And tonight would be only the beginning of her two-pronged attack.

Now that she knew he wanted her, she wasn't about to let him get away, at least not easily. He might refuse to tell her what the barriers were between them, but she was heading into his territory, and the answer was there. She just knew it.

By day, she'd take every opportunity to snoop around. By night, she'd drive Cole insane in bed. If she hadn't made him hers by the time she left Colorado, then maybe it was an impossible task. But she wasn't giving up without a fight.

The Evergreen corporate jet proved to be a luxurious way to travel. Increasingly, she had trouble believing that Christmas ornaments, beautiful though they might be, were financing this kind of perk. If nothing illegal was going on, and she trusted Cole's answer on that, then what explained the company's success?

If she found the answer to that, she might discover the big secret that Cole wouldn't reveal—the one that kept them from living happily ever after. She hoped it wasn't a dangerous secret, the kind that a person had to be killed for once they knew it. That was highly unlikely. Cole would never put her in danger. She knew that as surely as she knew he loved her.

She'd figured that out two seconds into their kiss. As a college student she might have confused love with lust. She wouldn't make that mistake now. He lusted after her, all right, but the passion of his kiss included a large measure of tenderness. Then she'd made him look at her, just to be absolutely sure.

He was in love and always had been. Ditto for her. If she'd ever doubted it, that doubt was gone. For some reason, he hadn't been able to figure out a way around the issue that divided them, whatever it was. She brought a fresh perspective, and—if she allowed herself to be honest—a tiny bit more analytical ability than Cole had.

Once she understood what she was dealing with, she'd find a way to make everything work out. They deserved each other, and they'd already missed out on ten years of happiness because she hadn't been proactive. She didn't intend to let them miss out on any more.

Throughout the first half of the flight, Cole kept glancing at her, as if still wrestling with the ethics of her suggestion. They couldn't talk about it, of course, because the flight attendant never strayed far. She served the meal and refilled their wine glasses. Then she cleared the main course and brought out dessert.

Taryn made small talk about changes in the tech industry since they'd been in school together. Cole participated in the discussion, but his mind wasn't on it. She could always tell those things. He was thinking about whether he was capable of a fling.

Poor man. He wasn't the kind who had sex with a woman for the hell of it. Even in college, they hadn't taken that step until they'd established a solid friendship. The thought of a short-lived affair would stick in his craw.

She didn't intend for it to be the least bit short. If all went according to plan, this affair would last for the rest of their lives. But she couldn't tell him that and tip her hand. She had to mislead him, which was heartbreakingly easy to do.

After she'd accomplished her goal, she would never lie to him again. She'd been touched by his willingness tonight to believe what she told him, even when it had been something as illogical as putting out the cat eighteen stories up. His trusting nature would serve her well in the days ahead, but in the long run, a man like Cole should never be lied to. That was taking unfair advantage of an endearing trait.

Toward the end of the meal, he smothered a yawn.

She glanced over at him. "You're tired, aren't you?"

"A little."

"Then take a nap."

His dark eyebrows rose. "Now who's the bossy one?"

"Just don't think you have to entertain me. If you're sleepy, recline your seat and rest up." She fought the urge not to smile. Little did he know she had ulterior motives for wanting him well-rested when they arrived in Gingerbread.

"Nah, I'm fine."

"If you say so. But I'm going to read for a while." She dug in her messenger bag and pulled out her tablet. Moments later, she glanced up from the screen. He was out. For all she knew, he'd been up all night worrying about her invasion of his database.

She couldn't help feeling remorseful about what she'd put him through, but apparently it had been for a worthy cause. He'd been pining for her as much as she'd been pining for him. She returned to the screen, but it wasn't nearly as interesting as the man beside her. Turning off the tablet, she leaned her head against her seatback and watched him sleep.

She used to do that all the time in college. Maybe his habits had changed, but at that time he'd required eight to ten hours a night, while she could get by on five. When she'd wake up in his bed and he'd still be dead to the world, she'd lie there and study his features—the high cheekbones, the elegant nose, the square jaw.

Sometimes she'd sketch that face. Tucking her tablet back in her bag, she took out the small sketchbook she carried with her, along with her favorite pencil. Although she'd never taken an art class and had no desire to study the subject, she sketched because it relaxed her.

After Cole had left MIT so abruptly, she'd ripped up every sketch she'd made of him. Then she'd regretted destroying them, because they'd captured him in a way photographs never had. Now she could create some more.

She became so lost in her work that she was surprised when the pilot announced they were landing. The flight attendant sat down and buckled up, which put her out of earshot.

Cole blinked and lifted his head. Then he glanced at the sketchbook in her lap. His gaze met hers. "You're still drawing?"

"Yep."

"You used to have a whole bunch like that. Well, I looked younger in them. In this version I notice a few extra lines here and there."

"Gives you character."

"Sure, it does." He chuckled. "Whatever happened to the other ones?"

"I tore them up."

He flinched. "Don't blame you." He lowered his voice. "That was a bonehead way to leave, but I had no choice."

"So I gather."

Regret darkened his green eyes. "That idea you had? It won't work."

She wasn't about to let him wiggle out of her trap. "I was twenty when I ripped up those sketches. I'm not that same girl. I've toughened up."

He smiled. "Maybe I haven't."

"Well, I can't speak for you. But personally, I think it would be a crime to waste the opportunity." She tapped the eraser end of her pencil against her lower lip, hoping to draw his attention there.

It worked. He watched as she caressed her lip with the eraser. "I'm worried..." He stopped to clear his throat. "I'm worried about fallout."

"Are you?" She nibbled on the eraser. "We never had that problem before. Everything stayed where it was supposed to."

He launched into such a violent coughing fit that the flight attendant called back to ask if he needed water. "I'm fine," he said in a strangled voice. "No worries."

"Here." Taryn took out the complimentary bottle of water she'd been offered during the limo ride to the airport and thrust it into his hand. "Drink."

He nodded and gulped some water. Then he sank back against his seat. "You need to warn me before you say something like that."

"That would take all the fun out of it."

He handed her the bottle with a grin. "Honest to God, Taryn. There's no one quite like you."

"I am somewhat of a special snowflake."

His eyes probed hers. "Can you promise me you won't melt?"

"Absolutely."

His voice dropped even lower. "Because you tempt me more than I can say."

"Back atcha. Oh, and I've been told that someone booked me into a room with a feather bed and a woodburning fireplace."

"Is that right?" His tone was casual but his expression was not. "How thoughtful."

"So what happens after we land?"

"I left my car at the airport, so I'll drive us to Gingerbread and...drop you off at the inn."

She didn't think it would go that way. "Will I need to check in?"

"Not tonight. I didn't want to disturb Mrs. Gustafson at this late hour, so I asked her for the front door key and your room key. You'll sign the register in the morning. You're on the second floor. You can go straight to bed."

She lowered her lashes. "That sounds lovely."

"Doesn't it, though?"

"I'll need some help with my bag."

"I bet you will. I suppose you'd like me to bring it up for you?"

She lifted her lashes. "Oh, yes, please. All the way up."

"Good Lord." He sucked in a breath. "What have I gotten myself into?"

"Nothing, yet. But I'm hoping before too long, you'll remedy that."

"*Taryn.*"

"If you keep feeding me these great lines, how can I resist?"

"The bigger question is, how can *I* resist?"

"You can't, and you know it." She smiled at him. "Surrender to the inevitable, Cole Evergreen."

Cole was going to do exactly that. He'd been a sucker for her smart mouth back at MIT, and nothing had changed. She still delighted in taunting him, and he wanted her more with every saucy word that passed her sweet lips. Luckily he found a twenty-four-hour drugstore on the way back to Gingerbread.

Because he had to concentrate on his driving instead of thinking about sex, especially on snowy roads, he resorted to a trick he and Taryn had come up with at MIT. Switching on the car radio, he found a station that played eighties tunes—the same music they'd memorized as kids. Then the two of them belted out the lyrics along with Duran Duran, a-ha and The Police all the way to Gingerbread.

Somewhere on that journey, as they laughed and sang together, he became twenty-two again, complete with reckless thoughts and powerful sex drive. When he'd first heedlessly plunged into a relationship with Taryn, she was the hottest, smartest female he'd ever met.

She was everything he'd wanted, with one tiny exception. She wasn't a witch, let alone a witch from the Winter Clan. He'd glossed over that detail, certain that he'd find a way around her inconvenient status as a non-magickal being. But then, he'd been called away on a family emergency and he'd never gotten the chance to return to college and figure out a way to address the problem.

Someday he might bitterly regret falling in with her plan. But that was someday, and this was now. A now filled with the kind of heart-pounding excitement he hadn't felt in a very long time.

After parking the sleek black sedan in a lot adjacent to the inn, he hauled her suitcase out of the trunk and they hurried, still laughing from their sing-along, to the inn's front porch.

She stood next to him, shivering a little, as he located the keys in his coat pocket. "I feel like a kid out after curfew."

"It's the music. We stepped in a time warp." He opened the front door and gestured for her to go inside.

"Exactly." She spoke in hushed tones. "It's just like that first time we spent the night together. Remember that?"

"I'll never forget it." He breathed in the scent of lemon oil and apple strudel. The main floor was dark except for a small light on the antique desk by the front door. Wall sconces glowed at intervals along the stairway leading to the second floor.

"I was so nervous." Taryn walked on tiptoe to the bottom of the steps. "I was afraid you'd think I was too skinny."

He followed her up the stairs, careful not to let the suitcase bump against the railing. "I was afraid I'd come too fast."

"Which you did." She giggled softly.

"Yeah, but I made up for it later."

"Yes, that's true."

"Saved my rep." That first time, he'd been so incredibly turned on by her he'd lasted about thirty seconds. But at twenty-two, his recovery time had been phenomenal. During the next go-round, he'd given her two orgasms.

"That was my first orgasm with a guy."

"It was? Wish you'd told me. We could have celebrated."

"I was too shy to admit it. I figured you'd think I was a dork. I wanted you to think of me as cool and sophisticated."

"I did."

"Really?"

"You were the coolest girl I'd ever met. You understood string theory." He paused. "Your room's at the end of the hall, on the right."

She headed down the hallway, her footsteps muffled on the patterned carpet runner. "I didn't want to be cool because I was smart. I wanted to be cool because I was sexy."

"You were sexy, too."

"You're just saying that."

"Nope." He followed her down the narrow hallway. Soon. Very soon. "Smart is sexy, at least to me, it is. Besides, you had a killer body."

"*Had?*"

"*Have*." He thought it was cute she was worried about that, especially when she had nothing to worry about. "Still. Even more so."

"Yeah, right. You're supposed to say stuff like that when you're about to see me naked for the first time in years. I'm nervous just thinking about it."

"You think you're nervous? I figure I'm destined to repeat that first night."

She reached the end of the hallway and turned back to

face him. "That's fine with me." She smiled as she looked him up and down. "As long as you repeat every bit of that first night."

His cock jerked in response to that seductive smile, and his heart hammered at the prospect of being inside that room alone with Taryn and a big feather bed. "I will, but I'm not twenty-two anymore. The second time might not happen as fast."

"I'm in no rush." She held his gaze. "We have all night."

Lust slammed into him with such force he stood there trembling.

"Do you have the key?"

"Yeah." He dug into his coat pocket and handed it to her. "You'd better open it."

Her eyes widened. "Are you shaking?"

"Yes." He clenched his jaw against the primitive urges rolling through him. "And if you don't open the door and go inside *immediately*, I'm going to take you right here in the hallway. Better move it, Harper, before we give Mrs. Gustafson the scare of her life."

Chapter 5

And *that*, Taryn thought as she quickly opened the door and walked into the dimly lit room, was why she'd never forgotten Cole Evergreen. No other man had ever wanted her so intensely, as if he might spontaneously combust if he couldn't have her in the next ten seconds.

Ten seconds was about all she had to drop her messenger bag to the floor, shrug out of her parka, and glance at the unlit fireplace and the giant four-poster bed that dominated the room. Then the door clicked shut, the lock shot into place, and Cole was there, spinning her around to face him. He made a sound low in his throat, something between a growl and a groan, and then he claimed her mouth.

If he'd kissed her this way in the hall outside her apartment, she might not have been so certain that he loved her. This kiss didn't have a lot to do with love, but it had everything to do with lust. That worked for her, because she was just as desperate for him.

They wrenched at each other's clothing, and didn't succeed in getting much of it off before he shoved her down on the feather bed. She still wore one leg of her jeans, and although his coat was on the floor and his shirt was unbuttoned, that was all he'd accomplished. With a soft oath he unzipped his fly and tore open a condom packet.

He no longer trembled. Instead he moved rapidly and deliberately to sheath himself. She sprawled across the bed, and he grabbed the damp crotch of her panties. With one swift tug, the seams gave way.

The thrilling sound of him ripping her panties from her

body nearly made her climax. He'd never been like this. She moaned, needing him, aching for him...and then he was there, surging into her with a powerful thrust that made her gasp.

His mouth hovered inches from hers. "I have you, now, my precious."

She would have laughed, because *Lord of the Rings* quotes had been inside jokes of theirs during college. But his wild assault had left her breathless, and *hot.* She'd never been so turned on.

He seemed to have achieved total immersion, but somehow he rocked his hips forward and settled himself deeper yet. "There. Right *there*."

The jolt of his penis set off her first tremor. "*Cole*."

His laugh was low and rich with satisfaction. "Ready for me, you are."

Hysterics and passion bubbled equally inside of her. "Not Yoda, too!" She gasped. "You're killing me here!"

"I'm distracting myself. Turns out I don't want a repeat of that first night, after all." He eased back slowly, setting off little explosions across her skin. Then he drove in again, filling her as only Cole could.

Her blood pounded through her veins as another spasm hit, and another.

"Ah, Taryn, you're going to come first." And he stroked her again, and again, and again.

Cupping his face, she pulled him down, needing his mouth on hers, because she was about to come, and if she yelled, she'd wake Mrs. Gustafson. He made love to her mouth with his tongue, mimicking the same steady rhythm of his hips. He required an embarrassingly short time to achieve his goal. As he swallowed her soft cries, she arched upward in a powerful climax. If he hadn't had her pinned to the bed, she believed she might have flown.

As her world spun and she quivered in his arms, his rhythm changed. Now his hips rocked with more speed and less care. Lifting his mouth from hers, he began to pant. "Yes...yes...now...Taryn...*now.*" With one final thrust, he drove home, his body shuddering with the aftershocks of his orgasm.

Sliding both hands under his shirt, she caressed his sweaty back. Her hands remembered the texture of his skin and the ripple of his muscles. He liked to be caressed after sex. She'd forgotten that. Each memory that surfaced was a treasure she'd kept locked away, but now she could uncover them all. Cole was back in her arms at last.

Cole's technique had lacked eloquence, but he was pleased with the end result. Brushing a kiss over her full lips, he eased away from her and gave her a Schwarzenegger *"I'll be back."*

"You'd better be," she murmured. "And next time I want it long and slow."

"Me, too." He headed for the little bathroom with its white antique fixtures. He'd never stayed here, but he'd toured the place. Whenever they had non-magickal folks visit Evergreen Industries, he put them up at the Nutcracker Inn. Everyone raved about it.

Good thing he wouldn't ever stay here, because now the place would be loaded with memories of Taryn. A sharp pain in the vicinity of his heart reminded him of the risk he was taking by falling in with her plan. These few days could turn him into an emotional cripple, but he was willing to pay that price.

Now that he realized no one else would do but Taryn, and Taryn was forbidden to him, he'd stay single forever. That might have sounded harsh to someone else, but to Cole, it made perfect sense. Marrying someone he loved less than Taryn would be unkind to them, and to himself.

Taking off his shirt, he walked back into the room and paused. She'd always been speedy at undressing, but she must have set a world record this time. Gloriously naked, she crouched beside the fireplace with a lit match in her hand.

The small flame illuminated her delicate features, and another pain sliced through his heart. So beautiful. She tossed the match into the fireplace and swore when it fell uselessly through the grate. Opening the box of matches, she struck another one.

Silly as it was, he wanted her to succeed, but he didn't give her method much chance. Focusing on the logs arranged in the fireplace, he timed his muttered incantation to her match-tossing. The logs caught.

"Yes!" She turned to him, her smile bright. "You were standing there thinking I wouldn't get it started, weren't you?"

"Actually, I thought you would." He'd simply increased her odds.

"Let's make love here in front of the fire."

"Why not?" He was touched that she'd ask, and that she'd used the phrase *make love* instead of *have sex*. They used to make love in front of the fire. His duplex had been a real find—a rental with a woodburning fireplace. He'd used magick to keep the blaze going while they were otherwise occupied.

An unmagickal fire required constant tending, which meant having sex by the fire was romantic in theory but inconvenient in practice. She'd never questioned the consistency of their fires. He hoped that was because she'd been too busy enjoying herself.

He wondered if she'd ever tried having hearthside sex with anyone else. If so, she would have discovered it didn't work quite the way it had with him. Selfishly, he liked knowing that their experience would stand out in her mind.

She rose from the hearth with an unselfconsciousness that showed she hadn't really been worried about revealing her body. He couldn't stop looking at her. She was the same, yet different.

The tiny mole positioned over her heart was still there, waiting for his kiss. But her breasts were more voluptuous now, and her hips flared a bit more, emphasizing her narrow waist. His gaze traveled the length of her slender legs. He had fond memories of those legs wrapped around his hips. She knew how to lock him in tight while giving him room to move. He didn't need much, just enough to create the right kind of friction....

She said something, but he was so lost in memories he missed it.

"Earth to Cole."

"Hmm?"

"Your clothes, Evergreen. Lose 'em. I'll fix us a bed by the fire."

He grinned at her and snapped a quick salute. "Aye, aye, cap'n."

"Smart-ass."

"Sweet-ass." How quickly they'd become comfortable with each other again. Ten years had vanished, replaced with the easy relationship he remembered so well. Taryn got him. Well, not completely, because she didn't know about the magick. That should have been a huge omission, but somehow, when they were together, it didn't seem to matter. They made their own magick.

By the time he'd shucked the rest of his clothes and located another condom, she'd spread a quilt on the floor and tossed a couple of pillows there, too. He walked toward her, his cock already standing at attention. "You made your bed. Now lie in it."

"I thought I would." Dropping to her knees, she stretched out on the fluffy quilt with the lithe movements of a cat. Then she glanced up at him. "Come on down."

"I will, but I just realized what's different. You're not squinting."

"No, I'm not. Want to see my bedroom eyes?"

"Absolutely."

"Watch this." She lowered her lids to half mast and her eyes took on a smoky quality.

His balls tightened. "That's good." He swallowed. "Very good." He started to kneel.

"Wait. I'm not done." Her gaze dropped to his feet. Then it traveled slowly up his calves to his knees, and beyond his knees to his thighs, until finally coming to rest on his pride and joy. At that point, she ran her tongue over her lips.

"Now you're done." He sank to his knees before she figured out he was shaking again.

"No, I'm not." She beckoned to him with a crook of her forefinger. "C'mere."

A stronger wizard would have refused the temptation she offered. He'd intended this session to be all about her. Apparently he wasn't as strong as he'd like to think he was. He stretched out on the quilt and allowed her to have her way with him, and it was so good the fire roared in the hearth.

She drew back, startled. "Why did that happen?"

His breathing wasn't very steady, but he gulped in air and managed a quick explanation. "Pine knots. They flare up."

"Oh." She wrapped her fingers around his bad boy and leaned toward him. "Sorry for the interruption."

"No, it's a good thing." He cupped her cheek, stopping her descent. "I was about to get carried away."

She glanced up at him with a seductive smile. "That's the idea."

"Not this time. I have a few plans of my own. Be fair. Take turns."

She hesitated.

"You used to really like some of the things I did."

Her eyes darkened and her breath hitched. "Yeah."

"Let me do those things again." He stroked his thumb over her cheek. "You know you want me to."

"Okay." She flopped back onto the quilt like a ragdoll. "You convinced me, Evergreen. Do me."

"You bet." And he proceeded to. Revisiting all his favorite Taryn places felt like coming home, and she rolled out the welcome mat for him. In seconds she'd abandoned herself to the process of being seduced.

By the time he put on a condom and slid into her, she was on the brink of climax. One firm stroke on his part, and she came. He muffled her cries with the flat of his hand and kept pumping into her.

"Again," he murmured.

She pulled his hand away, gasping. "I can't breathe."

"Then, here." Bracing himself on one arm, he cupped the back of her head and lifted her so she could press her mouth to his shoulder. When she came the second time, she bit him.

He didn't care. In fact, it made him happy to know she'd marked him. Eventually the mark would fade, but until it did, he'd have a physical reminder of loving Taryn.

Slowly she relaxed in his arms and he eased her head back onto the pillow.

She looked up at him, firelight dancing in her eyes as she massaged his back. "Amazing. Stupendous."

"Mmm." His own climax hovered, but he'd managed to keep the urge from overwhelming him. Holding her gaze, he eased in and out. "We've still got it."

She nodded.

"There's no one like you, Taryn."

"I'm a special snowflake," she murmured.

"Uh-huh. Very special."

"So are you, Cole."

And there was that pain, burrowing into his heart. He might carry that ache forever, but that was okay, too. The pain would remind him that, for a little while, he'd had Taryn to love again.

She grasped his hips. "Your turn."

"Not yet." He hated for this moment to end.

"We can do this again tomorrow night."

"I hope so." But he had no guarantee of that. His intuition was excellent, and it told him he'd better treasure this moment and not count on any more.

Her grip tightened. "I think I can come again. Let's do it together."

"All right." He'd mastered that little trick before. The secret was watching her eyes and timing his response to what he saw there.

He bore down and increased the pace. Yes, she was right with him. Her pupils widened. He slowly slipped the leash on his own response and his heart began to pound.

The glow in her eyes was impossible to misunderstand. She loved him. His eyes surely reflected the same emotion, because he loved her, too. And because he did, he had to let her go.

But in this moment, as they surged toward a shared climax, he was hers and she was his. He held nothing back as he drove in one more time. She arched against him and he pulsed within her, each of them silencing their cries and their words of love. Yet their eyes said all their voices could not. And the fire roared.

Chapter 6

Cole left long before anyone in the inn was awake, and Taryn understood why he'd done that. Whatever mysterious element was keeping them in limbo would naturally figure into his reluctance to let anyone here know they were lovers. She wouldn't give him away, either. She'd act strictly professional today at Evergreen Industries.

She hated that he couldn't stay to share the breakfast tray that had arrived outside her door, though. Cole had a sweet tooth—he preferred cocoa to coffee. She'd bet Mrs. Gustafson would have made him cocoa to go with the apple strudel and fresh orange juice.

Placing the tray on a small desk by the side window, she drew back the lacy curtains and peeked outside for the first time. Cole hadn't been kidding about the charm of Gingerbread. Judging from the slice of town she could see, it was a full-size version of the Christmas villages in Seattle shop windows this time of year. The architecture reminded her of Europe, with a fairy-tale element thrown in.

Old-fashioned lampposts each sported a wreath and a red bow. Every shop featured garlands in the window, and larger garlands hung at intervals across the snowy street. The late-model cars that drove by seemed out of place. Horse-drawn carriages would have fit in better. Then she saw one of those, with laughing people bundled up in blankets in the back, enjoying an open-air ride.

One lone high-rise building was visible above the peaked rooftops covered with snow. Evergreen Industries, no doubt. Beyond that, where the land sloped upward and the pine forest closed in, a snow-capped mountain pierced the blue sky. Although other mountains were visible in the distance, this one was quite distinctive. She decided it must be Mistletoe Mountain, which had been mentioned during her internet search.

Until now, she hadn't thought about what would happen if and when her plan worked and she eliminated whatever problem was keeping her from a happily ever after with Cole. Her business didn't require her to live in a certain place, which meant logically she'd be the one to move.

She let that idea percolate to see how she felt about it. Turned out she was perfectly okay with leaving Seattle if it meant being with Cole. The decision wouldn't even be that difficult. As much as she traveled, she could see her friends and family when she was between jobs.

But her home would be here in Gingerbread with Cole, wherever he lived. Come to think of it, she had no idea what his place was like, which seemed odd to her, considering they'd been naked together so recently. She'd ask him about it when he came to pick her up later that morning.

Remembering that she had to be ready soon, she tucked into her protein-free but delicious breakfast, took a quick shower in the claw-foot tub with its old-fashioned circular shower rod, and dressed in a clean pair of jeans and one of her nicer sweaters. Until she understood the corporate culture at Evergreen, she'd go with something a bit less casual than her usual techie outfit of old jeans, a faded T-shirt and a hoodie.

She was in the lobby chatting with Mrs. Gustafson about things to do in town when Cole walked in. Taryn might have been prejudiced, but the guy knew how to make an entrance. He swept in wearing that long black coat, a green wool scarf, and no hat. His tousled dark hair gave him a rakish look she'd never been able to resist.

"Ah, Cole!" Mrs. Gustafson, plump and graying, clasped her hands together. "Your guest is a delight. She's already in love with our little town. I hope you're planning to give her a tour."

Cole's bemused smile indicated he hadn't planned anything of the sort. "Uh, sure. Why not? But first we have some business to take care of at Evergreen."

Mrs. Gustafson waved a hand at him. "Well, I know *that*. The guests you bring here always have business at Evergreen. But Taryn has taken a real interest in Gingerbread, haven't you, dear?"

"I have." Taryn had to work hard not to laugh at Cole's uneasiness. "And I'd love a tour if we have the time."

Cole's green eyes flashed with amusement. "I'll see to it. Shall we go?"

"I'm ready when you are."

"Have fun, you two!" Mrs. Gustafson called after them as they left the cozy lobby.

"We will!" Taryn called back.

"Chatting up the landlady?" Cole said once they were on the front porch.

"Is that a problem?"

"No, I just…do you really want a tour of Gingerbread?"

"I wouldn't mind." She took a deep breath of the crisp air as they started down the sidewalk toward the parking area. "I like it here."

"Well, good…that's good."

She glanced at him, and his cheeks were ruddy. It could have been from the cold, but she suspected he was agitated. "You'd prefer I never come back here, right?"

"I can't stop you from doing that if you want to."

"But it makes you nervous."

"Yes."

"You're the one who raved about the Christmas cheer in Gingerbread. And sure enough, the place is charming. I have friends who would love to vacation here."

He sighed. "Then they should."

"I think so, too." She longed to assure him everything

would be okay, because she was going to figure this out, but saying anything like that would alert him to her covert plans. For now, he couldn't know what was in her mind and her heart. Soon enough, he would.

Getting into his sleek black sedan reminded her of their songfest the night before, but she doubted he wanted to repeat that. He was tense this morning, and she had a hunch as to why. He was second-guessing his course of action. Pulling out of the inn's parking lot, he drove slowly down the street. As they rolled along, Taryn checked out the shops.

Cup of Cheer bustled with morning activity. "Cute coffee shop," she said. "I suppose you never go there."

"No, but my sister Belle does."

"She still lives in Gingerbread?" Back in college, he'd mentioned two brothers and a sister, but she hadn't thought to ask where they lived now.

"We all work for Evergreen."

"Oh. That's nice." Or it could have been, except that if everyone had to keep the same damned secret, what kind of life did they have here? "Will I be meeting them?"

"We'll see. Depends on everybody's schedule."

"You don't want me getting chummy with your siblings, do you?"

He glanced over at her. "The thing is, they know you were my college girlfriend."

"Aha!" That pleased her immensely. "Then I'd be surprised if they didn't want to get a look at me. I would, if I were in their shoes."

"They probably do want to." He sounded resigned.

"Great. Then I will meet them." She settled back in her seat with a smile.

Cole, however, was not smiling. In fact, his profile resembled an ice sculpture.

She'd have loved to thaw him out. "You know, I realized this morning I have no idea where you live."

His throat moved as he swallowed. "It, um, doesn't really matter, does it?"

"It does to me. I'm not in the habit of taking my clothes off for a man when I have no idea where he lives or what his place looks like. Until this morning, I hadn't thought about that discrepancy. You do live in Gingerbread, I assume?"

"Outside of it, but yes, in a sense. It's the closest town."

"Will you let me see your place?"

"That's not a good idea."

"Why not?"

"Taryn, don't push."

"I hardly think it's pushing to want to see your home. Back at MIT we went back and forth between my apartment and your duplex all the time. I knew what was in your refrigerator and you knew what was in mine. Having no idea about your living space feels weird, Cole."

He sighed. "We're not at MIT. And I can't show you where I live."

She heard the note of finality in his voice and tucked that information away. Wherever he lived, the secret lived, too. If that weren't so, he'd have agreed to take her there.

Although she had a million more questions, she didn't ask them. He was already on edge. But she was about to enter a place filled with other sources of information.

As they approached the tall building she'd identified from her bedroom window, a portly man in a red jogging suit lumbered past on the snowy sidewalk. He had on a knit cap instead of a fur-trimmed one, but his white beard was very Santa Claus-like.

She'd decided not to make any more comments, but seeing the jogging Santa look-alike was a safe enough topic. "That guy we just passed looks exactly like Santa Claus."

A muscle in Cole's jaw twitched. "I know."

"Is he some local character?"

"Something like that."

"It's kind of cute, don't you think? A middle-aged guy

lives in Gingerbread and decides to take on the persona of Santa Claus. It's like the role players in old Western towns like Tombstone."

"Guess so."

"You don't seem to appreciate the charm of it, my friend."

Cole took a deep breath and looked over at her. "I'd forgotten that your brain is always analyzing, always evaluating, sifting and cataloging."

"Of course. So's yours."

He flicked on a turn signal and pulled up to a wrought iron gate with scrollwork incorporating an elaborate E. "I'm going to ask you to focus all that brainpower on the Evergreen database. Pretend you have blinders on and ignore everything else."

"Sounds like censorship, Cole."

He touched a button on the dash and the gates swung open. "That's because it is."

"For the love of God, what's going on in this building?"

Pulling into a parking space labeled with his name, he shut off the engine and turned to her. "I promise you that what goes on in this building is benign. There are no criminals here, no terrorists and no drug dealers. Nothing bad happens here, Taryn. Can you accept that and just do your job?"

"If it's nothing bad, why can't you tell me?"

"I can't tell you because..." He looked into her eyes and his throat moved. When he spoke, his voice was husky with emotion. "I can't tell you, not ever, and I really wish I could, because..."

"Because why?"

"Because I love you."

She gasped, shocked that he'd said it, but thrilled, too. "But I love you, too! And people who love each other share things they wouldn't tell anyone else."

"Not in this case." His gaze searched hers. "I need you to analyze the database. You're the person for the job—

maybe the only person who can do what I need done. Will you do that for me?"

"Yes, I will." He hadn't asked her to promise she'd wear those blinders. Maybe he secretly wanted her to find out what was going on.

Whether he wanted her to find out or not, she intended to. This was ridiculous. They belonged together, and she wouldn't let him throw their future away, at least not until she knew why he was so intent on doing it.

The lobby was decorated for Christmas, which she would have expected. A blue spruce that had to be thirty feet tall stood in the center of the two-story vaulted ceiling. Evergreen ornaments hung from every branch. Many of them gave off that mysterious glow she'd noticed in hers.

Display cases filled with ornaments lined the walls, and each ornament was labeled with the year in which it was manufactured. Taryn didn't have much time to look, but she'd swear at least one of them dated back to the 1600s. "Cole, some of those ornaments are really old."

"The company's been around a long time."

"Did it originate in Europe?"

"Yes, it did, in fact. Let's get you signed in." He guided her toward an ornate desk that looked as if it might have been imported from Versailles. Behind it sat a sweet-faced woman who could have been anywhere from fifty to seventy. She wore a red velvet dress, and the nameplate on her desk identified her as Jolie S. Garland.

Taryn wanted to ask her, with a wink, if that was her real name. But something about the woman's calm gaze kept her from doing that. Taryn suspected it was her real name, and she'd be insulted if anyone suggested otherwise. Whether she'd found her perfect job or the job had found her, she'd discovered the right spot for a person with that particular name.

Smiling, she handed Taryn a gold pen. "Sign here, Miss Harper, and I'll give you an access card."

Jolie reached into a drawer and came up with a sparkling gold card with Taryn's name embossed on the front and a magnetic strip on the back. "This will allow you to board the elevator, which will take you to the IT center on the twelfth floor. If you need anything, please come back to the lobby and I'll assist you."

"Thank you, Jolie." Taryn returned the woman's genial smile, but she had the distinct impression she'd been given a ticket to the IT floor and nothing else. Once she and Cole were inside the shiny gold elevator, she confirmed it with him.

"That's all you were hired to do." He unbuttoned his coat and loosened his scarf, but he stood on the opposite side of the elevator.

She found that significant—depressingly so. "I thought you might give me a tour of the building while I'm here." She hadn't really thought that, but it was worth a shot.

A ghost of a smile touched his lips. "Would you settle for a tour of the IT department? It's my favorite floor."

"I'm sure it is. But your parking space said you were the CEO. Who's in charge of IT?"

"I am, for now. I haven't found anybody I'd turn it over to, so I'm doing double-duty."

"That can't be easy. This looks like a huge operation. How can you handle the IT department when you're supposed to be the head honcho of Evergreen?"

"Obviously I'm not doing a very good job of it. You hacked in."

"You shouldn't let that bother you. As I said before, I know your MO. The average hacker wouldn't have nearly such an easy time of it."

"Nevertheless, you exposed my vulnerabilities. I want those protected."

That, too, was a telling statement. She was the woman who knew too much. He'd hired her to barricade him against future invasions, both business-related and emotional, and then leave.

The elevator came to a smooth stop on the twelfth floor. It hadn't stopped once since they'd left the lobby. Other people had to be working in this large building, and yet she'd never know it. Jolie S. Garland was the only employee she'd met. That was spooky.

"I gave the rest of the IT staff the day off to go Christmas shopping," he said. "I wanted you to be able to work undisturbed."

That meant he didn't want her talking to anyone. He'd done his best to isolate her from the rest of the workers at Evergreen. After they'd gotten so close at MIT, he should have realized the more he tried to deny her access to information, the more determined she'd become. If she hadn't believed her investigative plan was for his own good, she'd feel disloyal. But he'd refused to give her all the facts, and without those facts, she couldn't make an informed decision. Maybe, once she knew what the issues were, she'd agree with him that they had no future.

She seriously doubted that, though. Every problem had a solution. He'd been conditioned to believe this particular problem couldn't be solved. That wasn't a failing. Everyone had blind spots. Because she loved him, she would help him to overcome his.

After they left the elevator, he led her past several offices, but the hallway was ghost-town silent.

At the end of the hall, Cole opened a door into a larger office. An L-shaped dark walnut desk held multiple monitors, a top-of-the-line keyboard and a mouse pad in the shape of a round Christmas ornament. A Santa mug sat to the right of the keyboard, but that was it. No framed pictures, no flowering plant, no cluttered in-basket.

She glanced around. "Is this your office?"

"Used to be. I still work down here when I need to."

"Where's your regular office?"

"Fifteenth floor." He seemed reluctant to share that information. "Let me take your coat so you can have a seat and get started."

"Fine." She put her messenger bag on his desk and instantly the work space looked more welcoming. As she started to shrug out of her parka, her hands bumped his. He was helping her take off her coat. She froze. "I can do it."

"Right." He backed away. "Sorry. Habit."

Slipping off her coat, she turned to him. He looked positively miserable. "You can leave," she said. "I know how to turn on a computer." She smiled. "And I already know your password."

He laughed at that, although it wasn't a happy laugh. "So you do. Then maybe I will leave you to work for a while and I'll check on you later. I...uh...didn't realize that giving the IT staff the day off would have an unintended consequence."

"That we're all alone up here?"

His green gaze burned with frustration. "Exactly."

"Then go, before one of your siblings shows up and catches us in a compromising position."

Heat flared in his eyes. "I'll come back and check on you. Is there anything you need?"

"Besides the obvious?"

"Stop."

"Okay. I would love a good cup of coffee sometime in the middle of the morning. Is that possible?"

"I'll make it happen."

"Thanks. See ya." She made a shooing motion with both hands. She hoped his siblings did pop in to see her. She'd figure out a way to make that work to her advantage.

Chapter 7

Cole barreled down the hall and waited impatiently for the elevator. When it came, he was glad it was empty. He used his card and punched the number for the fifteenth floor. How could this have become so complicated? He hadn't factored in the possibility that she'd be as hot for him now—hotter, in fact—as she'd been before. And still in love with him, as he was with her. What a disaster!

Ethan got on the elevator as Cole got off. "Is Taryn in the building?" Ethan asked.

"Yes, and I hope you'll leave her alone to work."

Ethan laughed. "I will, for now. I have to deliver some ornaments to the Denver Chamber of Commerce. Their president read Lark's damned book, and the cheer level of their Christmas display is way down. But if Taryn's here when I get back, I'll stop in and introduce myself."

"Don't hurry home."

"I love you, too, big brother." The elevator door closed, obscuring Ethan's grin.

Cole blew out a breath and started down the hall. Then he remembered Taryn's coffee request and stopped at Belle's office.

She glanced up from her computer. "Is Taryn here?"

"Yes, and she's a coffee drinker."

"Cool! I like her already."

"She asked for a good cup of coffee mid-morning, and I thought, since you always go to Cup of Cheer around ten, you could bring back something for her."

"Uh, sure." Belle's gaze flickered. "I have some errands to run in town, though, and they could take a while."

Something was going on with her and these errands, but this time of year, Cole knew better than to quiz his family when they acted mysterious. For all he knew, she had been planning to buy his present that morning.

"How about this?" Her expression brightened. "She can walk down there with me. I'll buy her coffee, and then I'll send her back here while I run my errands. That way she can see what they have and get the flavor she likes. Will that work?"

"Guess so." Cole wasn't crazy about the thought of Taryn on the loose in Gingerbread. But he also wasn't ready to be alone with her again.

"Then we'll do it that way. I look forward to meeting her."

"You'll watch what you say, though, right?"

Belle's green eyes widened innocently. "You don't want me to tell her how destroyed you were when you had to break up with her ten years ago?"

He scowled.

"Don't worry, big brother. Your secrets are safe with me."

"Thanks." He remembered he wanted to mention seeing Kris. "Our wayward Santa was out jogging when we drove past. Taryn decided he's some guy who's into role-playing."

"That's good. Excellent. And I've been meaning to tell you that Louie, one of our elves, has designed Spit-Up Baby Susie. He thinks it's more realistic and should go into production ASAP."

"Have him send the prototype to me."

"You're not thinking of approving it, I hope!"

"No, but I'm curious to see how it works." Any distraction, including a vomiting baby doll, would be a good thing.

Taryn needed caffeine. Mrs. Gustafson's brew had worn off, and while Cole's whimsical database with its dopey categories like *"Lots of Toys for Girls and Boys"* was entertaining, Taryn needed hot coffee, and she needed it now.

When a green-eyed blonde wearing a trench coat tapped on the open door, Taryn hoped her visitor was there on a mission of mercy for the caffeine-deprived.

"Taryn, I'm Belle." Smiling, she hooked her purse more securely over her shoulder. "Cole said you drink coffee."

"I do. Is there a pot brewing somewhere in the building?" She wondered if Belle might give her access to a different floor. That would be exciting.

"Not really. Get your coat and I'll walk you down to Cup of Cheer. They make the best java in Gingerbread."

"I'm all over that." Taryn saved her work and powered down the computer. "I was about to send out an SOS."

"Trust me, I understand. Don't bother bringing your bag, though. This is my treat. Just make sure you have your access card."

"It's in my coat pocket." Taryn took her parka from the coat-tree in the corner. "Sounds like the Evergreen coffee room isn't up to your standards."

"There is no coffee room. Just a cocoa room."

"You're joking." Taryn followed her out the door. "Who doesn't have a coffee room?"

"Evergreen Industries." Belle headed briskly down the hall. She could walk fast for a short person.

Taryn had trouble believing the building had no coffee available. "Don't the employees complain?"

"Just me. Everyone else is fine with the cocoa. So I make the trek to Cup of Cheer every morning." She swiped her access card through the reader and the elevator opened.

"Thanks for inviting me along." Taryn noticed Belle's access card was the same as hers and Cole's. The only difference was in the coding and the name embossed on the back. What Taryn wouldn't give to have possession of that card for thirty minutes.

"I'm glad to do it. I'd walk back with you, but I have some

things that require my attention in town. I'm sure you'll find your way back okay."

Taryn laughed. "I can't imagine anyone getting lost in Gingerbread. Hiking around Mistletoe Mountain could be a different story, but I don't plan on doing that."

"That's good." They reached the lobby and Belle waved at Jolie S. Garland, who was still on duty. "That's a treacherous mountain. I'd stay away from it if I were you."

"I didn't bring my hiking boots, anyway." Taryn zipped up her parka as they started down the sidewalk that led to the heart of town. "What's your job at Evergreen?"

"I'm in HR."

"So you're in charge of the elves."

Belle's head whipped around. "What?"

"I figured you knew, but maybe not."

"Knew what?"

Taryn thought it was strange that Belle actually seemed upset. Maybe she was the sort of person who didn't like being the last to find out what was going on in the company. "Cole's put all sorts of goofy names in the database. It fits because you're a Christmas ornament manufacturer, but I had to laugh. HR is titled '*Elves*,' and customers are listed under '*Naughty or Nice.*' Like I said, goofy."

"Oh." Belle let out a breath. "I guess I did hear something about that system. Leave it to my geeky brother."

"He's one of a kind, all right."

"He is. Gotta love him."

Taryn thought it wise not to respond to that comment.

Belle switched the topic, which was probably a good idea. "You're from Seattle, right?"

"I am." For the rest of the walk, Taryn answered questions about her native city, one Belle had never visited. Cole's name didn't come up again.

The coffee shop seemed even busier than it had when Taryn and Cole had driven by first thing that morning. She and Belle had to stand in line, and Taryn took that opportunity to scan the extensive coffee menu. Belle kept looking around the shop, almost as if she were expecting to see someone. She seemed agitated.

The line moved slowly, and Belle continued to glance over each time the door opened. "Do you know what you want?" she asked as she continued to survey the crowd.

"I'm getting an extra-large eggnog espresso. That should do the trick."

"It should." She looked away again. "Aha. I just saw someone I need to talk with." She fished in her purse. "Here's my wallet. Order me a large double-shot peppermint latte, and I'll be right back."

"Okay." Taryn's heart began to pound as she realized the opportunity she had. What she was about to do was wrong. When she was caught, and she would be, she'd have no excuse other than the fact that she was doing it for love. But if she didn't overcome her scruples immediately, she'd lose her chance.

Opening Belle's wallet, she took out the golden access card and replaced it with her own. Then she tucked Belle's card in her pocket. Her heart was racing so fast she felt lightheaded. Belle hadn't returned by the time she'd ordered and paid for both drinks. She walked over to the window where the orders were coming out, and she waited. The crowd was so dense and Belle was so short that Taryn couldn't see her.

Taryn's coffee came up first, and right after it did, Belle appeared, her cheeks bright red. "All set?"

"I have mine." Taryn handed her the wallet, which by now felt like a ticking time bomb. "Thank you."

"You're welcome. Listen, you don't have to stay. I have to go in the opposite direction, anyway."

"If you're sure." Taryn could hardly wait to get out of there.

"I'm sure. Nice meeting you, and I'll see you later."

"Same here, Belle." With what she hoped was a smile and not a grimace, Taryn left the shop. Instantly she began drinking as fast as possible without scalding her tongue. The caffeine would give her the courage she'd need for what she was about to do.

Once she was out of sight of the coffee shop, she chugged the last of her coffee and tossed the cup in a nearby trash can. Then she picked up the pace, but she couldn't run. That would attract attention.

She slowed down again twenty yards from the Evergreen building. She couldn't pant when she called out a greeting to Jolie S. Garland. She would have trouble acting normal as it was.

Jolie smiled at her. "Did you get your coffee, dear?"

"Sure did. Drank it already. Back to work!" She kept moving. Her hand trembled and she had to swipe Belle's card twice before the elevator doors opened. Luck was with her. It was empty. And lo and behold, all the numbers were lit.

Her finger hovered over the button for fifteen, but pressing it would have been stupid. No doubt she'd run smack into Cole the minute she stepped off the elevator.

Wait a minute. Besides the fifteen floors above ground, there were five below. She hadn't been able to see those with her original access card. And everyone knew secrets were always hidden in the basement. She punched B5.

The car started its slow glide down, and her stomach began to churn. She reminded herself Cole had promised nothing bad was going on in this building, and Cole was incapable of telling a lie. Unlike her. She was both a thief and a liar. She prayed Cole loved her enough to forgive her.

The elevator slid to a stop and the doors rumbled open to reveal…a paint and body shop? She wasn't tremendously familiar with them, but she recognized the giant paint sprayers. Positioned in the middle of the area, its new coat of red gleaming in the overhead lights, was a giant sleigh. The curved metal runners had been taped, as had all the metal fittings. A workbench along one wall was lined with various sized brushes and a large can of paint.

No one was in the shop, so she crept forward and looked at the white label on top of the can. *Sleigh, Gold Pinstriping, Formula 896* had been typed on the adhesive label. Could this be a prop for an advertising campaign?

If so, she couldn't imagine why she wouldn't be allowed to see it. No wiser than before, she returned to the elevator and rode to the next floor. This time, as the doors began to open, she was greeted by quite a racket. Staccato tapping filled the space, as if dozens of tiny hammers were being wielded by...elves.

Stepping through the open doors, she stared at tiny people wearing pointy caps, green tunics and leggings, and shoes that curved up at the toe and were each decorated with a bell. They didn't notice her. Of course they wouldn't. Christmas Eve was drawing near and they were *making toys for girls and boys*.

She blinked, but the scene didn't change. Conveyor belts snaked through the two-story work area carrying finished toys to a wrapping machine. The toys emerged covered with bright paper and festive bows. Then they disappeared into a tunnel.

Slowly she backed into the elevator. This couldn't be real, and yet she was wide awake. She pinched herself to make sure. The secret, the one Cole had refused to tell her, was incredible, but she couldn't deny it now. Evergreen Industries, through some process she didn't understand but Cole obviously knew inside out, was responsible for making Christmas happen.

Cole glanced at the clock. Taryn would have her coffee by now, and he should probably contact her to see how she was getting along with the database. Texting her seemed like the best option. He'd begun composing one when his phone chimed. Noelle's name popped up on the screen.

He abandoned his text message and answered the call. "What's up?"

"You'd better get down here."

He'd never heard Noelle use that tone, which was part command and part freak-out. "Be right there."

Moments later he was in her office staring at the pictures coming from her surveillance cameras and swearing softly under his breath. "How did she get in there? Her access card was only coded for the IT floor!"

"Don't ask me, but we officially have a major security threat."

Cole's chest tightened. Deep down, he'd known this would happen. He should never have brought her here. "Do you have the cocoa ready?"

Noelle hesitated. "Yes."

"Will it work?" He was worried about Noelle's slight hesitation.

"It should."

"It will erase all memory of me and of this place, but nothing else, right?"

"Uh, yes."

He didn't like the faint tremor in her voice, which told him she wasn't all that confident about the cocoa. But even if the effects only lasted for a while, it would buy him some time, and it was better than nothing. "Get me some and bring it to my office. I'll go find her."

"I'll meet you there."

At this point, he didn't have to hide his powers anymore. Closing his eyes, he willed himself to B4, where Taryn was wandering through displays featuring the historical origin of the Christmas tree. He materialized next to her while she gazed up at a Scotch pine with candles attached to its branches.

"Having fun?"

She jumped and turned toward him, wide-eyed. "Where did you come from?"

He looked into her eyes. "I'm a wizard." In some ways, it was a relief to finally say it. "I can travel simply by wishing it."

"You're a..." She stared at him, her face drained of all color.

"A wizard. From the Winter Clan. As you've just discovered, we're in charge of Christmas."

"But you can't be. What about the North Pole? How does that figure in?"

"It's a decoy. The North Pole would be way too much trouble—no decent facilities at all up there. Colorado is much more convenient for our purposes."

"So this is what you couldn't tell me."

"That's right. And because you've breached our security, I have to take care of that. How did you, by the way?"

"I stole Belle's access card while we were in the coffee shop. Don't blame her. It's not her fault."

"I don't. If anybody's to blame, it's me for bringing you to Gingerbread in the first place. But I'll fix that." He held out his hand. "Hold on."

"Why?"

"We need to go to my office, and this is the quickest way." He gazed at her. "Trust me, please."

"All right." And she put her hand in his.

That simple act broke his heart. But he had a job to do, so he closed his eyes and willed them to his fifteenth-floor office. When the swirling stopped, he kept holding her hand. Anyone new to apparating needed some time to adjust.

She took a shaky breath. "Wow. How many Gs do you think we pulled?"

"Don't know. I've never tried to measure that."

"Next time you should. It would be fun to know."

"*Fun*? This isn't about fun, Taryn."

"Of course it is! This is a *blast*. I just found out the man I love is a *wizard*. How cool is that?"

"I don't think you quite understand."

"No, but I want to. Where do you live? Can you tell me now?"

He shrugged. "I suppose it can't hurt. The Winter Clan has a lodge up on Mistletoe Mountain."

"I knew it! That's why Belle warned me not to go hiking up there."

"You wouldn't have found it even if you had. We have it cloaked."

"Cloaked! I love it! What about the elves? Where do they live?"

"Their village is just below the lodge. They travel to and from the workshop through underground passageways." He looked into her shining eyes and frowned. "At this point any normal person should be hyperventilating and questioning her own sanity. Why aren't you?"

"You're kidding, right? This is me you're talking to, the woman who has read *Lord of the Rings* at least four times and has watched the movie more times than that. Cole, you're a *wizard*. Like Gandalf, only way sexier! I'm geeking out!"

"Knock, knock." Noelle appeared in the doorway holding an ornate silver mug on a silver tray. "I have the cocoa."

"Thanks, Noelle. You can set it on my desk."

She did. Then she walked over to Taryn and held out her hand. "I'm Noelle Frost, temporary head of security. I don't know how you breached our system, but I'm impressed. I wish I could get to know you better."

"Maybe you can," Taryn said.

"I don't think so." Noelle glanced at the cocoa and then at Cole. "It should be fine."

"What?" Taryn whirled around to face him. "What's with the cocoa?"

Cole stepped forward and grasped her shoulders. "It's

a special batch. I can't allow you to remember all you've seen, so the cocoa will erase those memories. Then you can return to your life, your family and your job as if this never happened."

"No, I can't."

Noelle cleared her throat. "I'll just head on back to my office. Call if you need me."

"I will," Cole said. Then he returned his attention to Taryn. "Yes, you can. It's the way things need to be."

"I didn't finish my work in IT."

"That's okay. I can do it."

"What if I hack back in?"

He shook his head. "You won't. I've asked Noelle to brew this batch so your memories of me will be selectively removed." He hoped Noelle had managed that.

"First of all, you may be a wizard and all, but that doesn't sound doable. I don't think it's possible to untangle my memories of you without screwing up all my memories from MIT."

"I believe it can be done."

"You mean you *want* to believe, but I can tell you're not a hundred percent sure."

"Taryn, listen to me. We have to try so you can live a normal life. I saw the pictures on your mantel. The burden of keeping a secret like this from those you love would be *huge*."

She gazed at him for several seconds. "Now I get it. The burden would be huge for you, because being open with those you love is so important. It's important to me, too, but if I have to keep a secret from my friends and family so I can be with you—it's no contest."

"Taryn, I—"

She cupped his face in both hands. "You are the best thing that ever happened to me. And now, on top of your brains, your sexy body and your intense love for me, you're a wizard. Do you think for one minute I'm going to dutifully swallow some iffy potion that might make me forget you? I intend to remember you for the rest of my life."

A tiny kernel of hope took root in him and began to grow. "You need to think this through very carefully. Snap decisions are never a good idea."

"I've been thinking it through for ten years, buster. And when I hacked into your site, I promised myself if I ever got my hands on you again, I would never let go."

He couldn't stop the smile from spreading over his face. "Really?"

"Really." She wiggled out of his grip and walked over to the desk. "Is this one of those fancy offices with a bathroom attached?"

"Yes. Do you need to use the facilities?"

"I do. Where are they?"

"Through that door." He was a little perplexed, but when a woman had to go, she had to go.

"Good." Taryn picked up the mug of cocoa and marched through the door he'd indicated.

"What are you doing?" He heard the toilet flush.

She came back bearing the mug and set it on the tray. "No more cocoa. You're stuck with me, Cole Evergreen. And you really need me, too, because you can't run this corporation and the IT department. I'll take that on."

Heart full, he gathered her in his arms. "I just plain need you. But I was so afraid I'd ruin your life."

She gazed up at him. "Then you don't know me as well as you think you do. Can we do that apparating thing again?"

"Why? Where do you want to go?"

"Your bedroom in the Winter Clan lodge. It's time I saw where you live."

He drew her closer. "It's the middle of a business day."

"Yes, but you're the CEO. Besides, I want to see your magic wand. You do have one, don't you?"

"Is that a loaded question?"

"What do you think?"

"I think it is. And that's what I love about you, Taryn Harper." Closing his eyes, he carried them both off to begin a life more magickal than he ever could have imagined. And he had one hell of an imagination.

* * * * *

SHE'S A MEAN ONE

RHONDA NELSON

NYT bestselling author, two-time RITA® Award nominee, RT Reviewers' Choice Award nominee and National Readers' Choice Award winner **Rhonda Nelson** writes hot romantic comedy. You can find her at www.readrhondanelson.com, follow @RhondaRNelson on Twitter and like her on Facebook.

For my fellow novella-mates, Vicki, Andrea and Kira.
I believe this book represents what makes us work as
dear friends and plotting partners—sheer magic.
Love y'all bunches!

Prologue

December 24th, 1996

Seven-year-old Lark DeWynter sucked in a startled breath, and then shut her eyes tightly. "He's not there. He's not there. He's not there," she repeatedly whispered. "And I am *not* crazy," she added, defiantly lifting her chin, a bit of a growl entering her voice.

The scent of sugar cookies and hot cocoa suddenly wafted around her and a low chuckle sounded from directly in front of her. "Of course you're not crazy, child," a merry voice said. "Whoever told you such nonsense?"

Lark's eyes popped open. And there he was.

Santa.

Just like he was every year. Red suit, black belt, snowy white beard tumbling from a rosy-cheeked face and the kindest, twinkling eyes Lark had ever seen. Just looking at him made bubbles of happiness burst in her chest.

Lark choked back a sob and flung herself at him, knocking a surprised grunting laugh from his big belly. She clung to him, profoundly relieved that he was real, that she wasn't crazy, but more than anything, that everyone else was *wrong*. "Oh, Santa!" she cried. "They don't believe me! They don't believe that you're real, but I know that you're real. I *know* that you are!"

"Whoa, there," he said. "What's all this about?" he asked, drawing her away so he could look down into her face. Concern clouded his gaze. "You're not supposed to cry on

Christmas Eve. You're supposed to be tucked away in bed, dreaming of toys and surprises."

Lark scrubbed a tear off her cheek and peered up at him. "But I never do that. I always wait for you."

His eyes softened and his especially pink lips curled into a warm smile. "That you do," he said fondly. "You're one of the very, very special few who do that, Lark. Did you know that?"

Her? Special? Really? "But they don't believe me."

He inclined his head, a grave expression on his face, though she sensed that he was merely pretending. "Ah," he said, as though giving it some thought. "Well, that's hardly surprising. Adults have a hard time believing in magic," he said. "Isn't that sad?" He cast a significant glance around the living room. "They can see the tinsel and the lights and the stockings, but the actual *magic* of Christmas?" He gave his head a tragic shake and tsked. "It eludes them, the poor dears."

She'd never thought about it that way before and for a moment felt pity for her parents and for sad Dr. Nancy, who had lots of wrinkles and smelled like mothballs. How terrible that they couldn't see Santa, that they didn't notice the occasional wink of a toy soldier, the flash of a smile from a nutcracker, the flutter of angel wings from the topper on their tree, the extra shimmer on many of the other ornaments.

There was one, in particular, that seemed to shine with an internal glow.

The snowman.

It was pearly white, like moonlight on ice, and seemed to change a bit from year to year. This time he had ivy sprigs on his top hat instead of holly berries, reindeer on the scarf around his neck in place of the snowflakes that were there the year before—even his expression changed. Some years he looked happier than others, when his eyes beamed with a mischievous twinkle. There were years, too, when he looked almost bored. It was odd, but in a strange sort of way it was comforting.

Naturally, that ornament was her favorite, and every year when it came time to dismantle the tree, she fought to keep him out. She had even gone so far as to hide him in her room. It seemed a tragedy to put away all of the decorations, but even more so when it came to her special snowman. He wasn't merely a "Frosty," Lark had decided, and had renamed him Mr. Cool.

She glanced at him now, where he hung front and center on the tree, nestled between a handprint reindeer and a green glass ball, and grinned when his raisin smile widened, his button eyes gleaming with encouragement.

An upside-down head suddenly emerged from the chimney. "Oy, what's the hold up? We're on a schedule here, Big Red," the little man hissed impatiently, the point of his cap dangling dangerously close to the flames. He cast a glance around the living room, stopping short when he spotted the pair of them.

"Oh. It's you." He rolled his eyes—which looked especially odd since he was upside down—and heaved a put upon sigh. "I should have known."

Lark smiled at the elf, despite his surly greeting. "Hello, Edgar."

"Edgar," Santa admonished with a significant arch of his brow. "What did I tell you?"

Edgar's guilty gaze slid away and his mouth flattened. "Christmas is for children," he said glumly.

"And what is Lark?"

He released a long breath and looked everywhere but at Santa. "She's a child."

"And what does that mean?" he prodded.

"She's more important than the schedule," he said, a hint of resentment creeping into his voice. Edgar reminded her of her older brother, John, who at thirteen was a champion door-slammer and could communicate his displeasure with a scowling huff of breath that never failed to make their mother grit her teeth.

Santa beamed at him all the same. "Excellent! You're learning."

Considering that they had the same argument every year, Lark thought Santa's optimism was impressive.

"Nevertheless," the older man said with a regretful grin as he returned his attention to her. "I'm afraid Edgar is right, my dear. Lots of houses left to visit before the dawn."

She nodded. This, too, was a familiar conversation.

He patted her on the head, turned and made his way over to the chimney, then withdrew a handful of glittery purple powder from his pocket and tossed it onto the flames, which instantly died down. Pausing before stepping into the fireplace, he shot her a look over his shoulder. "And, Lark, always remember this—believing is believing."

She frowned. Believing is believing? Didn't he mean *seeing* is believing? "But—"

He chuckled at her expression. "Anybody can see and believe," he told her, anticipating her next question. "But not just anyone can believe without proof. Those people are special, and you're one of them."

She smiled, pleased. "All right, then," she said. "See you next year, Santa."

"See you next year, Lark." He winked, then stepped into the fireplace and disappeared...permanently, it would turn out, from her childhood.

Chapter 1

Ethan Evergreen stared across the news desk at his nemesis, his archenemy, the perpetual thorn in his side, and couldn't decide if he wanted to strangle her or kiss her. Perhaps both, but in which order remained to be seen, he thought darkly.

"...and that is why it is *imperative* that children know there is no Santa Claus, that he's simply not real," Lark DeWynter insisted passionately, her pale violet eyes glowing with conviction. "Lying to them to perpetuate an increasingly commercialized tradition isn't just reckless, it's detrimental." She nodded once. "It devalues truth."

Yes, but whose? Ethan wanted to argue. It was the same tired old debate every year and had been for the past five. Santa wasn't real, children needed more honesty from their "moral instructors," imagination based on lies was unhealthy.

Blah, blah, blah.

He heaved an internal sigh. No doubt had anyone but Lark been making the claim he'd have gotten exceedingly bored by now.

But it wasn't just anyone. It was *her*.

Her, with her pale pansy-colored eyes—not quite blue, not quite purple, but an intriguing shade in between that put him in mind of a rare arctic flower of a similar hue. They were a little wide-set, almost kittenish, and fringed with dark, sooty lashes. She had a wide forehead—*undoubtedly to house that diabolical little brain,* Ethan thought uncharitably—and delicate cheekbones, which narrowed into an adorably sharp chin. And the mouth that sat above that chin? Of its own volition, his broody gaze dropped there and lingered, sending an unwelcome strike of heat directly into his groin.

Positively carnal, that mouth.

Ripe, naturally rosy and full, with a perpetual upturn in the left corner that suggested she was always savoring a secret joke, one he often imagined was at his expense.

She shifted and cleared her throat, which had grown slightly pink.

Ethan's gaze bumped up and collided with hers, and he resisted the immediate urge to recoil at the strength of emotion that slammed into him as a result of that seemingly innocuous non-contact—happened every time he looked at her, damn her. He had caught the faintest flash of longing in those startled eyes before she had disguised it with sardonic contempt.

He arched a pointed brow, one that told her he knew better, and had the pleasure of watching her lovely jaw harden. *Close, but no cigar,* he thought. He knew he hadn't really rattled her until she ground her teeth.

In a strange twist of what could be only considered wicked, vengeful irony, they were wildly—unhappily, miserably, potentially lethally—attracted to one another.

"Any rebuttal to Ms. DeWynter's argument, Ethan?" the toothy talk show host, Mavis, asked. She'd propositioned him earlier, letting him know exactly what she'd like under her tree this Christmas. As if he'd never heard that one before.

Meh. Not interested.

He never was this time of year; he routinely went through a three-month dry spell. It wasn't just because of the stress of being the official face of Evergreen Industries, or because he was busy designing and bewitching ornaments to help add Christmas cheer. But this year held even more pressure. This year he was running Grinch Control, making sure that said Christmas cheer stayed at a high enough level to maintain the magic because her *damned* book—*The Christmas Lie*—had zoomed to the top of every equally *damned* bestseller list. Add in the fact that Santa and Mrs. Claus were in the throes of a marital crisis and his job had never been more challenging. *Leave it to Kris to forget their twenty-fifth wedding anniversary,* Ethan thought with an inward sigh. *Bad form, Bearded Wonder. Bad form.*

No, much as it irritated and galled him to admit it...the sexual hiatus was because of her.

Because, after being around her, every other woman simply failed to capture his interest. For reasons that escaped him—penance for some unknown sin, possibly—Lark DeWynter utterly fascinated him. She was fire and ice, passionate but cool, with a razor-sharp wit and a mind so quick and fiendish he was often torn between being impressed, turned on and mildly terrified.

The rest of the time, he wasn't torn—he just felt all three simultaneously.

It was enough to drive any man insane.

Even more insane? He looked forward to it, looked forward to seeing her every year across the table.

And, of course, he'd offer a rebuttal. That's what he was here for, after all. Damage control. He smiled at Lark and assumed an expression indulgent enough to make her unusual eyes flash with irritation, then launched into his spiel. "Naturally, no one at Evergreen Industries is promoting dishonesty—"

She snorted.

Ethan upped the wattage on his grin. "Instead, we're in favor of indulging the imagination of children, of perpetuating a fantasy that feeds their creativity and builds family memories to last a lifetime." He leaned forward in earnest. "Listen, the way we look at it, kids are going to have the rest of their lives to learn about truths—some of them less palatable than others—and, knowing that, I don't think that it's fair to rob children of what's ultimately a very small window of opportunity to—" he lifted his shoulders and smiled helplessly "—believe the unbelievable."

"Aw, Ethan," Mavis said, pressing a hand against her chest, seemingly overcome by emotion. "That's just beautiful. What a lovely sentiment."

He heard it then, the faint grinding of enamel against enamel, and watched Lark's expression darken with fury. He grinned widely.

"Sentiment over truth?" Lark asked, her voice climbing, her eyes widening in outrage. "Really?"

Mavis purposely ignored Lark and looked at the camera. "I'm afraid that's all we've got time for today, folks. Stay tuned for *Cooking with Constance*. She's whipping up several tried-and-true holiday desserts over in the kitchen."

Ethan waited for the all clear from the producer, then carefully plucked the microphone from his shirt and placed it on the desk. He could hear Lark grumbling under her breath.

"Despicable sentimental bullshit. 'Believe the unbelievable,'" she mimicked scathingly, her sleek black brows winging up her forehead. "Sounds like a damned campaign slogan, not a valid argument."

Mavis laid a bejeweled hand upon his arm and leaned in to better display her cleavage. "Brilliant as always, Ethan," she said. "I'd love to hear more about those new ornaments you've designed for this holiday season." She arched a hopeful brow. "Got time for a drink?"

From the corner of his eye he caught Lark's smirk, right before she turned on her heel and headed off. Ebony curls tumbled over her slim shoulders and the ruffled hem of her hooker red skirt fluttered with each seemingly exaggerated swing of her lush hips.

"Um, no, sorry," he said, unreasonably annoyed by her hasty departure. They always had a second go at one another after these little on-camera feuds. "I've got to get back to Colorado."

Before Mavis could respond, he pivoted and made his way unhurriedly across the studio to the double doors that opened into the hall. From there he bolted, eager to catch up with Lark.

"Thought you were going for a drink," she drawled as he came up behind her.

"Look at that," he said, hurrying forward to get the next door for her. God, she was gorgeous. Just stunning. "You're so sensitive to my presence you knew it was me before you could even see me. I must ping the hell out of your sonar."

She snorted indelicately and shot him a look. "Don't flatter yourself. It's your cologne, fool. It's quite—" she wrinkled her nose distastefully "—distinctive."

"I'm not wearing any cologne," he lied. It was new, dammit, and he'd bought it with her in mind. He'd overheard her tell a makeup artist last year that she loved the smell of sandalwood.

That plump mouth curved into a provocative smile. "Right," she said. "Just like you aren't wearing pants."

He fell into step beside her. Why? Who the hell knew? "I am wearing pants," he replied. "It's underwear that I'm not wearing," he added, just to needle her.

She made a small choking sound and her gaze dropped to his crotch before darting back up again. "Why are you following me?"

"Who said I was following you? I'm leaving, same as you are."

She stopped short and pointed to the ladies' room door. "I'm not leaving. I'm going to the bathroom." She directed a red-tipped nail toward the other end of the hall. "If you'd wanted to leave, you should have gone in the other direction." She frowned, feigning concern. "Do you need me to draw you a map?"

Bullshit. He didn't need a map any more than she'd been

going to the ladies' room. He shook his head. "Not necessary," he told her, then leaned casually against the wall. He pulled out his cell and began to idly scroll through his email. "I'll just wait for you and follow you out."

"Surely you have better things to do."

He looked up and smiled benignly. "I don't, actually."

"Has it occurred to you that I might?" she asked tightly.

"Of course. But I hardly see how me following you outside is going to hold you up." He'd work that bit out later. For now, it was just enough to be this close to her, to annoy the hell out of her, to make her feel half as irritated and out-of-control as he felt right now.

Or any other time he was around her, for that matter.

Clearly he'd lost his mind. And instinct, however misguided, told him she was the key to finding it.

Chapter 2

Lark DeWynter braced her hands on either side of the sink, leaned forward and peered at her forehead. She was relieved to find that "Moron" wasn't written across it. She growled low in her throat, willed her rapidly beating heart to slow into some semblance of a normal rhythm.

"He's just a man," she told herself as she stared into the mirror. "Just a man. There is absolutely nothing special about him. He's got the same parts as any other man." She looked at herself, released a breath and whimpered, "Except that his parts are way more beautiful and compelling and hot and sexy than those of any other man I've met."

The stall directly behind her opened, startling her, and her gaze met a pair of twinkling dark brown eyes set in an equally dark brown face. "Mmm-hmm." The woman grunted knowingly. "That's the way of it, all right. The Curse of the Sparkly Penis."

Lark choked. The curse of the *what*? "I'm sorry."

The woman sidled forward and pumped the soap dispenser, then lathered her hands. "The Curse of the Sparkly Penis. Girl, you know what I'm talking about. There's always one, sometimes two or even three, if you're lucky," she mused, her expression turning thoughtful. "And when a man has the sparkly penis, there's nothing a girl can do. She's powerless. Everything about him just shines a little bit more. Because he's got the Sparkly Penis, see?"

Though Lark had never seen Ethan's penis to know whether it was sparkly or not—she snickered at the thought—her imagination nonetheless conjured up images of his undoubtedly impressive penis bedazzled with rhinestones and jewels, a little Christmas wreath proudly hanging from the root.

A bark of laughter bubbled up in her throat, making the woman next to her join in until they were both nearly bent double, tears streaming down their faces.

"There you go," the woman said, nodding approvingly, her gaze wise. "Next time that man's got you tied up in knots you just imagine him with a few rhinestones on his junk and you'll be right as rain, you hear me?" She mmm-hmm'ed. "Ain't nothing a few sparkles can't fix."

Lark giggled again. "Indeed."

A tentative knock sounded at the door. "Lark?"

Lark gasped and her new friend's eyes widened. "Is that him?" she hissed.

"Lark, is everything all right in there?" Ethan asked, anxiety tingeing his silky baritone. Heaven help her, the man had the *best* voice. Low and smooth with a soft rasp at the finish that put her in mind of tangled sheets and bare limbs, of candlelight and a whole hallelujah chorus of orgasms.

Oh, who the hell was she kidding? *He* did that to her.
Just him. Only him. Ever.

It was hardly fair to blame it solely on his voice, when everything about him made her want to forget that he was her biggest adversary. She knew that she was supposed to hate him, that she was a champion for all the confused children in the U.S., the ones like her who had suffered heartache and insecurity and been the target of countless jokes and ridicule for clinging firmly to Santa Claus delusions. But it was hard—so hard—because Ethan Evergreen did the one thing that no other man had ever been able to successfully do for any length of time.

He made her remember that she was a woman.

He made her belly ache with longing, her lips tingle with the anticipation of an imagined kiss. Her palms itched to touch his bare skin, to thread her fingers through that glorious dark chestnut hair, to run the pad of her thumb over the full, unbelievably sensual curve of his bottom lip. She wanted to lick, taste and suckle every beautifully proportioned inch of his body, but more importantly, she wanted him to do those same things to her.

On a rug. In front of a fire. In some remote cabin in the woods with no television, internet or cell phone reception. Indefinitely.

"We're fine in here," the woman called out to him.

After a long pause, he returned with, "Lark?"

Though secretly touched at his concern, Lark heaved a put-upon sigh, marched over to the door and pulled it open a crack. A beautiful, startlingly green eye stared at her.

"Ethan, for pity's sake, I'm in the ladies' room." She arched an imperious brow. "How about a little privacy?"

The green eye narrowed suspiciously and tried to peer around her. "It sounds like you're having a party in there."

Lark purposely shifted, obstructing his view. "So what if we are," she said. She flicked her fingers at him impatiently. "Shoo."

"Shoo? Really?"

"*Go away.*" She shut the door once more, and leaned against it, pressing a palm to her forehead.

"Mercy, he sounds pretty."

A wan smile curled her lips and she hung her head and laughed softly. "That's because he is."

"Then what's the problem?"

Another weak laugh. "*The* problem implies that there's only one."

"Chemistry is chemistry," she said. "Problems have a way of sorting themselves out when we stop thinking with our heads and start listening to our bodies."

That sounded awfully new age and open-minded, Lark thought. It also sounded like excellent advice…if it were in relation to anything other than Ethan Evergreen.

But him? Er, no. Her mind was constantly at war with her

body when it came to him. Inside of her, self-preservation went toe-to-toe in a bare-knuckled brawl with lust—right now, self-preservation was holding its own, but it flagged every time she was around him. That's why she'd bolted the instant the interview had been over. Ordinarily she would have lingered and they would have exchanged a few more barbs, then gone for a drink where they would have continued to flirt under the guise of a heated debate—one that inevitably would have been punctuated by a little laughter and a lot of longing—and then she'd come to her senses and leave in a huff, and he'd smile because he'd realize she was just running scared. That was the trouble, in a nutshell, Lark thought. He knew too much about her. Instinctively. Sometimes when he looked at her she was utterly convinced he'd just opened up her head and taken a peek inside. It was unnerving. And slightly comforting, which she'd no doubt need to ask her therapist about, she thought with a frown. Why in the hell would she find that comforting? That sort of invasion of her mind? Her very thoughts?

Possibly because, in an odd sort of way, she thought he *got* her.

Singular, that. No one had ever gotten her, not even her parents. She'd been *that* child, the fragile one with the delusions of Santa Claus, with the hyper imagination that had animated ordinary Christmas decorations. Even now, almost twenty years later, a doctorate degree under her belt, she still fought the delusions.

Hell, just that morning she'd caught a glimpse of a wink from a nutcracker in a store window.

And then there was her snowman, Mr. Cool, who she'd snuck outside and rescued from the garbage bin all those years ago when her parents had purged all the ornaments and decorations from the house. For reasons that escaped her, she'd hung on to him, unable to let him go. A sentimental weakness, she supposed. She'd tried several times to toss him into the trash or put him in a donation box, but she could never make herself do it. He presently hung from an artificial ficus tree, a lone reminder of her past, both the good and the bad.

"Lark?" Ethan persisted.

She groaned and massaged the bridge of her nose.

Her new friend finished applying a fresh coat of lipstick. "He's persistent, isn't he?"

Yes, dammit. "Like a dog with a bone."

She shot her a knowing look. "Then clip a leash on him, honey, and bring him to heel."

Ha! As if. She'd have about as much luck clipping a leash onto Ethan Evergreen as she would onto a rabid wolverine. And that's exactly what he would turn into if she landed that coveted slot on the *Ophelia Winslow Show*.

He'd *flip*.

Naturally, that thrilled her to her little toes. And sent the teensiest dart of panic into her chest. Ethan's family, steeped in Christmas tradition, had founded Gingerbread, Colorado—"Where Christmas is always in season!"—more than two hundred years before. His entire family worked for Evergreen Industries, as did many of the residents of Gingerbread. It wasn't merely a livelihood, it was a way of life. And she was threatening it.

The success of the book had brought plenty of media opportunities, but nothing as grand or potentially far-reaching as the *Ophelia Winslow Show*. The ultimate feather in her cap, it would be a game-changer. It would give her the opportunity to share her message with millions of dedicated viewers who considered Ophelia to be a virtual oracle on all things, from the best pair of women's pantyhose to the best facial cream on the market. Lark would learn this afternoon whether or not the show was a go and, with every second that ticked by, her anticipation and anxiety increased.

She shot a helpless look at the door and imagined the man on the other side of it—tall and gorgeous, with those unusually bright green eyes—and a snake of heat coiled in her middle, making her nipples tighten behind her bra, her muscles melt with desire. She closed her eyes tightly and beat back the urge to howl in frustration.

He was not helping matters.

To hell with it, Lark thought. She needed a drink.

She thanked her new friend for the advice, then squared her shoulders and exited the bathroom without sparing Ethan a single glance—the view from the corner of her eye was enough to make her pulse trip—and started down the hall.

"It's about time," he said, naturally falling into step beside her. God, he smelled good. Lickable. "I was on the verge of sending in a search party."

"You could have left."

He chuckled. "And miss the pleasure of your company?" he drawled, the smart-ass. "Never."

"Just out of curiosity, how long do you plan on following me?"

"Why?" he asked suspiciously, shooting her a sidelong glance. "Thinking of getting a restraining order?"

Lark felt her lips twitch. "No, but a Taser might be an option."

He feigned a gasp and tsked under his breath. "Bodily injury? Really? You wound me."

A laugh tickled the back of her throat and she rolled her eyes. "Please," she said. "Only if your Arrogance Shield has failed."

He pushed through the double doors, which led out into a small alley behind the studio. The smell of diesel fuel and garbage hung in the air—Eau de New York, she'd dubbed it, missing the scent of woodsmoke and cedar in her north Georgia home.

"Arrogance Shield? You've given me a superpower? Like a superhero?" He looked positively delighted, damn him, with that endearingly boyish grin. A deep dimple emerged in his right cheek, one that only made an appearance when he smiled with his whole face.

That dimple was downright dangerous, because it made her forget that he was the enemy, that she wasn't supposed to like him, much less want to tie him to her bed with tinsel and eat him up like a Christmas cookie.

"It was an insult," she reminded him pointedly.

His grin widened. "Only if I take offense. And I don't. How about a drink, Chickadee? Got time for one more argument before you fly south?"

Chickadee? That was a new one. He'd called her everything from Sparrow to Crow over the years, good-naturedly needling her because of her "bird" name. He wasn't the only one—she'd been getting ribbed since grade school—so she was used to it.

"Might as well," she said with a sigh. "I need to make sure my Bullshit Detector is up and running. Keep talking, would you?" She smiled sweetly. "You're my best diagnostic tool."

He gave her a small bow. "I am ever at your service."

Lark grinned up at him, charmed despite herself. "Yep. It's definitely working."

She inwardly girded her loins, thinking only a magical chastity belt would provide the kind of superpower she'd need.

Heaven help her…

Chapter 3

Looking more like he was leading her to the gallows than into a local pub, Ethan smothered a smile and held the door open for Lark, then waited for her to pass through before following her inside. He caught a whiff of something spicy and sweet, like cinnamon and vanilla, and felt his groin tighten. Honestly, *only* she could smell like a damned pastry and he'd find it a turn-on.

She picked her way through the lunch crowd and found a spot at a bar in the back, then slid her lush rear end onto a stool. A bit of the tension eased out of her spine, but it still hovered around her shoulders like a shadow she couldn't shake.

He empathized.

Odd that the source of his tension was the remedy, as well.

Just being around her wound him up, but it offered a bizarre sort of release, like he could suddenly let go of breath he didn't know he'd been holding.

He settled onto the stool beside her and signaled for the bartender, then ordered a shot of Jameson.

"Hitting the Irish this early?" she asked, a faint twinkle in her lovely blue eyes.

He shrugged. "Your sincerely misguided book hit the *New York Times* best-sellers list," he drawled. "We're celebrating. What are you having?"

She shot him a slightly exasperated look, one that somehow managed to be both sexy and endearing. "'Sincerely misguided,'" she repeated. "So I'm wrong, but since I believe it, you're willing to forgive me for my opinion?" She chuckled darkly and glanced at the bartender. "Give me a Jameson as well, but make it a double. I think I'm going to need it for this particular conversation," she added, a grim undertone shading her voice.

"Are you sure you want to do that? You know you can't hold your liquor."

She lifted her adorable chin. "I can hold it just fine, thank you."

He winced significantly. "Sincerely misguided," he repeated. "It's a theme with you, isn't it? Remember that I warned you when you start coming on to me."

She snorted. "Sure. Right."

"Last year, Minneapolis," he reminded her, bringing the tumbler to his lips.

She sucked in a small gasp and glared at him. "That was a combination of new medication and alcohol," she hissed. "And I wasn't coming on to you, dammit. I was a little unsteady on my feet."

"Yes, you were," he remarked, his lips twitching. "You were all over me." *Her soft breast against his side, her head on his shoulder, her arm around his waist as he'd helped her walk back from the hotel bar to her room.*

It had been an excruciating exercise in restraint, and they both knew he could have very easily taken advantage of her. He hadn't, of course, because when the time finally came for him and Ms. Anti-Claus to share skin on a mattress, he wanted her to be fully aware of what they were doing. He wanted her to want him, to make the *deliberate* choice, not one compromised by a new migraine medication and tequila.

She peered at him, squinting thoughtfully as though she were perplexed. "How do you do it?" she asked.

"Do what?"

"Carry around that *massive* ego. It's a miracle the weight of it doesn't cripple you."

He smiled. "Lift with your knees," he said, winking at her. "That's the trick."

She chuckled softly and rolled her eyes, slid a slim finger down the side of her glass. "I knew there had to be one."

"So how have you been?" he asked. "I'm assuming writing and promoting the book has taken up a great deal of your time."

"It has," she admitted. She took a sip of her whiskey and rolled it around on her tongue, savoring the flavor. "But in a good way, you know? I've logged less hours at the clinic this year, but I'm okay with that."

Because her message was more important. Because she believed what she said. It wasn't merely a talking point for her. She was genuinely passionate about protecting children, about preventing the heartache and pain she'd hinted at in her book.

Yes, he'd read it.

Theoretically so that he'd be able to refute it. But it had actually been out of blatant curiosity and the desire to know more about her. He wondered if she knew the insights she'd provided, if she was even aware of how much of herself she'd inadvertently left on the page. Probably not.

"What about you?" she wanted to know. "How's your year been?"

"Most recently, quite hellish," he told her with a pointed smirk.

"What?" she asked innocently. "But I thought all PR was good PR…"

"Not when you're the one handling it, I assure you."

"Come on," she teased, pushing her hair away from her face in the process. "It would ruin your Christmas if you didn't have me to argue with."

Yes, it would, damn her. "You mean fight with."

"That, too," she conceded.

"Ah, but the best part of fighting is making up, and we never seem to get to that point, do we, Chickadee?"

He watched a pretty blush bloom beneath her creamy skin and her pupils dilate. She took a bigger pull from her drink. "I saw the new ornaments for this season," she said, obviously deciding a subject change was in order. "They're quite lovely."

"Thank you. I've been pleased with them." That was an understatement. Other than his debut "Frosty" series, he'd been happier with this set than he had any other, and he'd been designing ornaments for the Evergreen Collection since he'd turned thirteen. Typically ornament design fell to the women in the family, but Ethan had inadvertently shown he'd had a knack for it when his little sister, Belle, had failed spectacularly at it. He'd come to her rescue and the rest, as they say, was history. He took a little needling from his brothers, of course—boys will be boys—but when his designs had started outselling all the others and had increased the company's overall bottom line, the ribbing had stopped.

Besides, it was his outlet. He could plead "artistic solitude," go to his studio and lock himself away from the rest of the world for hours. Being the smiling, perpetually upbeat and happy face of the company wasn't exactly an easy job, but it was expected and he was good at it. He didn't complain because he was certain that each and every member of his family felt the same way about their own roles.

But it was for the greater good of the Evergreen family, so...

"The inspiration?"

"*The Night Before Christmas*, the 1949 edition illustrated by Leonard Weisgard." Ethan loved Weisgard's work. He'd written and illustrated many books throughout his career that showed incredible technical expertise, but the sense of movement and the confident use of vivid colors were especially impressive. The style was less Victorian and more contemporary, particularly for the late 1940s.

A small line appeared between her brows. "I can't say

that I recognize that edition, but if the colors are as bold as your ornaments, I'm sure I'd like it."

He was sure she would, as well. "I have an extra copy," he said. "I'd be happy to mail it to you."

She looked intrigued for half a second, then practicality prevailed. "No, thanks."

Ethan smiled and leaned over, purposely crowding her personal space. Naturally, she didn't budge. "It's just a book, Lark," he confided. "Not propaganda."

"It wouldn't matter if it were," she said, deliberately lifting her drink to her lips. "*I'm* not drinking your Christmas Kool-Aid."

"Me neither," he said with a grimace. "Our wine is *so* much better."

Her mouth dropped open. "You're in the wine business now, too? Seriously?"

Ethan chuckled at her slack-jawed expression and shook his head. "No, but that's a thought. I'd never considered marketing it before. My father makes it just for the family."

An odd expression suddenly crossed her face. Seemingly embarrassed, she looked away.

"What?" Ethan asked, intrigued.

"What, what?" She adjusted the salt and pepper shakers so they were perfectly aligned. She liked order, he'd noticed. And right angles.

"That look."

She blinked innocently. "What look?"

"Cut it out, Lark," he said, smiling. "You know exactly what I mean. What was that look for?"

A slow grin teased her lips, consenting defeat. She let go of a small sigh. "Oh, all right. Since you refuse to drop it… It was the comment about your father."

He frowned. "My father? What about him?"

She shifted uncomfortably. "I'd, uh, never thought about you having one before."

Ethan blinked and a bark of startled laughter broke from

his throat. "Never thought about me having one before?" he repeated incredulously. "A father? Really?" he teased. "Did you think I'd sprung fully grown from Santa's bag of presents?"

"Or the loins of Satan," she quipped, chuckling softly, her eyes twinkling.

"Satan?" He shook his head, chewed the inside of his cheek. "*Wow*."

"I'm only teasing," she said, still laughing.

"It might surprise you to know I have a mother, too," he said. "And a couple of brothers, and a sister and grandparents and great-grandparents, aunts, uncles and cousins. A whole family tree that is quite large, multi-forked and healthy."

She was wheezing because she was chuckling so hard now. Her eyes had watered and, most significantly, the tension he'd noticed in her shoulders had melted away. She looked happy and relaxed and…gorgeous.

Her brow briefly folded in confusion. "Multi-forked?"

Ethan tossed back the rest of his whiskey and signaled for another. "Well, you know what they say about family trees that don't fork…"

Understanding lit her gaze and she inclined her head. "Ah, right. Well, I never said I thought your parents were closely related," she pointed out.

"No, only that you thought I didn't have any, and that, if I had a father at all, it was the Prince of Darkness."

She grinned at him, not the least bit repentant. "He's royalty, isn't he? Glass half-full, remember?"

The bartender slid him a new drink and he lifted it up to send a toast in her direction. "I prefer my glass completely full."

Her cell suddenly vibrated against the tabletop, drawing her attention. An instant smile bloomed over her lips and her eyes lit with excitement. "If this call means what I think it means, you're going to need a lot more *full* glasses."

Oh, hell. That didn't sound good. Inexplicable dread suddenly swelled in his gut.

"Well?" she asked by way of greeting. "Please tell me you've got good news."

Lark gasped delightedly and, impossibly, her smile widened. When she aimed it at him, it had a distinctly cat-in-the-cream-pot element that he found more than a little disturbing.

"This Friday? Wow. That was quicker than I'd imagined, but you know I'm ready."

He'd just bet she was. And whatever it was she was ready for was undoubtedly going to make his life hell and put him in full-blown defense mode.

Like there wasn't enough going on as it was.

He'd gotten a text message from his brother that featured a new picture of Santa and had the caption "WTE?" (What the Elf?) In addition to the twenty pounds he'd lost recently, he'd dyed his hair shoe-polish black and shaved his beard. Evidently trying to look more like Guido, the thirty-something ski instructor Mrs. Claus had recently started taking lessons from. Lord... Merry was on Cougar Patrol and Kris, the very epitome of Christmas, was rocking the "old Elvis" look.

Not good. *So* not good.

"Yes, yes, I know. I'm actually looking forward to seeing his face as well. As it happens, I'll get to do that in just a second." She was staring at him, the she-devil, looking absolutely triumphant.

The dread intensified.

"Oh, yes. We're having a drink. Yes, right here with me. Oh, yeah. I'm going to get to gloat in person."

Ethan feigned dispassion and tried to appear indulgent rather than curious, though admittedly she'd set the hook and was simply toying with him until she could scoop him into the net.

But that didn't mean he had to make it easy for her.

He glanced at his watch, deliberately noted the time with an exaggerated wince, then finished his drink. He was in the process of throwing cash on the bar and sliding off his stool before she realized what he was doing.

She started. "Sorry, Lisa. Gotta run. Will get back to you later this afternoon." She ended the call and arched an accusatory brow. "Where are you going? I thought we were having a drink."

"I've had several," he said, making sure he'd added a decent tip. "I've got to get to the airport."

"Please," she scoffed. "You have a private plane. You don't have to leave right now." She shot him a calculating look. "You're running scared. Hmm. That's disappointing. Never pegged you as a coward."

Ethan chuckled. "What am I supposed to be afraid of, Chickadee? You?" he goaded, purposely baiting her.

Predictably, those pretty violet eyes sparked with irritation. "Yes, actually, but I can see how you'd underestimate me." She tapped a thoughtful finger against her chin. "I wonder if you'll still feel that way after my special guest spot on *Ophelia* airs this Friday."

Ethan stilled and the dread that had been collecting in his middle hardened into a sickening lump. *Ophelia?*

The cat-in-the-cream-pot smile again. "Ah," she breathed. "Scared now, aren't you?"

Yes, actually, his mind whirling with the potentially catastrophic implications of her little bombshell revelation. With a platform like the *Ophelia Winslow Show*, she could quite literally *ruin* Christmas. She could squash the Christmas spirit to the point that the magic wouldn't work and the millions of children around the world who anxiously waited for Santa to arrive with their presents would be so disappointed that it could take *years* to overcome. A hit like that...

It could be the end of Christmas.

The end of life as he knew it, as his entire family knew it.

And it was Ethan's job to keep that from happening.

His gaze slid to her once more, his frantic mind flipping through the various ways he could thwart her plan. Ultimately, he settled on the most drastic solution. He sent a text to his driver, summoning his car.

The only way he would be able to keep her off that show would be to make it *physically impossible* for her to be there.

All righty then, Ethan thought, resolvedly. He'd just have to kidnap her.

Chapter 4

A prick of unwelcome sympathy pinched Lark's heart at the expression on Ethan's face. She'd never seen that look before—it was an almost panicked sort of dread—and the idea that she'd put it there didn't make her want to gloat at all. In fact, she had the irrational urge to comfort him, to tell him not to worry. For the briefest of seconds he'd looked impossibly alone, the weight of the world on his shoulders.

Which was ridiculous. He wasn't alone. He had his entire family—even the parents she'd never imagined him having—at his disposal, not to mention a cache of wealthy socialites waiting in the wings. (Yes, she occasionally Googled him. No, she wasn't proud, particularly when it came to her reaction to seeing him with any of the said socialites. Like she wanted to yank out their perfectly coiffed hair and break their fake fingernails.)

"Congratulations," Ethan told her, not a hint of the previous concern visible. He was his cool, unflappable self, the quintessential beautiful businessman. "I know you've been angling for an invitation there for years."

Yes, she had. She'd expected him to cry foul, to immediately launch a counterattack. His graciousness unnerved her. She shot him a suspicious look. "You know you won't be able to offer a rebuttal, right? I'm going solo on this one."

"Of course you are. The Powerful O doesn't do rebuttals, at least not during the same show."

"Ah. So that's your angle. You're going to try to weasel your way in after me, aren't you?"

"I don't know that 'weasel' is the right word," he drawled, shooting her a sidelong look. "Shall I walk you out?"

Still confused over his behavior, it took Lark a minute to catch his meaning. "Oh. You're really leaving?"

He glanced at her, his direct gaze tangling with hers. "Yes. I'd mentioned the airport, remember?"

Right. Yes, he had. She nodded, annoyed with herself. "You did."

He lifted a brow. "When's your flight? Can I give you a lift? LaGuardia, right?"

She nodded, torn. Her plane didn't leave for another three hours, but by the time she cabbed it over and made her way through security no doubt it would nearly be time to board. But there was no point in hiring a cab when he was headed to the same place, anyway. "Yes, you can, actually. If you're sure you don't mind."

He smiled at her, just the merest arch of his lips, and she felt it all the way down to her little toes. "Not at all."

"Excellent." Lark snagged her purse, then proceeded toward the exit, Ethan strolling along behind her. She could feel the weight of his gaze slide down the back of her neck and over her shoulders, and then linger on her ass. Another sparkler of need ignited in her belly, making her bite the inside of her cheek.

On second thought, being cooped up in the back of his limousine with him probably wasn't a good idea.

Ethan reached past her shoulder and pushed open the door with a mouthwateringly large hand. He was close enough that she could smell his cologne—something musky with a whiff of sandalwood—and could feel the heat of him behind her.

Yep. Definitely not a good idea.

"You know, I think maybe I should just—"

A soft, knowing chuckle slipped past his lips, as though he'd predicted this outcome. "Who's the coward now?"

Lark didn't know what she liked less—being predictable

or being called a coward—but since she was determined not to be either of those things, she smiled as the limo driver accommodatingly opened her door. She climbed into the back of the car, Ethan close behind her. Though he could have easily sat on the opposite side, he moved in right next to her, his powerful thigh brushing hers.

He was doing it on purpose. She knew it.

Maybe that was his game, she thought. Maybe he planned to drive her so crazy with desire that she'd ultimately snap and not be able to do the *Ophelia Show*. Instead she'd be locked up in a little padded room with no windows or sharp objects, a blubbering mess in need of a bath and a brush.

Was she overreacting? Yes, of course she was, but it was better than the alternative, which was letting him get into her head more than he already had—or, more importantly, getting into her body.

She scooted over.

He laughed again. *Bastard*.

"So what's next on your agenda?" he asked her. "Got anything lined up between now and the show?"

Lark didn't know why, but an alarm sounded inside of her. It was an innocent enough question, one that often came up when they were making the talk show and radio rounds, so she didn't know why the inquiry seemed off this time…but it did.

He turned to look at her when she didn't readily answer and a shocked brow arched over his right eye. "Really? You relish the opportunity to tell me about Ophelia, knowing there's absolutely nothing I can do about it, but now your other engagements are off-limits as well?" A bark of laughter erupted from his throat and he shook his head. "Wow. Talk about good sportsmanship. I guess the gloves are really off, aren't they, Chickadee?"

How was it possible for him to sound so confident and irritating one minute, then disappointed and vulnerable the next? More importantly, why did either of those things affect her so much?

Ultimately it was the disappointment she couldn't stand. Anybody who didn't welcome the opportunity to debate their position didn't hold a firm enough one, in her opinion. Ethan might have been a pain in the ass, but he'd never been one she resented or minded.

"Lisa is rescheduling everything until after Friday," she said. "It was part of the agreement with the producers."

He turned to look at her, his gaze even. "That makes sense. She's going to want a break in your message if she's going to launch it from her show. Think she's on your team?"

She smiled. "My team?"

He returned her grin. "You know what I mean."

She did. "Honestly, I'm not sure. I know she's read the book, but... Guess I'll find out on Friday, won't I?"

"I guess you will," he said. His gaze sharpened, making his green eyes appear impossibly brighter. "Tell you what. If you're free until Friday, why don't you come back to Gingerbread with me? I'll give you the official tour. Give you a tour of my design studio, show you how the ornaments are made. I can take you to Cup of Cheer for peppermint cocoa, and we can go snowmobiling on Mistletoe Mountain." He essayed another grin. "Even introduce you to my parents, if for no other reason than to prove I've got them."

If there was anything more shocking than his invitation—where the hell had *that* come from?—it was her actually wanting to accept it. The picture he painted struck a whimsical chord, sparked a yearning so strong in her breast it nearly stole her breath. It was crazy and wrong on so many levels that she didn't know where to start, but...

Lark shook her head. "I can't."

Another flash of something unreadable—disappointment? "Can't or won't?"

"Doesn't matter. The outcome is the same." She paused. "Why?"

"Why what?"

"Why did you ask?"

He looked away. "Selfish reasons," he said. "I figured if you were going to destroy my family and my town, then you should at least see it first."

Her chest squeezed. "That's not fair."

He lifted a shoulder. "I don't think it's fair that I'm not going to get a rebuttal, either, but that's the way it is. Put the shoe on the other foot, Lark, and tell me you wouldn't feel the same way."

"That's beside the point."

"Whose point?" he scoffed. "Yours?"

They were on the expressway headed to LaGuardia now, she realized, noting the signage. "I'm flying Bluebird," she mentioned. "Would you let your driver know?"

Yes, of course she would feel the same way, but that didn't change the fact that she'd landed the slot and he hadn't, and she'd worked too hard to get her message out there to miss an opportunity like this.

She couldn't afford to squander it on things like fairness and sentimentality.

Ethan leaned forward and muttered something to the driver. But when they reached the airport, to Lark's chagrin, he drove right past the terminal for Bluebird.

"He missed it," she said, wondering if the man needed his eyesight checked. "Just have him pull over. I'll walk back."

"I can't let you do that."

"What? Walk? Why the hell not? I'm not an invalid." She leaned forward. "Here is fine," she said. "Just let me out here."

"He's not going to do it," Ethan told her.

"Not going to do it," she repeated, getting as annoyed as she was confused. "What do you mean? He's going to circle again? He doesn't have to do that. I am perfectly capable of walking back to the correct terminal. Tell him to stop."

"Just remember that I asked you nicely, okay?"

She blinked. Asked her nicely? "What?"

"Not that it'll matter, but…"

Lark caught a blur—a flick of Ethan's wrist, a little burst of light—and then suddenly darkness pulled at her. She felt her cheek land against his chest, his arm come around her shoulder, and thought she heard a faint "Ho, Ho, Ho" before the world went black.

Chapter 5

Ethan hadn't expected the whole damned family to be home when he arrived with an unconscious Lark in tow, but had anything recently gone according to his expectations?

Six pairs of startled eyes turned from the grand dining room as he made his way past, stopping him in his tracks. He blinked, not entirely sure how he planned to explain himself.

He'd *acted*. That was his job after all. Damage control.

Naturally, it was Belle who spoke first, her trusty iPad in hand. Her lips quirked with sardonic humor. "Well, this is a change, brother. Ordinarily you don't have to knock them unconscious to bring them home."

"What are you talking about?" Cole asked her. "He never brings them home. He uses the lounge attached to his studio to *entertain*," he remarked, innuendo dripping from the last word. Taryn shot her new husband a scolding look and elbowed him in the ribs, which resulted in a startled grunt of pain and a wounded frown.

She turned to look at Ethan. "Is that who I think it is?"

"Probably." Though they were both geniuses, clearly in this instance Taryn was the smarter one.

"Who do you think it is?" Dash wanted to know, ever curious, a burn hole in his shirt from his latest glassblowing project. "Should we know who it is?"

Taryn ignored him. "Cocoa?"

Ethan nodded, relieved that someone seemed to recognize the gravity of the situation. "Yes, please."

To the Evergreens, cocoa wasn't just a hot chocolate beverage—it was a magical cure-all that could do everything from eradicate the common cold to wipe out memories, which was naturally its most important purpose.

"Protect the secret" had become synonymous with "Drink the cocoa." And since the secret had to be protected at all costs...

"Son?" his mother queried cautiously, clearly wanting an explanation.

"Ethan?" his father seconded.

"I'll explain later," he promised, then headed for the stairs to take her up to his apartment. The entire Evergreen family lived in the massive Art Deco–themed lodge, each member with a set of rooms to furnish and decorate as he or she pleased, and to escape into when too much togetherness threatened to drive one insane.

Togetherness was something the Evergreens lived, ate and breathed.

Ordinarily it was a comfort—nothing ever felt quite right when he was away from his family for any extended period of time—and, of course, like most magical families, theirs was stronger when they were together.

Right now, however, as the *entire damned family* trouped along upstairs behind him, peppering him with questions he didn't know the answers to, *"comfort"* was not the word that sprang immediately to mind.

He wished everyone but Taryn would go away. His new sister-in-law was *helping*—the rest of them were just being nosy.

"Shouldn't you be working on that new software program?" he shot at Cole. "Wrangling the reindeer?" he slung at Dash. "Feeding your caffeine habit at the Cup of Cheer?" he aimed at Belle, who blushed before a mutinous expression settled over her face.

"My work is in hand, big brother." Trekking along beside him, she dropped her pointed gaze to the unconscious woman in his arms. "Yours, however, seems to be in question."

"Oh, I'd say he's got it in hand," Taryn quipped. "Or *her*, rather."

"Her?" Dash repeated as they rounded the corner.

Belle suddenly inhaled sharply. "You don't mean... No. Surely not..."

Taryn hurried around him and opened his door. "Thanks," he muttered. He continued through his sitting room into his bedroom. He actually had a spare bedroom as well, but for reasons that were all too obvious, he preferred to deposit her onto his own mattress.

A tiny frown appeared between Lark's brows as she settled against his duvet and mewled lowly, stretched and then relaxed like a sleepy kitten into the pillows. Dark lashes painted half-moon shadows beneath her eyes and her skin seemed particularly creamy against his royal-blue bedding. Her hair tumbled in long curls away from her face save a lone curl that hugged the underside of her jaw. He ached to sweep that hair back and put his lips there, feel her pulse beneath his mouth. Taste it.

"Do you need a moment?" Dash asked, laughter in his voice.

"*Explain*." The single word came from his father and was delivered with calm but powerful authority, effectively silencing the rest of the room.

Ethan straightened and looked up, hoping his expression didn't reveal just how spun-out he felt. "This is Lark DeWynter," he said. "Author of—"

"*The Christmas Lie*," his mother finished, her gaze sweeping back over Lark's sleeping form. Her lips curled. "I didn't recognize her with her mouth closed."

A titter of laughter sounded through the room and Taryn turned her head to hide her smile.

"Ah," his father said, as though that were reason enough. "So you have the situation under control. Excellent."

Belle's eyes widened and she turned to her father. "You think this is under control?" she asked, her voice climbing. "He's brought our most vocal enemy *here*. Into our *home*." Her gaze swung back to Ethan. "Have you lost your mind? Inhaled too many paint fumes in your studio?"

Ethan resisted the urge to slap a Mute charm on his sister, but that would undoubtedly result in a magick war—and they'd certainly had their share of those, some of them especially epic—which might give him momentary satisfaction, but which would not solve the issue at hand.

"Why did you bring her here?" Cole wanted to know. Unlike Belle, his older brother wasn't questioning his judgment, but was merely looking to gather facts.

"Because she's got a slot on the *Ophelia Winslow Show* on Friday and I had to stop her."

A beat of shocked silence sucked the air out of the room before Cole gave his head a small shake. "No, no, that's not what I meant. Logic demanded that you'd have proper motivation for such drastic action—and the *Ophelia Winslow Show* is certainly that," he added grimly. "I mean why did you bring her *here*? To the house? Instead of putting her up at the Nutcracker Inn, or arranging for one of the Sugarplum cottages on Holly Lake? Belle's right," he said, glancing at their sister, who nodded triumphantly. "Bringing her here increases our risk of exposure."

"It was ignorant," Dash chimed in, blunt as always. Why use five words when three would do?

"I can't afford to let her out of my sight," Ethan improvised, thankful that his reasoning sounded believable.

The truth was it had never occurred to him to bring her anywhere but here. It had never entered his head to arrange for a suite at the Inn, or one of the gingerbread house replica cottages on the lake. The image of her like this—spread out on his bed, that gorgeous hair spilling over one of his pillows—had haunted him for so long that he hadn't considered an alternative at all.

Which in retrospect was—as Dash had so succinctly put it—ignorant.

Cocoa or not, it was a risk he shouldn't have taken. He could have just as easily taken a room alongside her at the Inn—the cottage scenario would have been more difficult—or assigned an elf to follow her. His gaze slid to Lark, who'd snuggled deeper into his mattress, and something shifted in his suddenly too-tight chest.

"Of course he couldn't have taken her anywhere but here," his mother said briskly, shooting Dash a scolding look. "And I don't appreciate any of you questioning his judgment on this matter. You should be ashamed of yourselves. While I'm sure the rest of us have things we don't like about our roles within the company—"

"Here, here," Dash grunted, shoving his hair out of his face. "Nothing sexy about shoveling reindeer shit."

"If I have to deal with one more disgruntled elf, I'm moving to Holland," Belle announced with grim determination.

"The eyestrain I deal with on a day-to-day basis is hardly a cakewalk," Cole muttered.

Taryn glanced at Belle and lifted an intrigued brow. "Why Holland?"

Belle smiled. "Because that's where the tallest people in the world live."

Taryn returned her grin.

"Be all of that as it may," their mother went on determinedly. "Do any of you want to trade positions with Ethan? Be the official always-smiling-even-when-he-doesn't-want-to face of the company? Make sure the Christmas cheer stays high enough to maintain the magick? Without it Christmas isn't the only thing that disappears, you know. So does our way of life. Our very purpose. Can you imagine the responsibility? The pressure he's under *every year* to make sure our family doesn't fail?"

Belle's expression had turned thoughtful and Dash's easy grin had flatlined, leaving him unnaturally somber. Both

Taryn and Cole were looking at him as though seeing him for the first time, as if he were some sort of science project under a microscope.

His father merely smiled, indicating this was a conversation he and Ethan's mother had had before.

"And this year, in particular," his mother went on with a significant eye roll. "Merry and Kris are in the throes of a marital crisis. Have you seen her lately?" she asked Ethan's father as an aside. "She's wearing hot pink lipstick and enough eyeliner to make a drag queen jealous. It's unseemly."

"That's nothing," Cole interjected. "Kris has dyed his hair black and shaved his beard."

"And bought a new Harley," Dash added. "I saw him on Yuletide Drive this morning. No helmet, by the way."

His mother inhaled sharply. "*Santa is breaking the law?*" She shook her head. "This is much worse than I thought," she said. She glanced at her husband. "You're going to have to talk to him."

His father shrugged helplessly. "I've tried."

"You'll have to try again. We can't have a…a *rogue* Santa," she finished.

Cole stroked his jaw. "Strictly speaking, it's Belle's job, correct?"

Belle glared at him. "Way to throw me under the bus, big brother. Appreciate it."

"Back to the issue at hand," his mother continued doggedly, her patience clearly wearing thin. "Ethan has this under control. I am confident in his ability and his judgment in this matter." She leveled a look at his brothers and sister. "Be grateful that the weight of this responsibility is on his shoulders and not your own and offer assistance as needed." She swept forward and kissed him on the cheek. "If I can do anything to help, just let me know."

"Me, too, son," his father added, and then the pair of them exited the room.

"You've always been her favorite," Belle grumbled. She looked up. "But she's right. I wouldn't want your job. Give me an unhappy elf any day over the continuing survival of Christmas and our legacy."

Dash grinned. "I'll keep my shovel, thanks. Least I can bitch and moan when the mood strikes."

Cole slung an arm over Taryn's shoulder and shrugged. "I like my job. We're here if you need us."

He knew, but he appreciated the sentiment. "Thanks."

"Me, too," Dash said. "Not sure what I could do, but if you need to keep her occupied, then a tour of the farm would probably be nice. Tourists love it, and Rudolph has really been putting on a show." He frowned thoughtfully. "Getting a bit of an ego, actually. I think having a fan club might have gone to his head." He slapped Ethan on the shoulder, and then with one last look at Lark, he shook his head and walked away, leaving just Belle.

"So...what's your plan?" she asked. "Aside from cocoa? I mean, I'm assuming since you hit her with a Sleeping Beauty charm she's not here of her own volition."

"No, she's not."

Belle frowned. "Eek."

"In my defense I asked her to visit first, but she said no. Had she been cooperative I wouldn't have had to..." He struggled to find the right word.

"Abduct her," Belle supplied.

"*Contain* her," Ethan improvised. "I can't let her go on that show, Belle. I can't do a rebuttal and with the success of the book, I'm already working twice as hard as I did last year. If Ophelia takes up her cause..." He shrugged. "I don't know that I can do enough damage control to save Christmas."

She nudged him admonishingly. "Why didn't you say something?"

"It's my job."

"You make it look easy."

He chuckled darkly and passed a hand over his face. "It's not."

Belle's gaze slid to Lark. "And it's her fault? This book she's written?"

"It's called *The Christmas Lie*, and she believes it, Belle. She's not a nut or a fanatic. Other than her penchant for trying to ruin Christmas and by default my life, she's actually quite nice."

His sister's gaze sharpened and then lit with an uncomfortable amount of understanding. "Oh, she is, is she?"

"Save it," he told her, annoyed with himself. "I've been arguing with her for years and I've done my homework here." He explained her history, her insistence as a child that Santa was real, that she could see ornaments move. He added that she'd even met an elf, that her family had placed her in therapy and stripped the house of any reminders of Christmas.

Belle swallowed. "Wow."

"I know."

"Yes, but how do you know? Did she tell you?"

Ethan hesitated. "Not exactly, but she alluded to enough of it in interviews and in her book that I was able to put the pieces together. I slipped her former therapist a little cocoa and reviewed her case history."

His sister was thoughtful for a moment. "Do you think she was telling the truth as a child? That she could really see the magick? I mean, lots of children can see Santa, but *elves*? *Animation*? *Like us*?"

"It's rare, but it happens," he told her. "I've got to do some more research."

"What do you hope to accomplish by bringing her here?"

The question startled him. "I want to keep her off the *Ophelia Show*, obviously."

His sister merely smiled, stared at him for a long moment. "That's your objective, E, but it's not your end goal."

Ethan's heart had inexplicably started to pound and his

mouth had gone bone-dry. "I don't know what you're talking about."

"Oh, I don't doubt that," she said with an infuriating little smile. "But I'm sure it will come to you." She leaned up and kissed him on the cheek. "And, oh, to be a fly on the wall when it does. I'll have Cook bring up some cocoa," she said as she turned to leave. "And Ethan?"

Still unaccountably shaken by his sister's cryptic little comment, he started. "Yes?"

"Did you bring her any clothes? Toiletries? Even a toothbrush?"

He blinked, and then he swore.

Belle grinned and shook her head. "Don't worry. I'll take care of it. I'll call Baubles and have him put some things together for her. You'll need to tell her that they're hers and pack it into some luggage."

He nodded. "Right. Yes. I'll do that."

"How long before the charm wears off?"

He winced as he thought about it. "Two, maybe three hours."

She smiled. "Then you'd better get busy."

Yes, he'd better, Ethan thought. He had to get his story straight—and the props to go along with it—if he was going to pull this off. Because cocoa or no, convincing Lark DeWynter that she was there by choice was going to be a hard sell.

And he had a lot riding on her buying it.

Chapter 6

Like a flower blossoming in the morning light, Lark awoke slowly, a feeling of contentment, of warmth and happiness, clinging to the instant smile that shaped her lips. The taste of chocolate haunted her tongue as she stretched and blinked sleepily awake…

…in a bed that wasn't hers, in a room she didn't recognize.

The carved mahogany canopied bed, draped in heavy royal-blue velvet, was something straight out of a fairy tale, and the room was equally opulent. A barreled ceiling gave way to watered silk, and heavy wooden paneling covered the walls. An enormous oriental rug—probably Aubusson—lay spread invitingly over the floor. Candlelight danced in sconces and firelight flickered from the massive marble fireplace against the opposite wall. The room was furnished with lots of beautiful antiques and comfortable, squashy chairs. It was gorgeous and masculine, and it had a lived-in feel. There were books and reading glasses on the table next to the window, a green silk tie slung over the arm of a chair. Wait a minute. She recognized that tie. It belonged to a man with eyes of the same color, and…

Lark sucked in a breath as she scrambled into a sitting position.

"Ah, you're awake," a familiar voice drawled.

Her gaze swung to the foot of the canopied bed. Ethan sat in one of the chairs flanking the massive carved fireplace—how in the hell had she missed him?—his feet propped up on a footstool, a cut-crystal tumbler of golden liquid in his hand. He wore a pair of jeans, a dark gray cable-knit sweater and an equally thick pair of gray socks on his feet. There was something about seeing him without shoes—or hell, even in jeans—that made her feel acutely off-balance.

He was formidable enough in a Tom Ford suit, but in casual wear? In what was obviously *his* room, in *his* house—which meant this had to be *his* bed—he was positively lethal.

And if this was indeed all of those things—his room, his house, his bed—then that meant she was in Colorado...and she had absolutely no recollection of getting there.

Lark frowned and gave her head a little shake. She had so many questions she didn't know which one to ask first. Her memory was muddled and fuzzy, and what should have been obvious answers hovered just out of reach.

"Um... How did I get here?"

Ethan grinned. "We flew," he said. "Honestly, Lark, I knew you'd had a little too much to drink, but I didn't think you'd had enough to forget a cross-country flight." He lifted a brow. "Do you want to shower before dinner? We've got reservations at eight."

Too much to drink? At the bar? But she remembered leaving the bar and heading to the airport. And after? She wracked her brain as she struggled to remember.

He stood and made his way over to her, lifted a pretty silver cup from the bedside table and handed it to her. "Here," he said. "My mother is a firm believer in cocoa and says there's nothing a little of it can't fix."

Lark unthinkingly accepted the drink and took a sip, still desperately trying to make sense of things. Oddly enough, she wasn't afraid or even terribly alarmed, but she felt like she should have been. It was weird...and, *oh sweet heavens*, this was the *best* cocoa she'd ever had in her life. It was creamy and rich—positively decadent. An immediate warmth spread through her limbs when it hit her belly.

"Mmm," she said. "This is good."

"I'm so glad you agreed to come out here with me," Ethan told her. "It was the honorable thing to do, all things considered."

She opened her mouth to argue, but the words instantly died in her throat. Truthfully, she didn't remember agreeing to come out here with him, but since she was here and she never did anything she didn't want to do, it only stood to reason that she had. Right? Right.

"Honorable?" She took another sip of cocoa.

"You know. Since I'm not going to get a rebuttal on the *Ophelia Winslow Show*, you thought it would be good for you to at least see my world and my town before launching your agenda from a platform that doesn't offer a quid pro quo." He smiled sincerely. "That was very fair of you. I appreciate it."

Once again the instinct to argue arose, but it died a swift death and she nodded. It *was* good of her. And it *was* fair. But...it didn't exactly feel right and, more importantly, it didn't explain how she'd gotten into his bed.

"Erm..."

Seemingly anticipating her question, he smiled again, this time a little sheepishly. "You passed out," he said. "I've never seen you drink that much. You were 'celebrating,'" he added with a significant look. "I had to carry you from the plane to the car, and then carry you into the house. I suppose I could have gone a few extra steps into the next room—" he jerked his head toward a door across the room "—but it was just easier to put you here."

Lark's cheeks burned. He'd had to *carry* her? *Really*? Rather than being alarmed that she'd ingested enough alcohol to incapacitate and give her memory loss, irrationally, she was more irritated over not being able to remember *that* part. Being carried. By him. In those mouthwateringly powerful arms. Her mouth close to his neck.

Need licked through her veins, making her aware of the

mattress beneath her and Ethan's exceedingly close proximity.

His eyes suddenly darkened and dropped to her mouth. "Unless you intend to stay in here, you need to stop looking at me like that, Chickadee."

She blinked, feeling her face warm even more. With effort, she swung her legs over the side of the bed and stood, forcing him to retreat a step. "My room is through there, you say?" she asked, pointing toward the closed door.

"It is. Because it was a spur-of-the-moment trip, my sister, Belle, arranged to have some clothes and toiletries delivered. If there's anything else you need, or if something doesn't fit correctly, let me know and I'll take care of it."

She blinked again, startled that she'd done something so out of character, something that had required someone else to think of her clothes and toiletries. Lark was an obsessive planner. She lived by her calendar. In fact, she'd gotten pretty anal about it, actually keeping track of her time to the point last year that she could graph it out and look at exactly how much time she'd spent working, sleeping, socializing—the woefully smallest sliver of the pie chart—and everything that fell in between. She couldn't decide if that was efficient or pathetic. Probably both.

"Thank you," she said, feeling even more at sea. "And thank your sister for me, too."

Another grin dimpled his cheek. "Oh, you'll be able to tell her yourself. I'm sure you'll see her around."

"Around where?"

"Here," he said, as though it should be obvious. "She lives here. Like I do. Like my whole family does."

Surprise rippled through her. "You live with your family?"

"Yes. We've each got our own set of rooms, of course—" he gestured to his "—but we're a tight-knit family, and the house is big enough to accommodate us all, so…" He shrugged. "It's nice."

Wow. She never saw her family. Her older brother had been resentful of her for ruining Christmas, and her parents had decided to homestead in Alaska right after she left for college. So much for going home for the summer. Though she'd occasionally gone to visit them over the years, they seemed entirely too nervous with her around for her to ever feel at ease. It saddened her to think about it, and she envied Ethan his close-knit family.

"You should wear the dress," he said, startling her.

"What?"

"To dinner. We're going to the Crystal Snowflake. It's nice. I think you'll like it."

She was sure she would, but she'd pick out her own clothes out of the clothes she hadn't picked out, thank you. She lifted her chin. "I think I know how to dress myself, Ethan."

His smile widened and those gorgeous bright green eyes twinkled with humor. "I'm sure you do."

Lark nodded and took another sip of her cocoa. She was strangely at peace, completely unconcerned about everything, including the fact that she'd journeyed to Colorado to stay with Ethan out of the goodness of her heart and in fairness to her upcoming visit on the *Ophelia Winslow Show*.

And though, deep down, it felt a bit out of character, Lark was certain it wasn't. And anyway, the cocoa was divine…

Though Ethan knew he was doing the right thing for his family and for everyone who enjoyed the magic of Christmas, he couldn't shake the guilt. Watching the cocoa work its magic and override that stubborn, bull-headed, opinionated woman's natural objections and tendencies had been as comical as it was…wrong.

But he didn't know what else to do. He absolutely *couldn't* let her go on that show.

The greater good, he reminded himself. Eyes on the prize.

Lark chose that moment to walk through the door and that last thought took on a whole new meaning.

Mercy.

"You decided to wear the dress."

Her lips curved. "How could I not? It's incredible. Your sister has excellent taste."

That she did. A deep purple, the dress was scoop-necked, with long sheer sleeves accented with crystal-studded cuffs. It hugged her curvy frame like a second skin, molding to the luscious swell of her breasts and clinging to her womanly hips. The hem stopped just above the knee—it was long enough to be appropriate, but short enough to reveal a serious amount of leg. She had paired it with black pumps and a matching bag, and with her hair hanging loose around her shoulders and her make-up a little more dramatic than usual, she looked…stunning.

Prior to her arrival, Ethan had been practically starving, but a hunger of another sort suddenly took hold of him. Longing coiled through his body, settling hotly in his groin, and his mouth actually ached for the taste of her. He wanted to slide his nose along the creamy column of her throat, slip his tongue over the swell of her breasts, sample the valley in between them. It took a supreme amount of effort to pull himself together and say something that sounded somewhat normal.

"You look beautiful," he said, his voice oddly rusty.

Those unusual violet eyes warmed and shifted away, almost shyly. Her? Shy? Had she gotten into more cocoa?

"Thank you." She nodded at him. "You look nice as well."

He chuckled. "This old thing?"

She rolled her eyes. "Old, my rear end," she scoffed. "The only thing that seems the least bit old around here is the furnishing, and in that case, it's a good thing."

"I like antiques," he said. "They've got character."

She nodded. "And better craftsmanship. I've got a few as well."

He'd just bet she did. He hummed thoughtfully under his breath and considered her. "I've often wondered about your lair," he said musingly.

Lark laughed, her eyes widening briefly. "My lair? You make me sound like a comic book villain."

"Well, I've never pictured you in a bat cave, if that helps," he said, chuckling. "More of a secret tree house, with a hidden elevator in the trunk."

She chewed the inside of her cheek. "Like a nest."

Ethan felt his grin spread. "Exactly like a nest."

She released a little breath. "I wish my parents had named me something simple, like Jane or Sarah," she said, giving her head a rueful shake.

"No, you don't," he told her. "You're neither of those. The bird name suits you. I like it." A thought struck him. "What's your middle name?"

"Lark is my middle name," she said a little too quickly. "Shouldn't we be going? You said our reservation was at eight." She checked her watch. "It's a quarter til now. How long does it take to get to the Crystal Snowflake?" she asked rapidly as she headed out the door, despite the fact that she had no idea how to locate the car, or the restaurant, or hell, even the front door.

Intrigued by her cat-on-a-hot-tin-roof response, Ethan followed her into the hall, where she drew up short. "Oh."

One direction must have looked the same as the other to her. Ethan smiled and guided her forward with a touch to the small of her back. "It's not nearly as daunting as it looks. This way," he said.

"It's...massive."

"I told you that my entire family lives here. There are too many of us to have any smaller of a place. We'd drive each other crazy. Still do sometimes," he added with a grim smile, remembering how they'd followed him upstairs earlier. "But the central staircase is just up and to the right. See?" he told her as they rounded the corner.

He heard her delighted gasp and felt a dart of pleasure land in his chest. It was his home, but it was impressive.

Particularly the central staircase.

Carpeted in thick jewel-toned colors with the Evergreen coat of arms cameoed throughout, bounded by rails and spindles intricately carved with garlands, pine cones and bows, the staircase was a testament to fine elfish craftsmanship. Creamy marble inlaid with subtle wreaths of holly leaves and berries blanketed the foyer floor and the enormous arched double doors matched the exquisite carving on the staircase.

"Wow," she said, running a reverent finger along the banister as they descended the stairs. "This is incredible."

Just wait until you see Mistletoe Mountain and Gingerbread proper, Ethan thought. Rather than use one of the elf tunnels that led directly to different parts of the town—their own magical subway system—as he normally did, Ethan had called for his car. To get the full effect of his little piece of earth, one needed to be aboveground. He was looking forward to seeing Lark's reaction to it.

"Thank you," he murmured. "So what's your first name then?"

She snatched her hand away as though she'd been burned. "I'd rather not say."

Ethan smiled. "I'd rather you did. Your reluctance is intriguing. It must be something ghastly if you're this determined not to share it." He paused. "Is it another bird name, I wonder? Like Falcon?"

She shot him a you've-lost-your-mind look. "Falcon Lark? Really? That's your best guess?"

"Not my best guess, just my first," he told her as he opened the front door. "And I've got the rest of the week to keep trying."

It was ridiculous how happy that made him, the excitement that tripped through his blood. He had a sense that something fantastic was near, but was still hovering just shy of his grasp.

It was the challenge, Ethan told himself. Nothing more. It was his determination to succeed.

And if he made a Christmas convert of her and finally managed to take her to bed and get her out of his system, all the better. He smiled.

Two Larks with one stone.

Chapter 7

With the "rest of the week" comment echoing in her ears and the faint hum of an alarm bell ringing along with it, Lark stepped through the huge double doors. If she'd been impressed by the house, then "blown away" was a more accurate description for the view that greeted her outside.

It looked like a scene straight from a greeting card.

Moonlight glittered with a luminous, almost otherworldly blue glow over rolling hills blanketed with snow. Enormous spruce trees, equally covered, their branches sagging beneath the weight, cast dark shadows in the night. Swans glided across a large lake, its center illuminated by a tall carved-ice fountain shaped like an angel tree topper, and twinkling lights from what had to be Gingerbread shimmered in the valley below like diamonds on a jeweler's cloth. She smiled, charmed despite herself.

"That's incredible," she said, giving her head a disbelieving shake.

"What? Hortense?"

"The fountain."

"Yes, Hortense. My brother Dash named her this year."

They descended the steps to what she presumed was his car, a sleek black Jaguar that suited him, and she waited while he opened her door. "So it's a tradition, then?"

"Yes."

She missed traditions. She'd established her own, of course—she always worked at the local soup kitchen on Christmas Day—but it wasn't the same as having one with a family. Though she'd tried to forget, she remembered that much about their early Christmases. Decorating the tree, making cookies for Santa the night before, eating a big pancake breakfast after opening presents. A needle of pain pricked her heart at the memory. She hadn't allowed herself to think about that in years.

"I named her last year," Ethan announced as he slid behind the wheel and turned the ignition, and then slipped the gear shift into drive.

"Oh?" she asked, thankful for the distraction.

"Yes."

"So who was she last year?" Lark asked. "Trixie? Tiffany? Celeste?" she drawled, immediately wishing she could pull the words back into her mouth.

He turned briefly to look at her, his expression a combination of surprise and delight. "None of the above, though I think it's sweet that you've been paying enough attention to my social life to read about the dates I take to charity events."

Crap. She feigned shock. "Those are the names of the women you've dated? Really? Wow. I had no idea."

He merely smiled. "Right. I'm sure you didn't."

"So what was her name then? The fountain angel?" she asked, eager to move past *that* particular topic.

He negotiated a bend in the road, one that left an unobstructed view of the little town as they grew closer. The lights were brighter and the colors more vibrant, and she found herself inexplicably leaning forward, eager to see more.

"Flossie."

A startled chuckle broke up in her throat and she turned to look at him. "Flossie?"

"Yes, Flossie," he said with a nod. "What's wrong with Flossie?"

"Not a thing." Lark looked ahead once more, surprised to see that they were just coming into town. Wide sidewalks lit by candy cane–like gas lamp posts lined a street called

Yuletide Drive, and live evergreen garlands festooned with big bows and curling ribbon were draped from posts, storefronts and even the grills of local cars. Christmas lights spun around trees, dripped from eaves and sparkled in windows. Life-sized nutcrackers marched along the streets, small people dressed as elves darted to and fro, looking busy and important and Christmas ornaments dangled from... *everything.*

An overwhelming wave of joy suddenly swept through her, followed by a delight so profound she could feel it expanding in her chest. It was the strangest sensation, a combination of relief and odder still...homecoming? There was a familiar shimmer to the ornaments, a certain glow and, as they passed a pair of tall wooden toy soldiers stationed outside a store called Baubles, she could have sworn that one of them actually smiled at her.

But it couldn't have. Because it wasn't a real person. *Logic, Lark,* she reminded herself, struggling not to panic. *Use your brain.* What was she doing here again? Why had she agreed to come here with him? It didn't make any sense.

"Is something wrong?" Ethan asked, his voice heavy with concern.

She started. "No, no. I'm fine. Just hungry," she improvised.

She could feel his gaze on her, the weight of it as he studied her, but thankfully he didn't push it. "Well, we've come to the right place, then," he said as he pulled the car into a space. "You're going to love the Crystal Snowflake. It's got the *best* cocoa in Gingerbread."

Lark chuckled. Unless it was laced with something alcoholic, she didn't think plain old cocoa was going to take the edge off. Between Ethan's perpetual sexiness pinging her sonar, the conflicting emotions about being here in Christmas Land and the niggling sense of something being not quite right, she was going to need something much stronger.

Ethan's fingers suddenly landed against her chin, turning her toward him, and his mouth met hers for the briefest of seconds, sending shockwaves of heat through her body. Her blood instantly boiled up beneath her skin, her breath caught in her throat and pleasure bloomed through her, petals of sensation so intensely hot and sweet she didn't know whether to kiss him again or weep. Probably both.

Lord, she was a mess—an absolute mess—and it was all *his* fault.

Seeming every bit as startled as she felt, he drew back to look at her, those singularly gorgeous green eyes lacking their usual irreverence and bravado. "I'd say I was sorry, but it would be a lie," he told her, his voice low and husky. "I've wanted to do that for years."

And she'd wanted him to do that for years. Lark knew that under ordinary circumstances she'd offer some sort of flippant remark, one that would be witty and slightly cutting, but for reasons that escaped her, the comment wouldn't come.

She swallowed, her gaze drifting of its own volition to his mouth. Her belly gave a little drop and longing ballooned inside of her. "Years, you say? Really?"

He nodded.

She hummed a regretful breath. "Seems like you'd have given it a little more effort, then. Maybe lingered a little—"

The smile that suddenly curled his lips did the same thing to her toes, and he leaned in, a mere hairbreadth from her mouth. "Critiquing me, Chickadee?" he asked, his strong fingers slipping into her hair. "You telling me there's room for improvement?"

A thrill whipped through her. "I'm not sure yet. It didn't last long enough for me to make a proper assessment."

"Hmm. I understand. I'll give it another go and you let me know how I do, okay?"

The next instant that supremely beautiful mouth molded to hers, slipped across her lips with expert skill—soft but firm and oh so hot—and his tongue dipped into her mouth and tangled around hers. The rest of the world just fell away, shrinking until there was nothing left but the two of them and a fog of desire so thick she could barely catch her breath.

A few moments later, hands trembling, Ethan drew back and rested his forehead against hers. "Well?" he asked, his voice slightly strangled. "How did I do?"

How'd he do? He'd practically set her underwear on fire and turned her into a melted puddle of goo. Parts of her were aching that she didn't know could ache, bits of her body were shaking that had never shaken before. And he had the presence of mind to ask for marks on his performance when she could barely string a coherent thought together?

Considering all of that, *she* was probably the one who had room for improvement.

Lark pulled in a breath and pretended to mull it over. "Better," she said. "Definitely better."

Ethan chuckled. "Hardly the ringing endorsement I'd hoped for," he said. "But I'm eager to improve and you know what they say about practice."

Yes, she did. And, heaven help her, she looked forward to working on his technique.

Chapter 8

"So you're giving her the guided tour this morning, eh, son? What's first on the agenda?" his father wanted to know.

"You should take her to the Cup of Cheer," Belle said, slathering jam on her biscuit. "They have the *best* peppermint cocoa," she confided with a look at Lark.

"You can get good cocoa anywhere in Gingerbread," Dash argued good-naturedly. He loaded a stack of bacon on his plate before passing the platter to Cole. "Don't waste your time there. Bring her out to the reindeer farm. They're beautiful animals. Very sweet. Most of the time," he added grimly. "That Rudolf..."

"Still having trouble with him?" their mother wanted to know. "I warned you about that fan club, but did you listen?" She shook her head.

Having paid attention to the Evergreen family chatter for the past few minutes, Lark's eyes widened. "Rudolf has a fan club?"

"He does," his mother confirmed, adding sugar to her cocoa. "And it's gone straight to his head. You wouldn't think fame could go to an animal's head, but it has." She tsked under her breath. "I don't know what you're going to do with him. But the deer is out of the barn now. It's too late to close the door."

"I've got it under control," Dash assured her.

"You should bring her to the offices," Cole suggested. "Show her Evergreen Central."

"Or," Taryn interjected with a secret smile, "you could

actually *ask* her what she'd like to do and let her make the choice."

Every pair of eyes at the table swung to Lark and waited expectantly. Her cocoa cup halfway to her mouth, her hand stalled. "Er…"

Ethan decided to save her. "She's my guest," he reminded them. "I have every intention of making sure that she stays entertained."

And if kissing her counted as entertaining her—and since this was his rodeo and he was making up the rules, it did—then he was already ahead by leaps and bounds. It had taken every iota of willpower he possessed to actually let her go through to her own room last night. And honestly, even now he couldn't explain why he'd done it. Why, when she was *right there* and for all intents and purposes, his for the taking…he'd let the evening end with a kiss.

He'd never thought of himself as particularly old-fashioned or chivalrous, but that was the only explanation his mind could produce that made any sort of sense. Watching her as they'd driven into town last night—seeing her expression go from awestruck wonder and delight to abject fear and despair, seemingly in a heartbeat… He couldn't imagine what she'd witnessed that could have put that haunting look on her face, but it had done something to him, seeing her that way. She was scrappy, a fighter. The Lark DeWynter he knew didn't back down, didn't run, but she would have last night if it hadn't been for the cocoa.

He was sure of it.

And that was ultimately the problem. He'd tricked her into coming here. For good reasons, he knew, but…

He couldn't trick her into his bed.

That was a different kind of betrayal, one he suspected would again put that terrible look he'd noticed on her beautiful face last night. He wouldn't be able to handle it, knowing he'd hurt her like that.

So he wouldn't. And that would be his penance. Not having her, when everything inside of him yearned with a need so powerful and magnetic that he literally *ached* with it. His gaze slid to her, over the lovely slope of her cheek, the upturned corner of her ripe mouth, and his groin tightened painfully, his chest squeezing with some peculiar emotion.

Fair enough, Ethan decided. Fair enough.

Having been to the Cup of Cheer for the peppermint cocoa—Belle had been right, it was divine—and out to tour the reindeer farm (where she thought she'd seen Rudolf's nose blink a few times, and yes, the animal had definitely developed a bit of an ego) Lark was presently strolling around Ethan's studio, which was housed on the very top floor of Evergreen enterprises.

It was not at all what she'd expected.

In the first place, it was a tall, sleek metal-and-glass building. One would assume it would be outfitted with commercial-grade carpet, serviceable paint, efficient work stations and low-tiled ceilings.

But, no.

Much like the rest of the village, the interior was more in keeping with a Swiss village motif. Lots of rich paneling, oriental rugs, framed portraits of Santa and Christmas scenes and, though she was trying to avoid stereotyping, there were lots of little people, some of them dressed in business casual, some of them dressed more like elves. Everyone wore interesting badges with their clearance level—Ethan's was gold, which indicated he had executive clearance—and everyone seemed extraordinarily busy and happy.

She stopped at a few sketches of birds—chickadees, doves, red and blue birds—and turned to look at him. "Is this what you're thinking about for next year?"

In the process of inspecting a new batch of ornaments—quality control, he'd explained—he looked up and smiled. "Ah, yes," he told her. "Do you like them?"

She hesitated. "I do."

He stilled. "You do, but?" he prodded. "I know there's a but. I heard it in your voice."

Of course he had. He heard everything, whether she said it or not. It was unnerving. Less so than normal, which she somehow knew but couldn't explain. Sitting beside him at breakfast this morning, sharing the first meal of the day with all of them and listening to them good-naturedly rib each other, talk about their plans for the day...

Something about it had made him *more* than the Ethan she knew. She was familiar with the rich, sexy executive, the one who argued with her, goaded and teased her, enflamed her. But he was so much more than that. He was part of something huge, a centuries-old heritage.

And he *did* have parents, she thought with an inward chuckle, and brothers and a sister, and they were all part of a team, one that was at odds with her own pitiful team of one. Somehow being here made her feel not necessarily less committed to her cause, but almost petty for clinging so tightly to it.

Though she was exceedingly reluctant to admit it, he'd been right about her visiting his little town, meeting his family, seeing just exactly what it was they all stood to lose when she went on the *Ophelia Winslow Show* on Friday. She was glad she'd done the right thing by coming here. She couldn't say that it had changed her position—though seeing that toy soldier wink at her had certainly rattled her last night, and there'd been a couple of instances already this morning that had made her question her eyesight—but it had certainly given her a more well-rounded perspective.

Kissing him, she told herself, had absolutely nothing to do with it. *Nothing,* she thought more forcefully, remembered heat snaking through her limbs. Nothing, nothing, nothing. She wasn't that shallow. She couldn't be. She wouldn't let herself be.

Not that he seemed inclined to do anything more than kiss her anyway, which had been both surprising and disappointing. He'd been flirting with her for years, priming her for what she could only imagine would be the best sex of her life and last night, when he could have pressed his advantage—hell, his bed had been *right* there—he hadn't. And after that kiss...

It had been quite...irritating.

Granted she wasn't exactly an expert on all things sexual, but she could generally discern when a man was attracted to her and that magnificent bulge against her belly last night when he'd given her a final farewell kiss, well... It had been pretty telling. She didn't know why he hadn't—

"Lark?" he prodded. "You all right?"

She blinked, momentarily startled. "Yes, just gathering my thoughts."

He rested a hip against the table. "Are you going to tell me what it is that you don't like about the birds?"

"Oh, they're beautiful," she said. "And it's not that I don't like them—I do." She struggled to find the words for what she was feeling. "It's just...I don't know. There's something different about them. They don't have that whimsical feel that all of your other designs have." She went to the case where all of his designs were displayed. "For instance, look at this teddy bear—there's a sparkle in his eye. And this nutcracker? There's something about his smile. He looks like he's in on a joke I'm not aware of." She moved farther down the case. "And this—" She stopped short.

Ethan frowned and followed her gaze. "Oh, that's Frosty," he said, smiling, as he moved to stand beside her. "He was my first ornament."

She reached out almost reverently and slid a finger over him. "I called him Mr. Cool," she said softly.

She'd called him—but— Ethan's heart skipped a beat. There'd only been a few hundred produced, nothing compared to his designs now, and she'd had one? "You had my Frosty?"

Her lips faltered with a smile. "Have him," she corrected.

"I rescued him from the garbage bin after my parents purged our house the last year we celebrated Christmas." She turned to look at him. "I've never told you that, have I? I mean, you know enough about my past to put things together—you're clever, after all—but that's what happened. I really *believed*, Ethan. My delusions were so detailed, so real, that I believed I talked to Santa, and his elf Edgar," she added with a rueful laugh. "I believed so deeply that my Mr. Cool even changed his clothes—his scarf would have holly berries one minute and snowflakes the next. I'd see toy soldiers wink, nutcrackers smile, angel wings flutter."

So he'd been right, Ethan thought, her confession tearing at him. She *could* see the magic.

And no one had believed *her*.

She lifted her shoulders in a fatalistic shrug. "I don't blame my parents," she said. "It's no wonder they thought I was crazy. Hell, there are still times when I'll catch a glimpse of something and think I'm crazy."

A *glimpse*, Ethan thought, his brain seizing on the word. That's what she was. A glimpse. One of those rare, rare children who could see the Christmas magick.

And, more importantly, could *still* see it.

That's what was missing from the birds. They were merely drawings at this stage, hadn't been enchanted with the magick. And that's no doubt what had happened last night. She'd caught sight of something and had immediately panicked, thinking she was experiencing a delusion.

His heart ached for her and he instinctively put an arm around her, pulling her close. How terrible it must have been to be so sure of your own mind, your own eyes, only to have the world convince you otherwise. Even your own parents. No wonder she'd fought as hard as she had. No wonder she was so passionate about her cause.

She relaxed into him, seemingly grateful for the support. "I'm so sorry, Lark," he said. "I—"

Her cell suddenly went off and she shifted away, almost

guiltily, and pulled it from her purse. "It's Lisa," she said, reading the display.

Lisa? Oh, hell.

"Hey, Leese," she said. "What's up?"

Ethan turned and discreetly muttered a few choice words under his breath.

Lark suddenly frowned. "Lisa? I can't hear you. We've got a bad connection. Must be the building. I'll give you a call back in a few minutes."

Oh no, you won't, Ethan thought. "Come on," he said. "We'll go downstairs and grab some cocoa and a cinnamon roll, and have a mini picnic by the lake."

She smiled. "Thanks, Ethan. That would be great."

He nodded and returned her grin. He had turned to leave when she stilled him with a touch of her hand. "And thanks for listening a few minutes ago," she said sheepishly. "And for not making fun. I appreciate it."

"Anytime," he said, his throat suddenly getting tight. He'd been on the verge of telling her the truth—that she hadn't been crazy or delusional, that she'd been right. A cardinal sin among their kind.

Protect the secret.

And yet, for the first time in his life, he deeply resented that edict. She deserved to know the truth—to know that she was special, not damaged. And yet he couldn't tell her.

Because what if she didn't believe him? What if she decided he was the one who was delusional and it only reinforced her own position in her own mind? There were too many what-ifs, too many things that could spell disaster for his family.

And while he could argue that he could tell her now, give her that peace of mind for however brief a moment and then hand her the cocoa, wouldn't that be crueler? To fully open her eyes to the magick and then take it back? Ethan swallowed.

He'd be no better than everyone else who hadn't believed her.

He couldn't do it.

And honestly, at this point, he didn't have a frigging clue what he was going to do, other than spend as much time with her as possible, show her his world…and keep his hands to himself.

Chapter 9

"That was *amazing*," Lark said, feeling the rush of excitement and the burn of adrenaline tripping through her veins as she climbed off the back of the snowmobile. "Absolutely incredible."

In the process of dusting the snow off the front of his pants, he looked up and shot her a smile. "I'm glad you liked it. I told you you would."

"Yes, you did. You were right," she said. "Feel better?"

He nodded, the wretch. "Yes, I do, actually. You'll have to come back soon and I'll teach you how to drive."

A bubble of sadness burst inside her at the thought of leaving the next morning. The past few days had been so unbelievably bizarre. She'd spent practically every minute with Ethan, which had been a combination of fantastic and torturous. Or as she liked to call it...

Her own personal hell.

She'd known deep down that there'd always been something special about him—aside from the off-the-charts attractiveness—but seeing him in his element, watching him in his studio and at his family home... He was a genuinely great guy. He had a wonderful sense of humor; he was an excellent conversationalist; he was witty and clever and, as she'd learned recently, he had more willpower than anyone she'd ever met.

She knew he wanted her—*she c*ould feel it when he looked at her, when those startlingly green eyes raked over her body. She could feel his longing in her damned bones. But despite the fact that she'd all but crawled into bed with him, he'd very politely—and regretfully—kissed her good night at her bedroom door.

And that had been all.

For the life of her she couldn't understand it. It didn't make the least bit of sense. They were both adults, both consenting and, after tomorrow when her *Ophelia Winslow Show* aired live, it was entirely possible they'd no longer be friends. Or even frenemies, as they'd been up to that point.

Which, of course, depended on what she said when she actually went on the *Ophelia Winslow Show,* and the truth was...she was no longer sure what that was going to be. Everyone's perception was their own reality. And the Evergreens? Christmas tradition, Christmas spirit...it was their way of life. It was the only way they knew. And the town, with Baubles and Cup of Cheer and the Toy Shop and all the beautiful decorations? It was more than charming—it was *special*. She could feel that, too. The air here was different, and it seemed to shimmer and glow a little more brightly.

Oddly enough, she'd felt more at home here in the last few days than she had in Georgia, where she'd lived her whole life. And, sad as it was to admit it, she liked Ethan's family more than she did her own.

"I thought we'd eat upstairs tonight," Ethan said, opening the back door for her. A blanket of heat from the house wrapped around her and she smiled as Cook pressed a cup of cocoa into her cold hands.

"Mustn't get chilled, dear," she said.

Lark murmured her thanks, wrapped her fingers around the pretty little cup and took a sip. The rich flavor spread over her tongue and into her limbs and she sighed with pleasure. Man, she was going to miss this stuff.

"Is that okay with you?" he asked. "Dinner upstairs?"

Lark nodded. As much as she enjoyed the meals with his family, tonight she'd just as soon be alone with him. "That sounds good to me," she said.

"Great," he said, smiling at her. "Why don't we both have

a shower, thaw out a little bit, and then we'll open a bottle of wine and have dinner?"

An image of his naked and body, water sluicing over supple muscle and masculine hair, suddenly materialized in her mind's eye, rendering her momentarily mute.

"Chickadee?" he prodded with a smile, as though he knew exactly what she was thinking.

Lark lifted her chin and nodded stiffly. "Sounds great." Having learned her way around the house at this point, she set off toward the door that would lead her to the central staircase.

"I'll be along in a few minutes," he called after her. "I need to talk to Belle."

All too aware of how little time she actually had left with Ethan and the Evergreens, Lark hurried upstairs and quickly showered. She took a little more time with her makeup and hair than she normally would have, and she donned a long nightgown and robe instead of actual clothes. She'd expected to find Ethan in the sitting room when she entered, but he wasn't there. Puzzled, she crossed the room and carefully nudged his door open.

"Ethan?"

Peering inside, she saw him sprawled in one of the chairs in front of the fire, his hair damp from a shower, his chest and legs bare, a mere towel fastened loosely around his waist.

And it was sagging.

He was asleep, she discovered, and something about seeing all that beautiful masculinity in vulnerable repose, gilded by firelight, made a wave of longing swell deep inside of her. Her mouth and eyes watered simultaneously, and her heart thundered in her ears.

She crept closer, unable to help herself, her feet moving quietly along the carpet.

Mercy, he is beautiful, Lark thought. High cheekbones, lashes long and obscenely curly for a man—why hadn't she ever noticed that? His dark locks were uncombed, looking as though he'd merely toweled them dry. A teensy bit of golden stubble shaded his jaw.

But ultimately, it was his mouth that did her in.

A little too full for a man, but incredibly beautiful, it was sin incarnate, wicked and carnal. Suddenly it wasn't enough to just look at it—she *needed* to taste it.

She bent low, carefully touching her mouth to his, and she knew the exact instant he awoke, because that wonderful mouth moved beneath hers, coaxing her closer, and one hand crept up and cupped her neck while the other grasped her hip and pulled her into his lap.

A shivery thrill eddied through her as she landed against him, deepening the kiss. Like butter over a hot bun, she melted over him, her soft to his hard…and mercy was he *hard*. She could feel the long, stiff length of him against her bottom and her feminine muscles clenched in response, sending a rush of dewy warmth over her folds.

Ethan suddenly drew back and pressed his forehead against hers, his expression agonized and futile. "Chickadee…" he breathed. "You're killing me."

"Yeah," she said, smiling. "But you like it."

He chuckled and kissed her. "Yes, I do."

"You know where you'd like it better?" she murmured, threading her fingers through his hair.

"Where?"

She gestured across the room, where his giant bed loomed invitingly. "On a mattress."

He chuckled again lowly, and then his eyes darkened with desire, flashed with purpose. He wrapped her up in his arms and headed for the bed. "I believe you're right."

Excitement and anticipation bubbled through her, pushing a laugh out of her throat. "I'm sorry, I didn't catch that. What did you say?" she queried lightly as her back landed against velvet and his warm body landed against hers.

"I said I believe you're ri—" He stopped, smiled darkly

and drew back to look at her. "Trust you to home in on that little comment," he told her. "You like being right, don't you?"

She rocked her hips against him and arched her back, her sensitized nipples straining against her gown. "Beats the hell out of being wrong."

Ethan pressed his hot mouth against her neck, sucking the air from her lungs, and she squirmed against him, desire and desperation winding through her, making her impatient. She'd been waiting for this for *years*, had been thinking about it for *years*... She loved the feel of him beneath her hands, sleek muscle, smooth and warm and oh so wonderful. She tugged at the loose towel, tossed it aside and then palmed his length.

Ethan sucked in a startled hiss and parlayed with a long suck of her pouting nipple. He flexed against her, his slippery skin working against her palm.

"I've got a clean bill of health," he said, as he pulled the robe and gown impatiently off her body, baring her to him. "You?"

Lark bent forward and licked a path up his throat, curved around his jaw and then nipped at his earlobe. "Clean. Protected. *Now*," she said, opening herself to him.

Ethan threaded his fingers through hers, pinned her hands over her head, and then entered her in one long, beautiful thrust.

The breath vanished from her lungs, her feminine muscles clamping tightly around him while the rest of her body went strangely limp, and every cell in her being sang with joy, with impossible recognition.

Her startled gaze met his equally shaken one and for the briefest of seconds she saw something there that made her want to weep—something so pure, so sweet and so genuine there wasn't a name for it. Affection? Yes. Love? Maybe. But it was more, too. Bigger.

And then he drew back and pushed into her again, and

again and again, harder and faster, angling deep, the engorged head of his penis hitting that one elusive spot that elevated a garden-variety orgasm to something akin to a religious experience. Like a storm gathering force in the distance she could feel it swelling within her, and she welcomed the feeling.

Like a crack of lightening, she came, her entire body feeling gloriously illuminated and electrified. She sucked in a breath and couldn't let it go. Every muscle atrophied with pleasure and then let go with a soundless scream, and as the hot, sweet rain of release washed over her she knew without a doubt that she'd never be the same...

Lark DeWynter was unquestionably gorgeous.

Lark DeWynter naked beneath him, her hot, tight little body squeezing around him in a violent orgasm?

Indescribable. Beyond words.

Dark hair fanned out over his pillow, pale, creamy skin, rosy-tipped breasts absorbing the force of his thrusts, the tiny, almost heart-shaped mole beneath her jaw...

He'd been so proud of himself for resisting her the past few days, of being able to stop at a kiss when what he really wanted to do was kiss her all over, lay her out on the rug in front of the fireplace and learn every curve of her body. Every indention, every freckle, every taste.

And had she not kissed him awake—before he could put his defenses in place—and not sat in his lap, putting that delectable part of herself so close to the part of him that wanted her the most? He might have been able to keep it together.

Might being the operative word.

But she hadn't. She'd tasted like cocoa and desire, familiar yet exotic, and he'd wanted her, just wanted her. And now, as her greedy hands slid over his body, her muscles contracting around him to create a delicious draw and drag between their bodies, Ethan knew he'd *always* want her— there would be no getting her out of his system.

He'd been an idiot to think he could resist her.

She was part of him, as important as any vital organ, and the idea of her leaving in the morning, of not telling her the truth, of allowing her to continue to believe that she was delusional…

He couldn't let any of that happen. He just couldn't.

He didn't know how he was going to fix it, how he was going to make everything work out, but there had to be a way to be honest with her *and* protect his family.

But one thing was for damned sure, Ethan thought as his balls tightened and every hair on his body stood on end—a prelude to what he instinctively knew would be the best orgasm he'd ever had in his life—there was no way in hell he was going to make her drink any more magick cocoa.

Every decision she faced going forward would be made with her own mind, one that he hoped she checked with her heart first.

Chapter 10

Pleasantly warm, with a feeling of contentment deep in her bones, Lark smiled sleepily and stretched a hand toward Ethan's side of the bed...only to find it empty. They'd skipped dinner and reached for each other repeatedly during the night, talking, dozing, and then making love again.

Goodness...

He *definitely* had the Sparkly Penis, and if this was her curse, she'd count herself lucky. He was a phenomenally attentive lover, paying particular attention to parts of her she'd never realized were sensitive. The crease of her upper thigh, the bend of her knee, hell, even the spot just above her elbow.

Though they'd avoided the subject of her leaving and her impending spot on the *Ophelia Winslow Show,* she knew they'd turned a corner, come to some sort of unspoken agreement. While she hadn't necessarily changed her opinion on lying to children about Santa Claus, Lark had to admit she'd gotten swept back up in the Christmas spirit by being in Gingerbread. But more importantly...she'd gotten swept up in Ethan Evergreen.

If Ophelia came round to her way of thinking, then the effect on Ethan and his family—who she'd come to adore—and the little town of Gingerbread would be jeopardized... and she just didn't think she could do that.

In fact, she didn't just think it—she knew it.

It suddenly seemed imperative that she tell him that to put his mind at ease. She'd noted the worry in his face over the last few days, and it had tugged at her then, knowing that she was responsible for it.

Determined to find him, Lark rolled out of bed, donned her robe and made for the door to the sitting room. She'd just put her hand on the knob when she heard the low, heated murmur of voices and something made her pause and listen.

"I'm not going to do it, Belle. I can't. I just wanted to give you fair warning," Ethan said.

"Fair warning?" Belle echoed, sounding incredulous. "You call letting me know a few hours in advance that you're going to let her leave here and go and destroy our family *fair warning*? Really?" She exhaled a pent up breath. "Look, brother, I know you're in love with her—we all do—but that doesn't change the fact that you have a job and part of that job is protecting the secret. And to protect the secret, she's *got* to drink the cocoa."

Drink the cocoa? What the hell? Lark thought, her heart beginning to pound.

"Listen, I adore her," Belle went on. "I think she's great and I think any woman who can go toe-to-toe with you deserves your respect and your heart. But...she's got to drink the cocoa."

"No more," Ethan insisted. "It's been terrible watching her struggle with what she knows and what the cocoa makes her believe. I can't do it to her," he insisted. "She thinks she's crazy, Belle. *Crazy*," he emphasized. "Because she can see the magick. She's a *glimpse*," he told her. "I confirmed it with Edgar—Kris was too busy trying to decide on his tattoo to listen to me," he said, sounding exasperated. "But Edgar remembers her. Do you have any idea how hard it's been for me to know the truth and not tell her?" he asked, his voice climbing with frustration. "I can't do it to her, Belle. I won't. I'm not going to let her continue to believe she's delusional when *I* know the truth. I know she's *special*."

A glimpse? Special? See the magick? Surely she'd misunderstood. Surely she—

"Edgar remembers her?" Belle asked.

"He does," he confirmed. "But even if he hadn't, I still would have known. You should have heard her when we were in my studio. She systematically pointed out the magick in each ornament. She even knew there was something wrong with next year's collection because she *couldn't* see it. She knew." He let go of a breath. "And that's good enough for me."

"Say you tell her the truth and let her leave without altering her memory, and she thinks *you're* delusional and goes on the show. Then what? You'd risk everything? For her?"

Ethan was quiet for a moment and she could sense his anxiety, his determination, his agony. "I trust her," he said simply, bringing tears to Lark's eyes. "And I'm going to believe in her, because no one else ever has, Belle. And she belongs here. With me."

Yes, she does, Lark thought. And she was going to prove it once and for all.

It took Ethan less than ten minutes to confirm that Lark had snuck into her room from the hall, collected her things, and asked Cook to arrange for a ride into town because she wanted one last peppermint cocoa before she left. From the Cup of Cheer she'd rented a car and driven herself to the nearest airport, where she'd promptly switched her ticket out for an earlier flight and left.

Ethan was so stunned he was numb.

He couldn't imagine what would have made her sneak away like that without saying goodbye...unless she couldn't bear the thought of telling him that she was still planning to go forward with her platform on the *Ophelia Winslow Show.*

Much as he wanted to be angry at her, he couldn't, not when his own intentions—however well-motivated—were in question.

But that still didn't change his job, which was to protect his family. He wasn't going to lie to her, but at the very least he wanted to plead their case. With that thought in mind, he readied the jet and two hours later found himself in Atlanta, at the studio, where the show had already gone live.

His gaze locked with Lark's just as Ophelia finished her introduction.

"I have to tell you, Ms. DeWynter, I absolutely love Christmas. I love the presents and the food and the joy and camaraderie. I love making cookies with my kids and decorating the tree, and doing crafts. I love the scent of pine and cinnamon, the excitement that hovers in the air. The *humina humina* from a little time under the mistletoe," she added, drawing a tittering laugh from the audience. She paused dramatically. "But I have to say there are aspects of your argument that particularly resonated with me."

Oh, no, Ethan thought, his heart jumping into his throat. He wracked his brain for a solution. A mute charm? A quick power outage? A—

Lark smiled reassuringly at him, and there was something in that grin that made him pause. "There are certainly aspects of my book that I find valuable, too, Ophelia—in particular, honesty—but I have come to appreciate the value of a child's imagination, the innate certainty they have of their own minds and their own realities. Rather than squashing the innocence of that early creativity, I think we should indulge it."

Ophelia blinked, clearly taken aback by Lark's very obvious change of heart. "But in the book you say—"

Lark grinned, picked the book off the table and held it up. "I know what I say, and when I wrote the book I was sincere—" her gaze locked with Ethan's "—but I was *sincerely wrong.* Let me tell you a story," she said. "Once upon a time there was a little girl who believed in Santa Claus—believed so thoroughly that she could talk to him and see his elves and see toy soldiers smile and nutcrackers wink and angel wings flutter. She had a great imagination, but one that frightened her parents, so her parents took away

Christmas and set up regular appointments with a therapist. The girl grew up believing Christmas was bad because it had caused her so much grief, and she believed that it was the Christmas lie, in particular, that was so harmful." She paused, swallowed, her eyes shining with tears. She lifted her shoulders in a tiny shrug. "But what was the harm, really? How long would the little girl have continued to believe the unbelievable? Another year, maybe two?"

With tears in her eyes as well, Ophelia handed Lark a tissue.

She took a bracing breath. "It's my professional opinion now that it would have done less damage for the little girl to have a harmless fantasy than for her to believe there was something wrong with her, that she was defective in some way. And her family would have been stronger as result of having Christmas tradition. Because what is Christmas if not a tradition?" she asked. "The things you mentioned, Ophelia—the making cookies and the wrapping presents, the special dinners, the mistletoe. Those are traditions, and traditions are built to bond a family. They make them stronger."

Ophelia wholeheartedly agreed, as did the rest of the audience. Ethan's phone lit up with text messages and the app his brother had designed to measure Christmas spirit glowed brighter than it ever had.

All because of her.

"You know we have Mr. Christmas himself in the audience, right, Ophelia?" Lark asked her.

Ophelia's brows lifted and she scanned the crowd until she found Ethan. "Ethan Evergreen," she said, smiling. "Why don't you come up here and join us?"

He was glad she'd asked because he was ready to rush her stage and wasn't eager to get thrown out. He mounted the steps, his gaze on Lark, and then reached out to shake Ophelia's hand. "Thank you for having me," he said.

"Pleasure." She grinned. "So this is quite a turnaround.

Ms. DeWynter is typically your biggest adversary, wouldn't you say?"

Ethan reached over and took her hand, threaded her fingers through his. "Yes, she was. But you know what they say about your enemies," he said leadingly.

Ophelia noted their hands with an "mmm-hmm" and arched a knowing brow. "Keep your friends close, and your enemies closer."

"That's a good one, but it wasn't the one I was thinking of," Ethan told her.

"Oh?"

"Yes. The best way to get rid of an enemy is to make them your friend." He squeezed Lark's hand. "But I've got an even better solution."

Lark's eyes widened as Ethan suddenly slid to one knee in front of her and the audience went absolutely wild.

Ophelia was smiling so widely she could barely talk. "And what's that?"

Ethan looked at Lark, his gaze searching hers. "Make her your wife." He essayed a grin. "What do you say, Chickadee? Will you marry me?"

"I believe I will," she said with a watery smile. She bent forward and kissed him, and then she drew back. "And you won't even have to make me drink the cocoa to do it. I heard you this morning," she whispered. "Thank you for believing me," she said, a tear slipping down her cheek. "You can't know what it means."

Ethan returned her smile, gesturing significantly at the audience. "Oh, I think I've got a pretty good idea."

"Ho, ho, ho," she murmured with a chuckle, and kissed him again.

* * * * *

HIS FIRST NOELLE

KIRA SINCLAIR

Double winner of the National Readers' Choice Award, **Kira Sinclair** writes passionate contemporary romances. Her first foray into writing fiction was for a high school English assignment. She lives out her own happily-ever-after with her husband, their two daughters and a menagerie of animals. You can visit her at www.kirasinclair.com.

I'd like to dedicate this book to an amazing group of women—Andrea Laurence, Rhonda Nelson and Vicki Lewis Thompson. Working together on this project has been one of the highlights of my career... well, you know, except for the tooth fairy and bloody teeth. Love you guys!

Chapter 1

"We have a problem," Noelle Frost said, not bothering to knock before barging into the one room she'd been avoiding since returning to Gingerbread, Colorado.

Dash Evergreen's sharp green eyes swiveled to pierce straight through her. Noelle felt his loaded gaze catalogue everything about her body in mere seconds. From the severe cut of her black business suit down to the compact body that she considered her greatest weapon and spent hours honing. This man knew all of her weaknesses and strengths. Her knife-edged longings and pulse-pounding fears. Dash Evergreen absorbed it all and then dismissed her. Found her wanting.

Although that was nothing new.

Born of two rival clans, she'd never been completely accepted by either. She might have been raised in Gingerbread, Colorado, as a member of the Winter clan, but her Summer-blue eyes were a visually dynamic reminder to anyone who cared to look that there was a part of her—however small—that was different.

And not even the fact that her father was head of security for Evergreen Industries and a highly trusted member of the clan had stopped people from holding her at arm's length. Or the other kids from teasing her.

There had been a time in her life when she'd thought Dash was different. That he saw beyond all the conflict and accepted her for who she really was.

But then, there'd been a time when she was young and naive, too.

Noelle ground her teeth together and tried not to let his dismissal hurt. But even after eight years, her ex-husband still had the ability to wound her with nothing more than a simple glance. But she'd be damned if she'd let him know that.

Her years of CIA training had prepared her for deep-cover operations. She could kill with her bare hands, slip into some of the most secure facilities undetected and rub elbows with the elegant and elite.

Apparently that training was also useful when trying to protect herself from the man who'd broken her heart.

She'd been back in Gingerbread for several months, utilizing those skills to fill in for her father while he was recovering from a heart attack and emergency open-heart surgery. So far, she and Dash had managed to avoid each other. Mostly.

Unfortunately, thanks to this latest snag, it was going to be difficult to continue to do so.

Noelle knew just how much Dash hated to be disturbed when he was in his hot shop, and frankly, if she'd had any other choice she would have waited until he was through.

Dash all hot and sweaty, his muscles all slick and gleaming, had always been her weakness.

Pushing farther into the room, Noelle glanced around. Nothing much had changed. She could see the orange-red glow the fire emitted through the square opening in the furnace. Huge metal implements that looked more like they belonged in a medieval torture chamber rather than Dash's private lair had been placed on the tables scattered around the room.

He didn't glance at her as she moved closer to get a better look. One wide palm rolled the hollow metal rod back and forth across the raised platform of the workbench. A glowing ball of molten glass twirled in front of him as he worked it, poking, prodding and coaxing it into the shape he wanted.

Color had already been added, a breathtaking swirl of blues that reminded her of a cloudless summer sky. With quick movements, he pulled a long finger of glass from the spinning globe. A flick of his wrist here, a quick snip there. The ornament would be gorgeous—as every piece Dash produced was. For the briefest moment, Noelle fought the desire to have the ball hanging on her own Christmas tree.

But it wasn't for her.

With practiced movements, he separated the piece from the pipe and stored it in the annealer, which allowed the glass to gradually cool without cracking.

While she'd never used any of the equipment in the room, she was intimately familiar with every piece. Dash had spent hours explaining to her just what they were used for. He didn't let many people into this space—not even his brothers or sister. At the time that access had made her feel…special.

Apparently all he'd really wanted was inside her panties. Noelle couldn't fight down the twist of a sickly smile as it crossed her face. She might have been impressed with his talent and turned on by the heat of his sweat-slicked skin, but her parents had raised her right. She'd still held out until he'd asked her to marry him.

If she'd known the high price of agreeing to that handfasting she probably would have saved herself the trouble and just let him have her here. Maybe then it would have just been hot sex instead of a soul-crushing disaster.

Dash stalked back across the room toward her, a soft, worn T-shirt clinging to his impressive chest. Damp patches arrowed down leading straight to the valley where she knew a six-pack was hidden. Tattered jeans clung to narrow hips, the thighs so threadbare she could see through to the bare skin underneath.

Most women would probably swoon at seeing Dash Evergreen in a perfectly tailored three-piece suit. And he definitely knew how to rock that look. But this, *this,* was what she dreamed about. Not the perfectly polished businessman or the responsible member of the Winter clan ruling family.

Nope, her fantasies were filled with the man—his dark hair disheveled and slightly damp and his green eyes snapping from an internal fire he worked hard to bank around most people. But she'd seen it. Knew the dangerous edge, the prowling restlessness and the burning passion.

Noelle's muscles began to quiver, a fine tremble that she seriously hoped he wouldn't notice. Dammit! What was it about this man that cut through every single shred of self-preservation she possessed?

As if she hadn't learned her lesson.

Her head might have, but apparently her body still craved more sweet punishment.

He stopped in front of her, arms crossed over his wide chest. The hard line of his jaw tensed. A single muscle ticked rhythmically just below his left ear. The only sign that he was thoroughly pissed that she'd interrupted him.

Tough.

"We have a problem," she said again, modulating her voice to something crisp and professional even as awareness and need crackled across the surface of her skin.

"So what's new? All we seem to have lately are problems. Let Cole or Ethan handle whatever it is. My plate's already full preparing the sleigh and overseeing the packaging."

She didn't want to hear the thin line of weariness buried deep inside his words, but Noelle couldn't help it. Fine lines of strain flared out from the corners of his eyes, and the faint smudge of exhaustion bruised just below them. What was the idiotic man doing in the hot shop when he should obviously be in bed catching up on some much-needed sleep?

Exasperation flickered through her, and she almost stepped closer, intent on running her hand down the slope of his shoulders and convincing him to get some rest. But somehow she managed to stop herself. It wasn't her job to care about him anymore. Hadn't been for a very long time.

Unfortunately, what she was about to say was going to add to the strain. But there was nothing she could do about that.

With a deep breath she said, "Kris has decided not to take the sleigh this year."

The dark slash of his eyebrows winged up in confusion. Noelle completely understood. That had been her initial reaction, as well.

"What are you talking about? Of course he's taking the sleigh. How the hell else is he going to get around the world in twenty-four hours?"

At her sides, Noelle clenched her hands into fists. He wasn't going to like this any more than she had.

"He wants to take the Corvette."

The moment the words left her mouth, Noelle cringed, preparing for the inevitable explosion. But it didn't come. Instead, Dash blinked at her and waited...possibly for a punch line that would never come.

Silence stretched between them. Noelle's gaze darted across his face looking for any clue to his reaction, but there really wasn't one. His face was thoroughly blank.

Just as she thought the tension building between them might actually crack like one of his pieces of glass, he said, "The damn thing is yellow. Yellow."

His voice dipped down, the smooth, even cadence going slippery with horror and temper.

"How the hell are we supposed to hide a yellow convertible flying across the sky?"

Dash had really hoped she'd been kidding. He should have known she wasn't. Just the fact that she'd entered his domain after months of avoiding him should have been clue enough.

Noelle Frost certainly wouldn't have come all the way down to the lower levels of the lodge just for some sick joke.

That wasn't her style. Actually, he couldn't remember the last time he'd seen her crack a smile, let alone laugh.

It made him sad, but there was nothing he could do to change it. She wanted nothing to do with him, and that was probably for the best.

There'd been a time when he'd known every nuance of Noelle—her body, her mind, her soul. She'd shared pieces of herself with him she'd held in check from everyone else. And he'd done the same.

But eight years was a long time, and she wasn't the quiet, passionate girl he remembered.

Nope, now she had a hard edge to her that made him want to tear into whatever had put the wary caution in her soft blue eyes. She insisted on keeping her beautiful dark hair pulled ruthlessly into a knot at the nape of her neck. And the holster resting beneath the cut of her suit coat… the first time she'd popped it open and he'd gotten a look at it he'd wanted to rush her to the nearest room, lock her inside and make sure there was never a reason for her to need the damn thing.

When she'd walked into his hot shop just now, he'd first thought she was a figment of his imagination. Breathed to life from the thoughts whirling around inside his overly tired brain. He needed sleep. The weeks leading up to Christmas were always his busiest. But no matter how exhausted, the moment his head hit the pillow and his eyes closed images of Noelle were burned into the backs of his eyelids.

And if he did manage to drift off, those images would change from still photographs to flickering images with movements that left him panting and frustrated with a raging hard-on he couldn't do anything with.

So, to exorcise his demons, he'd come down to the one place he always found peace. But she'd even invaded there. He hadn't realized the ornament he was working on was the exact color of her eyes until it was too late.

And then she'd been standing there, her mouth tight and

her eyes burning as she watched him work. Did she remember the feel of his hands on her body as he'd tried to teach her how to work the glass? Did her body ache with memories and unfulfilled needs?

There was no way to know by looking at her. The CIA had worked her over well. Her expression was always perfectly, pleasantly blank. Initially, he'd thought it was him. But then he'd realized that was her new default position. Or it had been when she'd first returned. After a few months some of the severe reserve had begun to fade. He'd seen her let her guard down, a little, with Belle, Taryn, Lark and his brothers.

The mask was still firmly in place with him.

Although he wasn't really surprised. Their history didn't exactly breed open friendliness. The passion that crackled between them had always been too explosive for that kind of easy camaraderie. They burned hot, just like the furnace at his back.

But now wasn't the time to think about any of this. Not if what she was saying was true.

"Surely to God someone can talk some sense into the man. A Corvette? The damn thing is barely bigger than a Tinkertoy. How does he expect to get all the deliveries packed inside?"

Noelle's eyebrow swooped up into a silent version of "did you really just ask me that?"

"Yeah, yeah. Magick. But we both know there are limits to what I can do. Especially less than two weeks before Christmas. Maybe if I'd had a year to prepare...the cloaking spell alone is going to be almost impossible."

She sighed, the heavy weight of it lifting her shoulders and breasts tight against the dark cut of her jacket. "I know. But...I've already spoken to Cole, Ethan and Belle. With all the other 'issues' going on, we're agreed that it's probably in everyone's best interest to accommodate this request."

Irritation rolled through Dash's chest. "The man is having a midlife crisis and the rest of us have to pay the price?"

The mountain was already buzzing with the muted whispers of gossip mingled with suppressed panic. He had no idea what they were going to do with a Santa who'd taken up jogging and refused to eat cookies. In a few weeks millions of children would be leaving him enough to counteract twenty years' worth of exercise.

And he didn't even want to think about the snowy white beard the man had shaved off. At least that could be fixed with some strategically glued stage makeup.

Making a damn car fly was going to be the last straw.

Even if Dash was a little miffed at being left out of the family discussion—probably because they already knew what his answer would be—he grudgingly recognized their point. Everyone was walking on eggshells around Kris. Personally, Dash thought it was useless. The guy's wife was going to leave him. Everyone could see it. The sooner he accepted the reality and moved on the better it would be for everyone.

Dash's wife had walked away from him without even bothering to tell him she was leaving. He'd managed to survive. Somehow. So would Kris. Just not in a Corvette flying across the sky.

If this crisis had struck at any other time during the year, Dash would have dug his heels in and refused. He would have forced everyone—Kris, Cole, Belle, Merry—to deal with the reality of what was happening.

But it was two weeks before Christmas, and the last thing they needed was for Kris to go comatose with heartache. Hell, he could barely remember the first few weeks after Noelle had left. They were a whiskey- and fire-fueled haze. And he had the scars to prove alcohol and molten glass were a lethal mix.

Noelle watched him, patiently waiting for his reaction. It was one of the things he'd always loved about her, the way she'd instinctively known when he needed space for the wheels to spin and had always given it to him. Unlike his brothers and sister, she didn't push.

Which was good, because if she had he probably would have balked on principle alone.

Picking up the nearest handy object, a pair of metal tongs he used to shape the glass, he threw them across the room. The metallic rattle as they hit first the wall and then the floor was less than cathartic.

Noelle didn't even blink at his outburst, which only made him regret the less than helpful gesture.

Her smoky voice, the sound of it making him think of flickering fires and her lithe body spread out across the soft surface of a white rug, swirled across his skin. "Feel better?"

"Not particularly."

A smile, all the more enticing because of its rarity, teased at the corners of her lips. "Yeah, me either. Although I do feel guilty for leaving a dent in the wall of my father's office."

"Your office."

Noelle's startled gaze collided with his. Her mouth went slack with surprise before she snapped it shut again.

"My father's. I'm only here temporarily."

"Yeah, that's what you keep saying."

Was it wrong that he wanted her to stay? Had always wanted her to stay. But she hadn't. She had a life outside Gingerbread, one that she was pretty damn good at apparently. One that he knew nothing about.

The spike of sadness surprised him. Reaching up, he rubbed at the ache of it in the center of his chest.

"Fine. Let's go figure out how to make a damn car fly."

Chapter 2

Noelle tried not to pay attention to the way his body moved, but it was difficult not to notice. Especially when she had to quicken her strides, forcing out two for every one of his, just to keep up with Dash. Even in her four-inch designer heels the top of her head hit just even with his chin. Unfortunately, it gave her a great view of the dimple there.

Jerking her gaze away from him, Noelle forced herself to pay attention to what they were doing.

"Sir, Kris had the car delivered to the barn fifteen minutes ago."

From the expression in the elf's eyes it was clear the general consensus was that this was an idiotic idea. Noelle didn't disagree...they just didn't have many other options.

With a nod, Dash followed the tiny man around the back of the lodge to the huge structure waiting there. *Barn* was a misnomer. It might have looked like one on the outside, but it resembled a warehouse on the inside.

On one end were large bay doors that would be rolled up so the sleigh could be brought out and loaded. Noelle's gaze swept across the ancient vehicle. It had been used for centuries. The wooden boards and gold-leaf paint seemed laced with magick. The runners gleamed beneath the fluorescent light. She used to creep inside the sleigh, curl up on the soft velvet seat and pretend she really did belong here.

She hadn't seen it in years...and until that moment hadn't realized how much she'd missed the outward sign of her heritage. A little prick of longing shifted inside her, but before she could do anything about it, Dash was striding off across the cavernous space.

The Corvette stuck out like a sore thumb. Not because they didn't have modern conveniences. The clan kept a huge fleet of vehicles available for use by anyone.

A crowd stood around staring at the huge yellow monstrosity. Their heads barely reached the top of the low-slung car. Several of them whispered back and forth to each other. Off to her left, Noelle heard a bleating sound that seemed to echo the consternation swirling around. Apparently the reindeer weren't oblivious to the fact they'd just been replaced.

The crowd split, clearing a space for them to pass.

Dash frowned. "This is a bad idea," he mumbled beneath his breath. If the elves loitering around weren't blessed with preternatural hearing, she would have been the only one to hear his words. Big pointy ears had their advantages.

"Maybe, but we're doing it anyway," Noelle countered in a loud voice filled with as much certainty as she could muster.

Shaking his head, Dash ordered the staff to clear the area. Everyone fell back, although they didn't completely disappear. Small faces filled the large bay opening.

"Why don't you try the cloaking spell first? Let's make sure we can hide this monstrosity before I try to make it fly."

Logically, she knew he had a point. But that didn't stop the infinitesimal tremor she felt. Her magick had been... finicky. For months she'd been working hard to cover up her issues. She'd been lucky. But it looked like that good fortune was about to run out.

She felt sick with nerves. The sensation wasn't completely unfamiliar. There had been plenty of times she'd felt the same churning mix of anxious apprehension, usually moments before she plunged into a deep-cover assignment. Those jitters never lasted for long because she knew she had the skills to handle the situation.

She didn't think she had what she needed to pull this off.

Growing up, she'd struggled to keep up with the rest of her classmates. The spells and casts they could do in their sleep she'd had to fight for. She'd spent hours practicing, determined that she would not let herself be different from the rest of the kids. But she was. And everyone knew it.

This was it. The moment everyone realized she'd been lying from the day she'd come back. They were about to get firsthand evidence she didn't belong with the Winter clan. The Evergreens would decide she couldn't fulfill her position and kick her out. Her father wasn't strong enough to resume his duties yet. He'd lose his job, and while the Evergreens wouldn't boot him to the curb, he needed his job. He needed something to fight for in order to get better.

Well, it had been a good ride. She'd actually lasted longer than she'd expected.

Here went nothing. Closing her eyes, Noelle pulled out her wand and concentrated on the car in front of her. In her mind's eye she recalled every detail so the memory was as complete as possible. The glaring color. The glint of light on the chrome. The squeak of brand-new tires against the coated concrete floor.

Whispering words in an ancient language only a few remembered, she started at the hood and moved backward, imagining the entire thing disappearing beneath a blanket of nothing.

She breathed evenly, drawing on the surge of light that kindled deep in her belly and radiated out.

A murmur started behind her, the sound of it growing to the point of annoyance. Didn't they realize she needed to focus?

Beside her, Dash shifted. His arm brushed against her. And she reacted. That single moment shattered her concentration as everything inside her centered on the man next to her. The picture in her mind was no longer of the car, but of Dash as he'd worked the ball of blue glass with expert precision. The bunch and pull of his muscles. The glowing heat on his skin.

A strangled sound erupted from Dash. Smothered laughter. Noelle's eyes popped open and she stared blindly at the car. A very blue Corvette.

"Well, it's definitely an improvement, but not quite what we were hoping for."

Dash tried desperately to smother the laughter, but he wasn't succeeding very well.

"At least we don't have to worry about flying lemons anymore." His foot connected idly with the tire. "Blue would work well...if Kris was traveling through the sky on a warm summer afternoon."

A choked gurgle erupted from Noelle. Dash jerked his gaze away from the car and back to her. She stared at him, horror and hurt filling her eyes for the briefest moment before that damn mask slammed back over her expression.

But he'd seen it.

"Jesus. Elle." His voice was low, full of the regret rolling through him. He took a single step toward her, planning to wrap her in his arms and soothe away the damage he'd unintentionally caused. But she stumbled backward, shaking her head.

Dammit! He knew how touchy she was about her powers. Knew how much she'd struggled growing up. But it had been easy to forget those old insecurities and assume they were long gone. From the moment she'd come back, Noelle had been nothing but competent, confident and efficient.

But that didn't excuse what he'd just done. He'd hurt her, and that was the last thing he'd ever wanted to do.

"You know that's not what I meant. My mouth gets me in trouble."

Her eyes flared. Her gaze dragged down to his mouth. A hot blast of need shot through him. Part of him wanted to follow through on the unwitting invitation. He'd wanted to kiss her from the moment he'd walked into the Evergreen boardroom and seen her sitting in one of the dark leather chairs.

He could make her forget, soothe the emotional wound he'd just inflicted. Coax her to forgive him with his tongue instead of words. But that tactic hadn't exactly worked well for them in the past. Anytime she'd gotten upset about something, his solution had always been to distract her with sex. To remind her just how compatible and perfect they were together.

Instead, he rolled his head, stretching tight neck muscles, and tried to find the core of control that was slowly slipping through his fingers.

"Don't beat yourself up over this, Elle."

"Don't."

He wasn't sure whether she was talking about the nickname or his pacifying words.

"It's a difficult spell. Even the most powerful from the clan would struggle. Besides, you almost had it right until the last moment."

Her gaze collided with his. "What...what do you mean?"

He shrugged. "Half of the car had disappeared and then it...was back. And blue."

Eyes wide, her beautiful mouth fell open. It only made him want to kiss her more.

Slowly, a brilliant smile melted across her face. It was like watching the best sunrise, the ache of it difficult to take. It lit up her eyes, making them shimmer just like his glass.

God, she was gorgeous. And he loved to see her happy. There was a time when his whole existence was tied up in drawing out that smile. Even then she'd been so serious and intent.

"I did it?" she whispered.

This time when he moved closer she didn't pull back.

"Yep. What happened?"

Her teeth clicked together. Her gaze jerked away. And a

soft burst of color seeped across her skin. "Something distracted me."

Reaching for her, Dash ran his hands down the curves of her arms. Why did she have to be wearing that jacket? He wanted to feel her skin.

"Okay. Then why don't we try again?"

Turning her back to face the car, he flicked a glance over his shoulder and found Montreal, his head elf, in the crowd. Dash silently flashed his right-hand man the order to have the area cleared and knew it would be followed.

Wrapping an arm around Noelle's waist, Dash let his palm settle across the taut expanse of her tummy.

"What are you doing?" she asked, her voice low and husky. The sound of it burned across every nerve ending in his body, but he ignored the reaction. That was not what she needed right now. Or wanted.

"Helping you."

"I don't need your help."

"Probably not, but you're going to get it anyway. Relax."

A harsh sound that was a combination of disbelief and jagged humor escaped her.

She shifted, probably completely oblivious to the fact that the tiny movement rubbed her rear straight across his groin. If she kept it up she was going to get irrefutable evidence of just how much he still wanted her.

Dash tightened his hand, holding her still. Her spine stiffened, and then she slowly began to melt against him. Her head dropped to his shoulder and she let him take her weight.

Her arms hung limply at her sides, her fingers still wrapped tightly around her wand.

Bending, he brushed his lips against the delicate shell of her ear and whispered, "Close your eyes."

She did, the softest sigh slipping through her parted lips.

Dash bit back a groan.

He touched her throat, unable to stop himself from running the pads of his fingers down the slope of her exposed neck. But he forced himself to continue, over her shoulder, down her arm to the hand holding her wand.

Twining his own fingers with hers, he raised her hand and pointed the slender blade of wood at the car.

"Start again."

She shook her head, the round point of it rubbing against his chest.

"I've got you, Elle," he promised. "It's only you and me here."

Her ribs expanded under a deep breath. She held it in before slowly blowing it out again on a steadying stream.

This close to her, he could feel the moment her powers surged to the surface. The glow of it was intoxicating. He'd never understood how she couldn't get it.

Her entire life she'd struggled against being different. She'd tried desperately to fit in. The problem was she couldn't. She *was* different. That was what he'd loved about her.

Unlike everyone else, her power was fueled not just by the cold core of Winter, but also by the bright sunlight of Summer. Together, the best of both worlds entwined inside her. Her skin glowed with the force of what she held deep inside.

She was one of the most powerful witches he'd ever met. She just didn't trust herself…or accept what was there. She fought to close off the piece of her that she didn't think belonged, which only drained her energy instead of feeding it.

So he'd help her tap into that potential. At least for today.

"Do you feel that?" he whispered. "The ball of energy churning deep inside you?" His hand flexed where it rested over her belly. "You must. I can feel it, and I'm only holding you."

Slowly, his fingers spread wide, slipping farther out across her body. "Let it go."

A small sound of refusal squeaked out of her.

"Yes," he argued. "All of it."

He could feel her struggle, not just in the tensed muscles pressed hard against him, but in the twisting center of her power. She was trying to cut it in half, to cordon off what she thought wouldn't help her.

"No. Don't fight it. Don't try to force that warmth down. I want to feel it, Elle." His mouth grazed her skin and his breath slipped across the sensitive spot just behind her ear. "Let me," he growled.

The burst of it nearly knocked his hands away from her body, but his muscles instinctively tightened and held on. Heat rippled down his body. Wherever they touched burned, but it didn't hurt. In fact, it felt heavenly. Like the warm cocoon of his hot shop.

He was so preoccupied with the revelation of just how powerful she really was now that the lock holding her Summer magick captive had burst open that he hadn't been paying attention to the car.

It was gone. Or, rather, it appeared gone. If he reached out, his hands would still brush across metal.

Unlike before, when the car had disappeared an inch at a time, one burst of energy and it had vanished.

"Elle," he murmured. "Open your eyes."

She did, her eyelids dragging slowly up as if weighted with sleep. He remembered that sated, drowsy, satisfied expression and wanted it again. More than his next breath.

Her gasp of surprise had him chuckling.

She whirled in his arms. One moment she was completely pliant and the next she was shoving at him like he'd suddenly turned into a serial killer.

Shocked, Dash let his arms drop from around her body and stumbled back a step.

The accusation that filled her expression slammed against him.

"What the hell do you think you're doing, Dash Evergreen? I really don't appreciate you playing with me. Aren't you a little old to be pulling that kind of shit? Grow up."

He opened his mouth to argue with her, but he had no idea what to say. How could he? What the hell was she talking about?

Spinning on her heel, the hard click of her stilettos hitting the concrete floor blasted around him like gunshots. His own temper flared. Before he could think through the implications of his actions, he was striding after her. Grasping her arm, he whirled her back to face him.

She glared, the sharp cut of her beautiful eyes slipping straight between his ribs. "What the hell are you talking about?"

Her teeth ground together as if she didn't want to dignify his question with an answer. Too bad. He shook her shoulder, not hard enough to rattle anything, just to make her realize he had no intention of letting her go until she explained what she meant.

"That stunt back there. I have enough bullshit to deal with right now. I don't need one of your pranks piled on top of everything else."

"Prank? What prank?"

"All that husky whispering and those touchy-feely hands." She dropped her voice down into a growling register. "'I've got you, Elle. Let it go.'"

A sharp breath pulled in through her teeth. For the briefest moment he thought he saw the glitter of tears in her eyes, but she blinked and they were gone.

"What the hell did you hope to get? Me falling back into your arms?"

He did not appreciate her harsh laughter.

"Why let me think I was doing all of that?" Her hand swung to encompass the car, still perfectly invisible. "If you were just going to do it your damn self."

She thought he'd cloaked the car. The realization did

nothing to bank the anger flickering through him. It increased it. Why did she constantly underestimate herself?

His voice was silky and dangerous when he said, "That was all you, Elle."

She scoffed, the harsh sound scraping across his eardrums. "Yeah, right."

Jesus, he wanted to shake some sense into the woman. And then he wanted to strip her completely bare and revel in her heat and fiery passion.

"I. Did. Nothing," he bit out.

"I felt it." She flung the words at him like an accusation. "The burst of energy. I felt it." Her voice wobbled. Her chin quivered. Her throat worked overtime, trying to swallow.

And the anger just…evaporated.

He didn't mean to, but somehow his fingers tangled into her hair. His palm cupped the nape of her neck. Closing the space between them, he tipped her face and made her look at him.

The slick sheen of tears covering her eyes nearly sent him to his knees.

"God, I hope so," he rumbled. "That was you, Elle. The piece of yourself you've kept locked down for as long as I've known you. That was you finally letting all of your power free."

His control stretched to the breaking point, Dash couldn't hold back. No longer remembered why he should even try.

His mouth slammed down over hers. He wanted to be gentle, knew he should hold back and coax her. But couldn't find the willpower to do it. Not when he'd struggled to keep his hands off her for months. Not when it had been so long since he'd tasted her.

He might regret the moment, but not now.

Her squeak of surprise quickly morphed into a groan. Her mouth opened beneath the probing force of his. She let him in. More than that, met him measure for measure.

Her tongue tangled with his, taking just as much as she

was giving. Hands tugged at his hair, coaxing him closer. She went up on tiptoes, pressing her body flush against his.

The past and the present melded together. The taste of her was just the same, peppermint and sunshine.

But the moment his hands brushed against the cold leather of the holster tucked between her shoulder blades cold reality came crashing down around him.

They both jerked back. Panting, they stared at each other. Dash didn't know what to do or say. His body wanted her, so much that he throbbed with the pain of it.

But this wasn't the girl he remembered. The one he'd fallen in love with so long ago.

This was the woman who carried a gun everywhere she went. The one who'd left him.

Chapter 3

God, she shouldn't have kissed him, Noelle thought later that evening. Rubbing her hands down her face, she tried desperately to wipe the memory from her brain. Yeah, like that was going to work.

Even hours after walking away from him, she couldn't seem to think of anything else. Her body still buzzed with energy and ached in all the right places. It would have been so easy to get swept up in the moment and give in to what they both obviously wanted.

And if she'd shared that kind of unbelievably overwhelming kiss with anyone else, she probably wouldn't be pacing restlessly inside her room, but instead stretching languidly next to a warm male body.

Dash had been the one to make her body light up like a damn Christmas tree. He'd always been the one to do that. The only one. She'd dated and even taken lovers since she'd left him. But none of them had made her feel as raw and alive as Dash always had.

With a growl of frustration, Noelle yanked open her bedroom door and stalked out into the silent hallway. It was almost dawn. No doubt she'd need copious amounts of Diet Coke to keep her eyes open today, but for now, whenever she put her head down on the pillow all she could think about was rolling across the bed tangled in Dash's arms.

Maybe a walk would clear her head and exhaust her body enough that she could at least get a few hours of sleep.

Like the barn, from the outside the lodge resembled a quaint ski cabin. But the place was big enough to house the entire Winter clan. The elves had their own village close by, protected by magick just as the lodge was.

Everyone had their own apartments but shared common spaces—the dining room, a game room, a movie theater, and a huge living area with soaring ceilings and a man-size fireplace. The lower floors housed the communications and security hub and Dash's hot shop.

At this hour the hallways were quiet and deserted, or at least she thought so, until she rounded a corner and ran smack into someone. Belle's high-pitched *oomph* and rounded green eyes greeted her.

"Noelle," Belle said, her voice filled with anxious surprise.

"What are you doing wandering around in the middle of the night?"

Belle's gaze jerked sideways, refusing to meet hers. Noelle had enough interrogation experience to know when someone was hiding something.

Her sharp gaze catalogued Belle's attire, the same outfit she'd worn earlier but a little more rumpled. She clenched her fist around the familiar Cup of Cheer mug as if it was a lifeline. The shop had been closed for hours.

Noelle's eyebrows quirked up and a smile threatened the corners of her lips. If she was reading the signs correctly, Belle Evergreen had just returned from a midnight tryst. For weeks she'd wondered just what the youngest Evergreen had been up to. *Coffee breaks, my ass.*

"I won't tell your brothers," Noelle promised.

Belle's startled gaze flew to hers. "What are you talking about?"

"As long as you're not spilling company secrets, I don't care who you're sleeping with, Belle. And neither should your brothers, although we both know they're likely to go all caveman the moment they find out. So, I won't be the one to tell them."

Her entire body sagging with relief, Belle flashed Noelle a brilliant smile. "I appreciate it."

With a shrug, Noelle left Belle standing in the hallway. It was none of her business, and women had to stick together.

The encounter with Belle gave her something else to think about as she wandered around. Eventually she hit the ground floor. She told herself it was simply to check in with her nighttime team. But she never quite made it that far.

For some reason her feet stopped outside the closed door to Dash's workroom. Light shone through the crack at the floor. He was inside. Of course he was. This was where Dash came whenever something was bothering him.

Toward the end of their marriage it had upset her that more and more he'd sought out the hot shop instead of her. She'd woken up countless mornings to an empty bed, her heart a little crushed. Maybe if it had been another woman, she could have fought, but it wasn't.

She had felt him slipping through her fingers and hadn't known how to stop it. The more he'd hurt her, the more she'd withdrawn. The more she'd withdrawn, the more he'd disappeared. Looking back, she could see the vicious cycle their marriage had dissolved into. Maybe if they'd been older...

But they hadn't been. Leaving Gingerbread and taking the position with the CIA had been what she'd needed. The chance to challenge herself in ways that didn't require the use of magick. Considering she'd spent all of her youth struggling to become as adept at using it, it seemed like a good idea to try living without it. She'd had to learn how to rely on just her intelligence and physical strength.

And she'd been damn good at her job.

What surprised her was that so far she wasn't missing her work with the CIA. The long hours, isolation and cloak-and-dagger existence had been starting to wear on her. And she hadn't even realized it until she wasn't part of it anymore.

She'd left the lodge certain it could never be home. But

the moment she'd walked back inside it had felt...right. Where had those misfit feelings fled to?

And then what had happened this afternoon with the car?

Noelle wasn't entirely certain what to make of that. Had it really just been *her*? Part of her wanted Dash to have given her a little boost, but looking into his deep, honest eyes, she hadn't been able to believe he was lying to her.

But what did that really mean?

She had no idea.

Thinking about that burst of heat that had spread through her like she'd mainlined hot cocoa brought her full circle to the man who'd been holding her. The spread of his hand low across her belly. The way his fingers had rested right beneath the curve of her breast. His fingers entwined with hers. The unavoidable buzz of need.

God, even now she wanted him. Her body was begging her to open that door, forget everything that was between them and give in to the need.

Her hand rested on the knob, indecision freezing her muscles.

No. She couldn't do this. This man had destroyed her. Broken her heart and let her walk out of his life without even a single word asking her to stay.

Her hand dropped uselessly to her side. But before she could turn away, the door jerked open. Dash was framed there, blinking at her like she was a mirage he was trying to clear away from his brain.

"Elle?" he asked, his voice low and fluid.

His hand wrapped around her arm, holding her in place when everything inside her urged her to run.

"What are you doing up?"

She could have told him she was just checking in with her team. Or that she hadn't been able to sleep and was wandering. But she didn't. She didn't say anything. She couldn't. Her throat refused to work. All she could do was stare up into his eyes, the hum in her body steadily increasing as if someone was ruthlessly turning up the volume on her desire.

His skin glowed with heat. Several damp strands of hair clung to his forehead. He needed a haircut, but what else was new? His dark hair was always just this side of too long. It had been a running joke. Slowly, she reached up to push the mess away from his face. She wanted to see him.

The moment she touched him she knew it was over. All the struggle to pretend she didn't still want him. Dash Evergreen had always been her weakness.

"Elle?" His fingers tightened around her arm, biting into her.

She knew what he was asking, but she didn't really have an answer. Shaking her head, she swiped her tongue across her suddenly parched lips.

The groan that rocketed up from his chest made her tingle in the strangest places. Before she could blink, they were both back inside his shop. The door slammed shut behind them and her back hit the hard surface.

Caught between the thick slab of wood and the towering height of Dash's body, she couldn't think. Didn't want to.

His mouth devoured her, touching everywhere. The hard press of his lips trailed across her exposed collarbone. For the first time she questioned the intelligence of prowling the halls in the tiny shorts and tank top she liked to sleep in. Until the tip of his tongue slipped beneath the low edge of her shirt to find the tight tip of her breast.

"Oh, God," she breathed, her fingers clenching his hair to hold him close.

Her body was on fire, as surely as the banked furnace pumping heat into the room.

She didn't protest when he grasped the hem of her shirt and pulled it straight over her head. She played tit for tat and made his own damp shirt disappear.

God, the man had a body. He was rock-solid, hard muscles beneath her questing fingers. Bulging biceps from all the glass work. Abs that made her want to lick him everywhere.

Her own mouth grasped for any patch of skin she could reach, greedy for the taste of him after so long. His skin was salty-sweet. She'd always loved him best when he'd come straight from the shop. It had taken her a long time to convince him she didn't want him to shower after he'd been down here.

The familiar smoky scent of the fire clung to his skin. She breathed it in, filling her lungs and holding him close.

Grasping her hips, Dash boosted her into the air. Her legs wrapped around his waist, bunching tight as she clung to him. She reveled in the feel of him sliding against her.

The hard ridge of his erection settled exactly where she wanted. Her own hips ground against him, pulling a ragged sound from between his lips. The brush of heated breath whispered across her skin.

Throwing her head back, she delighted in the feel of him.

"Jesus, Elle," he groaned against her belly, her own muscles tightening beneath the caress.

But his mouth moved away, and suddenly there was nothing but cool air touching her skin. His hands bracketed her face, scraping hair off her forehead. He stared up at her, the intense glitter of his green eyes nearly her undoing.

"Do you have any idea how much I want you? I can't get you out of my head. Haven't been able to since the moment I caught you sneaking out of your bedroom window when we were eighteen. The tempting swell of your ass in that tight little skirt as you shimmied down the drainpipe. Your tart mouth when I came out of the shadows to order you back inside."

Strangled laughter burst from her chest. "The way you tailed me to the Gingerbread party and interfered with every guy I tried to hook up with."

"None of them were good enough for you."

"Oh, and you were?"

The words were out before she thought about the consequences. With regret, she watched the manic heat fade slowly from his eyes.

"Hell no."

He tried to set her down, but Noelle just shook her head and tightened her thighs. "Oh, no you don't, Dash Evergreen. You are not going to light my body up like the Fourth of July and then send me back to my room unsatisfied. I've been fighting this since the moment I walked back into Evergreen Industries, and I'm tired. I don't want to do it anymore. I want you."

To prove her point, she arched her back, letting the door take all of her weight as her body went off center. His hands scrambled to hold her, but she wasn't worried. Dash would never hurt her, at least not physically. She trusted him with her body and always had. It was her heart he'd screwed with. But as long as she could keep that piece of herself out of this...

Her legs flexed, driving her body higher, before she relaxed and brought them even tighter together. The soft cotton of her shorts rubbed perfectly against his denim-encased length. The combination of rough and soft nearly made her whimper.

It had been so long. She was close enough that if she rubbed in the right place she might just go off. But that wasn't what she wanted. If she'd wanted quick and easy she could have done that for herself.

Noelle wanted Dash deep inside her, filling her up and rubbing in all the right places.

"I tried to do the right thing, Elle," he ground out. "But no matter what, I just can't seem to succeed. Not where you're concerned. You trump every one of my good intentions."

"I don't remember asking you for good intentions, Dash."

With a snarling growl of surrender, Dash wrapped his arms around her back and spun. Swiping his arm across one of the metal tables in the middle of the room, she heard the clatter as tools hit the floor.

She hissed when her naked back hit the cold steel. He didn't wait, but followed her down, keeping their bodies locked tight together.

He ripped her shorts from her body, literally tearing them straight down the seam. Some small part of her wanted to protest, but she didn't. How could she when the gloriously naked heat of him descended on her?

He played with her, teasing fingers slipping through the evidence of her desire. A strangled cry erupted from her lips when he finally plunged inside. Her entire body bowed off the table, searching for more and delighting in the pleasure.

He drove her to the brink, leaving her gasping and whimpering, but he wouldn't let her go over. The moment she got close he'd back off, pressing featherlight kisses across her belly, down her thighs and over her eyelids.

Good thing she didn't need to see to feel him. He wasn't the only one who could dish out a little torture. Her fist wrapped around his hard length, remembering just what would drive him insane. She dragged several gasps and guttural groans from him.

They were both delirious, completely consumed with each other. If he'd asked her to walk across hot coals at that moment she would have done it. Done anything. If he'd just give her what she wanted.

"Please, Dash. Please. I need you. Now."

He panted, his ribs expanding and contracting erratically beneath her hands. "I know. God, baby, I know."

Grasping his hips, Noelle widened the cradle of her thighs and settled him right at the entrance to her body. A snarling sound of relief slipped through his parted lips just as he flexed and thrust deep.

The sound that ripped from her throat was part ecstasy and part torture. They fit together perfectly, just as she'd remembered.

It was overwhelming—more than she'd expected. Her chest tightened even as her body began to completely unravel. Both of them were too close to the edge to be gentle or deliberate. Instead, they came together in a flashing pump of hips, the glorious friction of bodies and brutal slice of long-denied passion finally finding a delicious outlet.

Her throat constricted just as her body spasmed. The dark spiral of release tried to suck her into oblivion, but she wasn't ready to let it have her. She waited for him, holding out so that she could feel the swell and pulse of his release deep inside her. And when she had it, she finally gave in. Wave after wave of pleasure washed over her. It was too much. It wasn't enough.

Dash sank down beside her, their arms and legs tangled in a knot she didn't have the energy yet to unravel.

Noelle lay there—the cold press of metal at her back and the heat of him draped over her like the warmest blanket on the harshest winter night. Her chest heaved, and every cell in her body seemed to quiver, energized and newly alive.

She didn't realize she was crying until Dash lifted himself onto an elbow. The smile of satisfaction that stretched his face faded.

Swiping a thumb across her cheek, he said, "Hey, hey. What's this?" and held up a single glistening tear.

Chapter 4

Dash hated to see her cry.

Hated to be the reason for Noelle's tears.

And he'd been responsible for quite a few of them in their relationship.

Gathering her in his arms, he rolled around until his back was against the table and Elle was pressed tight to his chest.

She tried to bury her face in his shoulder, but he wasn't having any of that. Part of the reason they'd crashed and burned was because they hadn't taken the time to communicate. He wasn't making that mistake again.

Because now that she was back in his arms, he wasn't sure he could let her go. It had nearly crushed him the first time.

Tipping her chin up, he forced her to look at him.

"What's wrong?" he asked, trying to make the words as gentle as possible.

"Nothing."

Her tears might have stopped, but he could still see the tracks where they'd been. Swiping his thumb through the ghost of them, his mouth tightened. "That isn't nothing, Elle. Talk to me. What did I do?"

Her gloriously blue eyes went wide with surprise. "Nothing, Dash. You didn't do anything. Well, at least nothing wrong. It's just been...a long time since I've felt that...connected to another person." She pulled against his hold, trying to duck and cover her face. "I was a little overwhelmed."

The tight ache centered in his chest began to ease.

"That was pretty intense."

She laughed, the sound of it rolling across him. Her body relaxed, going pliant. Folding her arms across his chest, she cradled her chin on her hands and looked at him through the cover of her lashes.

"It was always intense. You and I. The bedroom was never our problem."

A low chuckle curled up from his belly. "No. Definitely not. Maybe I should have handcuffed you to the bed. Kept you there, naked and waiting for me."

She frowned, but he still saw the brief flash of interest before she extinguished it.

"Oh, absolutely. Because forcing me to do what you wanted would have solved all our issues. Why *not* handcuff me to the bed? You wanted me to give up all my dreams for yours anyway."

"What?" he asked, his voice incredulous. "I never asked you to give up your dreams, Noelle."

"Please. You wanted me to be the perfect Winter wife. Bake cookies, serve cocoa, never complain and wait patiently for you to decide to come home."

His fingers tightened around the curve of her hip. She winced, telling him he was holding on too tight, but he couldn't make his hands uncurl.

"What do you mean wait for me to come home? You make it sound like I was screwing around on you."

How could she possibly think that? Hell, even at twenty he'd barely had the energy to keep up with her. Not when he was struggling to handle the responsibilities and pressures of his new position with the clan as well as a new wife.

"No. I actually think I would have preferred it if you were. Do you know how much it hurt to wake up alone in an empty bed and know you'd rather be here instead of with me?"

He'd had no idea. Stunned, his mouth opened and closed without anything coming out.

"You shut me out, Dash."

The shock was quickly devoured by long-repressed outrage. "And your solution was to leave? I was working all the time, Elle, trying not to drown beneath my stressful and exhausting job. My wife, a woman I loved desperately, seemed more and more unhappy the longer we were together. I couldn't figure out how it had all gone to shit so quickly. Or how to fix it."

His jaw flexed. He could feel the tension whipping through every muscle in his body but couldn't force himself to relax. The tears were back in her eyes, glistening across the bright blue surface. He should let it go, but he couldn't make himself shut up.

"You didn't even say goodbye. I came back to the lodge and you were just…gone. Not even a note, just an empty closet and a missing suitcase. It was weeks before I realized you weren't taking a break. You were never coming back."

Unable to stay this close to her while the memory of that pain ripped through him all over again, he wrapped his hands around her hips and lifted her off.

Grabbing his jeans, he slipped the worn denim over his hips. Turning to search for his shirt, he was in the middle of buttoning the fly when he caught a glimpse of her from the corner of his eye.

His hands stilled. She stood there, completely naked and utterly vulnerable. A contradictory mixture of the girl he'd fallen in love with and the woman she'd become. She might not have on the suits she liked to use as armor, but her body was still perfectly straight. Her shoulders were tight and her chin was tipped upward in a challenging show of confidence. But deep inside her eyes he could see the shadow of her insecurity and doubt. And something else—the slice of pain that he recognized because he wore the same damn scar.

"I heard you," she whispered, so low he almost didn't pick up the words.

Taking a single step closer, he said, "What?"

"I heard you. That night. Talking with Cole about our handfasting. *You* were the one to insist on the ancient practice, wanting to honor the custom of our ancestors. But the year and a day was coming up, and you weren't talking about making the union permanent. You were going to leave me."

"What?" he asked again, his heart suddenly lurching painfully inside his chest. A scathing protest was hot on his lips, but the words died before he could speak them. The look of utter devastation crumpling her face was difficult to argue with.

She truly believed what she was saying.

"I barely saw you. When you weren't working you were here." She flung her hands around his workroom. The bitterness in her voice cut straight through him.

He wanted to protest that he hadn't been hiding away inside his shop, but he knew the words would be lies. He had come here to avoid the fact that his marriage was crumbling and he had had no clue how to stop it. At the time he'd convinced himself he was giving her space.

But the reality was he'd had no idea how to handle what was going on between them, and he'd used the hot shop to pretend everything was okay when it clearly wasn't.

"When you did actually come home we inevitably ended up fighting."

Or channeling that pent-up frustration and passion into ripping each other's clothes off, but he didn't mention that. He didn't think that reminder would be helpful just now.

"I was so afraid I was losing you. I couldn't be what you wanted. I didn't fit in with the other women. I burned every batch of cookies I tried. I even managed to screw up cocoa." She threw her hands up into the air, letting them fall back around her in frustration. "It takes a whole lot of talent to screw up hot cocoa, Dash. It's milk, chocolate and a tiny bit of power. But I couldn't even manage that.

"You didn't want to spend time with me, and frankly,

I didn't blame you. I hated myself. The harder I tried, the more I just managed to screw up and push you away.

"When I heard you talking with Cole about what your options were at the end of the year and a day, I knew you were planning on leaving. Hell, I would have left me, too. Rather than put us both through that humiliating ordeal, *I* left. It was easier that way."

Dash let his eyes slide closed. He breathed in through his nose and out through his mouth, using the warm weight of it to ground him. It was either that or give in to the pounding need to scream at the universe.

When he thought his emotions were back under control, Dash opened his eyes and stared straight into Elle's churning gaze. "I had no intention of ending our marriage, sweetheart. But I thought you might. Especially after you screamed that our handfasting was a mistake."

He tried to keep the ache of her words from his voice, but didn't quite succeed.

She gasped. "I didn't…" Her words trailed to nothing. He could see the memories as they flashed back across her mind. The moment she remembered saying the words to him in a blinding fit of angry tears.

"I didn't—" she tried again, but the statement didn't come out any clearer the second time around.

Her throat worked hard as she tried to swallow. Soft hair whipped around her face as her head jerked back and forth in denial.

The third time went better. "I didn't mean it."

With a sad smile tugging at his lips, Dash closed the space between them. She stared up at him, her eyes filled with a jumble of emotions so tangled up together he couldn't pull one from another. He knew exactly how that felt, to be so tied up in knots that you didn't know what the hell you felt.

Running the pad of his finger down her cheek, he whispered, "Apparently you did."

* * *

Noelle stared at the computer screen on her desk. There were words and numbers. Information she was supposed to be absorbing and managing. She didn't see any of it.

The only thing she could see was the expression on Dash's face right before he'd walked away from her last night. As if she'd ripped out his heart and fed it to a reindeer.

Her own chest still ached with the realization that she'd hurt him.

And right now, she had no idea what to do with that knowledge. What did it mean? What did last night mean?

Could they go back and start again? Was that even a possibility? Would he forgive her for leaving, and could they work out the issues that had driven a wedge between them in the first place?

What about the life she had back in D.C.? And while everyone else seemed to accept her presence here, there was still a part of her that didn't feel like she belonged. Not when she was struggling with the simplest requirements of her job.

She could direct her personnel, devise security protocol and implement diversionary tactics with no problem. But that wasn't all the Winter clan needed from their head of security.

Eventually they were going to figure out she wasn't qualified for the job.

And then what?

"Baby girl." A loud booming voice echoed outside her office door. Well, actually, it was his office door.

"Daddy," she said, a smile lighting her up inside. The sight of him always made her happy. Especially after the scare of almost losing him.

He was the only parent she had left. The only family, really, since she wasn't close with any of her Summer relatives.

Pushing up from her desk, Noelle allowed herself to be wrapped inside the warmth of a crushing hug. Her father was tall and broad-shouldered. Silver was finally starting to thread the dark, burnt-toast-brown of his hair.

He was her rock and always had been. Bigger than life and indestructible. Getting the phone call that he'd collapsed had nearly sent her to her knees.

Although he was definitely looking better these days.

She almost offered him the chair she'd been sitting in, but before she could he dropped onto the hard chair across from her. He settled back, the plastic creaking ominously beneath the bulk of his body.

"How's my gorgeous girl today?" he asked.

"Good. Fine. How are you?" she asked, trying not to put unnecessary emphasis on the words but failing miserably.

The doctors kept telling her that he was going to make a full recovery. Sure, he'd have to make some lifestyle adjustments, but that was typical after suffering a massive heart attack that required emergency open-heart surgery. At least his skin no longer had a sallow look.

He gave her a weak smile. "Good. Just came back from physical therapy in the village. Those are some sadistic bastards. I thought I was going to puke right there on that damn treadmill."

Shaking her head, Noelle said, "They're trying to make your heart stronger, Daddy. Do what they say."

Frowning, he grumbled something beneath his breath, but she couldn't hear it. Maybe it was better that way.

Pushing up from the chair, he leaned across her desk and touched his warm lips to her forehead. "Just wanted to check on my girl since I was walking through. I'm going back to the lodge to take a nap."

Flipping her hand in goodbye, Noelle watched her father disappear back out the door.

She wasn't happy. Not once did he ask her about work. And he hadn't since the day she'd agreed to take over for him. At first she'd thought it was simply because he didn't have the strength to think about it. Now she wasn't so sure.

Growing up, work had been his life. It bothered her that he didn't seem to care about it at all anymore.

But she wasn't quite ready to push him on the issue.

Shaking her head, she turned back to the spreadsheet open on her screen. At least his visit had accomplished one thing—she'd stopped thinking about Dash and last night.

Although the reprieve was short-lived. A couple hours after her father's visit, the walking distraction himself breezed into her office.

Noelle looked up, startled. She'd been back for months, and Dash hadn't come into her office in all that time.

She wanted to berate him for interrupting her concentration, but the words died in her suddenly dry throat. Gone were the work clothes he'd had on yesterday, replaced by the kind of brilliantly tailored clothes the citizens of Gingerbread expected from the VP of Evergreen Enterprises.

The man could fill out a suit. Maybe it was knowing just how hot and sweaty he could get beneath the veneer of civility the expensive material provided, but Noelle felt like she was about to start drooling.

It didn't help when he reached behind him and closed her door. He leaned heavily against the wood, his intense gaze running across her from tip to toe. Her body responded, going all liquid and needy.

After he'd walked away from her last night, she'd expected him to go back to pretending she didn't exist. Apparently, that wasn't the plan anymore.

"What are you doing?" she asked, her voice much more breathy than she'd meant it to be.

"Look, we could throw accusations at each other all day. The reality is there's plenty of blame to spread between both of us. We were young. We made mistakes. But last night proved there's still something there."

She'd be lying if she said the heat that flared inside his eyes didn't kindle something deep in her own body. Those blazing green eyes sent a flood of tingles ripping across her skin. He could make her a puddle of mush with nothing but a glance. Had always been able to get to her like that.

At one time she'd seen her response to him as a weakness. Another power that tied her irrevocably to him and made her vulnerable.

Now she recognized it for what it was. The kind of physical connection that was rare in the real world.

"I don't know about you, but I'm not willing to ignore it."

Pushing away from the door, he stalked across her office. Spinning her chair, he planted his hands high on the arms, caging her in.

"I can't keep my hands off you, Elle. And I'm tired of trying."

Tipping her chair backward, he let the springs take her off center. Her feet left the floor, and the world felt like it was falling out from beneath her.

The hard length of his thighs bracketed her own. She stared up at him, unable to do anything else. Her heart thudded desperately against her ribs.

Licking her tongue across her lips, she watched as Dash groaned. His eyelids slid closed. A pained expression crossed his face, and his entire body shuddered as if he'd been punched in the gut.

When his eyes opened again she was the one gasping. Heat and savage need filled her, spilling over her in a shower of sparks. No man had ever looked at her that way—not even Dash when they'd been together before. Now he looked as if his world might end if he wasn't buried deep inside her within the next sixty seconds.

All the doubts she'd been harboring fled, at least for the moment. How could she think about anything else?

Never in her life had she felt so beautiful and perfect and…necessary.

Fisting her hand in his crisp white shirt, she wrapped her legs around his hips and used her leverage against him. She jerked and had him tumbling against her body. The chair creaked in protest, but she didn't care. Not when his hot mouth found her and seared a path up her throat.

He was crushing her, but she still wanted him closer. She couldn't breathe and felt a little light-headed.

They tore at each other's clothing. She shoved his half-opened shirt away from his chest and leaned up to sink her teeth into his shoulder. He grunted and then groaned when she licked the tiny dents she'd left behind.

"Wicked little hellcat," he breathed, retaliating with a nip at her earlobe.

She laughed, the effervescent sensation bubbling up through her chest.

His hand was slipping up her thigh, pushing it relentlessly toward her waist. She was panting. Desperate. Her body raw and aching.

The door burst open behind them.

"Holy shit," someone said.

Instincts and training kicked in before Noelle's brain could pause long enough to consider what was happening. With a heave of her body, she shoved Dash away from her. Her hand was at her side and the gun from her holster pointed at a wide-eyed Cole before she could blink.

"Holy shit," he said again, holding up his hands in the universal sign of surrender. His eyes were wide, but mirth glittered dangerously inside them anyway. For the briefest moment, Noelle contemplated the merits of shooting him. Not to hurt, just to wipe the knowing smirk off his face.

However, she was intelligent enough to realize firing on her boss wasn't smart, not even if he was her pain-in-the-ass ex-brother-in-law.

She watched his eyes travel from the dark barrel of her gun down to the man lying at her feet.

Dash's bemused expression would have been comical if it wasn't also accompanied by an edge of irritation. She wasn't sure whether it was directed at her or at his brother. Probably both.

Holstering her weapon, she held out a hand to help him off the floor. She realized her mistake about five seconds too late.

Instead of bringing them palm to palm, his hand slipped higher, wrapping tight around her wrist. And it was his turn to tug. She probably could have stopped it, although not without possibly hurting him.

She sprawled against him, sending them both collapsing to the floor. His hard body cushioned hers, absorbing the shock and giving her a safe place to land.

One hand tangled in her hair while the other clamped around her hips, holding her hard against his still aroused body.

"What do you want, Cole?" he growled without taking his eyes off her.

"Uh..." Cole shifted behind them. She couldn't see him, but could hear the scrape of his feet against the deep green carpet.

"You have about sixty seconds before you're going to get an eyeful you probably don't want," Dash warned.

"Never mind," Cole finally said.

"Smart man." How could eyes smolder and twinkle at the same time? Noelle had no idea, but somehow Dash managed to pull it off.

Before the door to her office could close, Dash said, "By the way, your head of security is taking the rest of the afternoon off. And so am I."

There was a pause. Noelle felt it more than heard it, could practically taste the tension wafting off Cole.

"Whatever, man. I hope you know what the hell you're doing."

She tried not to let the disapproving edge in his voice bother her. But it did. Cole didn't approve of what was going on between them. But then, what was new?

While none of the Evergreen family had ever said anything, there were plenty in the Winter clan willing to voice their dissatisfaction with the match. Dash was an Evergreen and could have any girl he chose.

No one wanted him with a half-Summer witch.

She tried again to scramble away, but his hold hadn't loosened. Cole was long gone when Dash leaned forward and whispered against her cheek, "I know exactly what I'm doing."

Chapter 5

Dash had spoken some big words. Now he just hoped he could back them up. He'd stormed away from Noelle and his hot shop last night, furious and hurt all over again. It had been a defense mechanism easily deployed. But the moment his temper boiled away only misery was left.

He couldn't do it. For months he'd been walking around this place trying to pretend it wasn't killing him to see her, talk to her, smell her damn perfume whenever he walked down the hallways. It was a lie, and it wasn't getting him anywhere.

It certainly wasn't saving him the agony.

And touching her, tasting her, losing himself deep inside her again only made it worse.

Somewhere in the early morning hours he'd realized he had no intention of making this easy on her. She wanted him, responded to him, just as fiercely. He was going to use every weapon in his arsenal to convince her she belonged with him, with her clan.

And he wasn't above engaging in a few dirty tactics, namely of the physical variety. He hadn't been completely kidding when he'd threatened to handcuff her to his bed naked. If he wasn't half-convinced she'd know how to escape...

His body was still humming from the frantic release they'd found together on the floor of her office. It hadn't been nearly enough. The next time they were together it would involve a bed and uninterrupted hours that he'd use to explore all of her.

However, when he'd whispered that plan in her ear she'd gone from pliant to ramrod-straight in his arms. The afterglow hadn't lasted long before she was shoving him away again and ordering him out of her office. She had too much to do to leave right now.

He'd wrung a compromise out of her. They'd have dinner alone together in his apartments.

Which meant he had hours to fill until then. Striding through the enchanted tunnels that led from the lower levels of Evergreen Industries up the mountain to the lodge and elf village, Dash turned a corner and came up short.

Gabriel Frost was hunched over, his wide shoulders practically bowed halfway to the floor.

Dash's first instinct was to rush forward and help the man. The last thing he wanted was to tell Noelle her father had suffered another heart attack. But his brain quickly dismissed the fear as his eyes registered just what he was seeing.

Three elves huddled close to the man. Dash recognized them immediately. They were part of Gabriel's trusted team. No, they were part of Noelle's trusted team. What the hell were they doing powwowing with her father in the tunnels?

Sensing something was off, Dash slowed his steps and hid in the shadows.

"There are no problems?"

"You mean aside from Kris's midlife crisis, Merry's snit, Cole's hacker discovering our secret and Ethan going toe-to-toe with Lark DeWynter on television?"

Gabriel sighed, his shoulders lifting as he pinched the bridge of his nose. "But those issues have all been handled. Well, all except Kris and Merry, but that will run its course eventually."

One of the elves grunted. "Kris is demanding he take the Corvette instead of the sleigh."

The three glanced at each other, exchanging the kind of look that carried the weight of shared agreement.

"When are you coming back, sir? Noelle is struggling. She's had trouble with several of her spells, although so far she's been able to hide it. But that can't last forever. And when the Evergreens learn she isn't capable of performing the job..." The tiny voice trailed off ominously.

"Not yet," Gabriel growled. "She isn't ready to admit this is where she belongs. Until she is, she'll leave again the minute I return to my duties. I won't let her do that."

Dash gasped, the full extent of what was going on finally hitting him.

All four heads jerked around, the shadows not strong enough to hide him from their direct gazes.

The three elves shrunk backward, dropping their eyes to the ground.

Straightening from his slump, Dash moved into the light. Grasping for the mantle of authority laid across his shoulders at a young age, he strode forward.

Sweeping the three with a heavy stare, he said, "What kind of trouble is she having?"

One of them stubbed his toe into the packed ground, his mouth tightening in the kind of sealed line that indicated he wasn't saying a damn thing. Dash appreciated the man's loyalty to Noelle, although it wasn't helpful at this precise moment.

The other two exchanged a glance. Through silent agreement, one stepped forward. "They're minor issues. We thought at first it was simply because she'd been away from us for so long and needed to get reacquainted with her power. But it's been several months, and she's still having issues."

Frowning, Dash murmured, "The cocoa."

The elf nodded.

"Thank you for telling me." Thinking back over the way she'd cloaked the car yesterday, that ball of energy and light erupting from her core, maybe what had been holding her back would no longer be an issue. But just in case...

"I saw her cloak an entire car yesterday. Whatever happened before, I don't believe there'll be any more problems. Since that's the case, I'm going to keep this information quiet."

Dash didn't miss how their shoulders slumped with relief.

"However, if there are any issues, I want your promise you'll come to me immediately."

"Yes, sir," they said in unison.

"Excellent. You may return to your duties."

Without even a nod, the three disappeared.

Alone, Dash swung his gaze over to Gabriel's. He half expected to find Noelle's father cringing just as the elves had been. He should have known better. Gabriel hadn't risen to head of security by cowering. He'd been a trusted friend and colleague of Dash's own father and often an adviser to the Evergreen children as they'd stepped in to take the reins when their parents had retired.

However, the man would find intimidation tactics that had worked on Dash as a teenager no longer carried any weight.

"What do you think you're doing, Gabriel?" he finally asked.

The older man's mouth firmed with determination. "Whatever I need to to keep her here. If you'd taken better care of her eight years ago she never would have left."

The blow was meant to hurt, and it definitely hit the mark. Especially after Dash's conversation with Noelle last night and realizing she'd been scared and upset and bruised. By him.

Gabriel visually braced for an argument, but Dash had no intentions of giving it to him. "You're right."

The other man's mouth opened, but before words could tumble out he snapped it shut again.

His ex-father-in-law studied him for several moments before jerking his head up in silent agreement. "So, what are you going to do?"

"Let me just make sure I understand what's going on first. I'm going to assume you're medically cleared to come back to work?"

Gabriel nodded again, his jaw going rigid beneath the white fuzz of his beard.

"When?"

Gritting his teeth together, he said, "Six weeks ago."

Something twisted deep inside Dash's belly. If Gabriel had told Noelle he was fine six weeks ago, none of the past few days would have happened. It made him physically ill to think he might have missed his second chance with her because he was being a blind, stubborn ass.

Blowing a calming stream of air out between his parted lips, he had to let go of the what-ifs and focus on what was in front of him.

Gabriel must have taken his shaky silence as a bad sign, because he blurted out, "Don't tell her. Don't cost me my little girl again."

He could tell Gabriel hated himself a little for the pleading, watery tone in his voice, but Dash didn't really blame him. If their roles were reversed, he'd most likely be the one begging.

He had two choices. March back up to her office, tell her and possibly watch her walk away again. Or let Gabriel continue to deceive her. Just for a little while. Until he had enough time to convince her this was where she belonged. With him.

It had already been six weeks. What could a few more days hurt?

As much as the weight of it settled over him like a tiny burr beneath a reindeer saddle, there was really no question what his decision would be.

Licking his lips, Dash said, "I don't want to lose her either, Gabriel. I still love her."

He brought his own eyes up to meet his ex-father-in-law's steady, understanding gaze.

"I know you do, son," Gabriel said.

"We're having dinner tonight. With a few more days I might be able to convince her to stay no matter what."

"So we won't tell her."

It had been three days since the afternoon in her office. She and Dash had spent more time together in those three days than the last three weeks of their marriage. Even when she was working he was constantly finding reasons to find her.

And she was doing the same thing. Popping over to the barn pretending to do a security check. Her favorite place to catch him was still the hot shop. There was just something mesmerizing about watching the man work. It was the only time he was completely...himself.

She knew he enjoyed his job with Evergreen Industries and took his responsibilities for the Winter clan seriously, but those things weren't his passion.

As much as she tried to just let things unfold the way they should, Noelle couldn't quite shake the tension that was steadily building deep inside her.

She was falling for him all over again. Which wasn't exactly true. It implied that she'd let him go at some point, which was far from the truth. There was a piece of her that had always—and would always—love Dash.

It was too soon to worry about what would happen tomorrow or next week or three months from now. But the permanent knot lodged in her tummy didn't quite agree with the carefree attitude she was trying to adopt.

She was worried about her father, but for the first time since she'd gotten the phone call that he was ill, she was happy his recovery was taking longer than expected.

If he told her he was ready to come back to work then she'd be forced to make a decision. And she wasn't sure which one she'd make.

"Ms. Frost! Ms. Frost!" The low voice filled with panic

hit long before the tiny man burst through her open office door.

Agitation turned sourly through her stomach, but Noelle pushed it away. No sense getting freaked out before she even knew what the problem was. And whatever it was, she'd handle it. She'd managed every other shit-storm so far.

The man doubled over, gasping for breath as he pressed his hands to his knees. Sucking in oxygen, he panted, "We… have…a problem."

"I already figured that out, Roscoe. Take a deep breath and tell me what's going on."

Shaking his head, he didn't wait for that. Grasping her hand, he began tugging. Noelle tried to resist, but the elf was damn strong. And she was wearing four-inch heels and a tight pencil skirt. She really didn't want to end up sprawled across the green carpet with her ass in the air.

So she followed, patting her side just to make sure her gun was still tucked next to her ribs.

The moment she tumbled out the main doors of Evergreen Industries it became patently obvious a gun wasn't going to help.

She wasn't the only person standing outside gaping up at the bright blue afternoon sky. And the obscenely yellow car streaking above the town like a banana.

"What the hell?" she screeched out.

Beside her, Belle muttered beneath her breath, "Fruitcake. Just…fruitcake."

Behind her, Cole burst through the doors, Ethan and Dash hot on his heels. Dash's gaze rounded with shock before narrowing into a roiling temper. His skin flushed a dangerous shade of red, the kind of color that reminded her of the glow of his furnace. She really hoped he wasn't angry with her, although he had every right to be.

Ethan stared up into the sky and then burst out laughing. Cole shot him a cutting glare. Ethan tried to smother his reaction, but didn't quite succeed.

Cole's eyes blazed, the only sign his temper was close to exploding. Slowly, his gaze scraped across the street in front of them, which was crowded with the citizens of Gingerbread.

With a growl, he swept a cutting glare across his brothers, sister and her. Noelle felt the cold prickle of it slide down her spine like ice. "In my office. Now."

Accepting the fact that they'd follow his order, he turned to the phalanx of elves scattered around them. "Get a communication link up to them and tell them to get their asses back down here before I shoot them out of the sky."

No one believed he'd actually do it. That would create a bigger mess than they already had. But he was definitely pissed, and if Kris and Merry were smart, they wouldn't push him.

Everyone piled into Cole's office.

Today, instead of crossing his arms over his chest and leaning against the far wall, Dash sank down beside her on the love seat. He didn't look at her, but the hand he dropped onto her knee steadied her in a way she hadn't expected. Or known she'd needed.

Squeezing, he gave her a jolt of comfort and support before pulling his hand away. Noelle drew in a deep breath, using it and the heat radiating off him to soothe her jangled nerves.

"This is a clusterfuck," Cole muttered, leaning his head back and scraping his hands through his hair. Ever the worrier.

"It isn't that bad," Ethan, the eternal optimist, countered.

"You're kidding, right?" Belle asked, her own voice going up into the squeaky range. "This is bad. Very bad."

"I didn't say it wasn't bad, just not a mortal wound."

"Weeks before Christmas," Belle groaned. "Seriously, someone needs to knock some sense into those two. Whatever the ho, ho, holy crap is going on with them needs to stop. Now. Before they ruin Christmas completely."

Cole rubbed his hand over his face, jumbling up his words, although not enough that she couldn't understand. "Agreed. But first problems first. What are we going to do about the entire town seeing a damn flying car?"

Ethan shrugged. "That's easy. I'll arrange a free Evergreen Industries event for the town. Hot cocoa and cookies for everyone. Holiday outreach to the citizens who support us. We can hold a toy drive. It'll be great PR."

Only Ethan could spin a huge cover-up into something positive. And as much as the idea made Noelle want to vomit, it was a good plan. A great plan, actually. If only she wasn't the one required to supply all the cocoa. She'd struggled to make a batch strong enough to wipe Taryn's memories...how was she going to manage to produce enough to wipe the entire damn town?

Before she could open her mouth to come up with a protest, Cole's hand dropped from his face, and he stared at Ethan, hope flickering deep in his eyes. It caught and grew.

"You are brilliant, Ethan," Belle said.

"I know," Ethan said, spreading around his charming, egotistical smile.

Oh, shit. She was in serious trouble.

Her hands trembled. To hide the weakness, she clasped them together and dropped them into her lap. Dash silently reached over and covered them with one of his own. He might have meant to help with his gesture, but it didn't. In fact, the tremors increased, moving up her arms and engulfing her entire body.

She had to stop this. She had to speak up and tell them she couldn't do it.

Her mouth opened, but before the words could fall from her lips, the door to Cole's office burst open.

Kris walked in, his normally jolly expression thunderous and cheeks red for a completely different reason than Christmas cheer. Merry, quiet as always, slipped in behind him, her eyes cast down to the dark green carpet.

"What were you thinking, Kris? How could you take the car out like that? What did you think would happen when the entire town saw you?"

Kris bellowed. Behind him, Merry cringed, placing her hand on his arm in an attempt to cool the temper that was clearly about to erupt.

Somewhere in the back of her mind, Noelle registered the utter violation of Santa lore as she watched him completely lose his shit. Although, without his beard, paunch and snow-white hair, it was a little less weird.

"What did I think? What did I think?" he asked, stalking toward Cole and slamming his hands down onto the desk. "I was thinking that I should take the car for a test drive before I attempted to fly it around the world on the most important night of the year. I was thinking a quick trip up and down wouldn't hurt. I was *thinking* that the cloaking spell would hold."

Noelle gasped. Her eyes squeezed shut and her head dropped back against the curved edge of the love seat.

"What are you talking about?" Cole asked, his voice steady as he ignored Kris's burst of emotion and focused instead on his words.

"Everything was fine until I got above Gingerbread. The car shuddered and then it was…there. Nothing I could do about it at that point. I headed back as quickly as I could, but…"

"There's no hiding a flying car the color of a school bus," Ethan muttered.

Kris nodded sharply.

For the first time since they'd sat down, Cole's gaze swept over to her and Dash. "What the heck is he talking about?"

For the second time, Noelle prepared to spill her guts and tell the Evergreen clan just how unqualified she was to hold the position they'd given her. This problem was too big for her to continue pretending. But before she could, Dash's hard voice blasted into the room.

"The cloaking spell wasn't ready." His eyes glowed with banked heat. "If you'd bothered to tell us what you were planning, Kris, we could have told you that. The spells cast over the sleigh and reindeer have been in place for hundreds of years. They require only small infusions of power each year as a kind of booster for the magick that lingers inside each item."

Everyone else in the room might have been buying the line of bullshit he was selling, but Noelle knew better.

This was all her fault.

Chapter 6

The moment they were alone in her office, Noelle spun on him. "What were you thinking?" she cried, slapping her hands onto his chest and pushing him backward with the force of her words and her displeasure.

"I can't do it, Dash. I could barely pull off the cocoa for Taryn. There's no way I can make a batch big enough for the whole damn town. By tonight."

Horror and dismay edged her expression. In that moment, Dash's only concern was to calm her down. They weren't going to get anywhere with her spun up into a panic.

Grasping her arms, he pulled her tight against his body and covered her mouth with his. She fought him, struggling to yank her lips away. Capturing her chin, he held her in place. Slowly, her body overruled her brain, and she began to melt. The gradual transition was entirely erotic and threatened to pull him down into the moment right along with her. The soft sigh that brushed across his lips was almost his undoing, but somehow he found the strength not to succumb. Elle needed him right now. The passion building between them would have to wait.

When he was certain she wasn't going to revert the moment he let her go, Dash pulled back.

She blinked up at him, her eyes glazed with passion and her lips slick and temptingly swollen.

Sliding his hand around to the nape of her neck, he locked her in place. Slowly, reason returned. He hated to watch it seep back into her expression. Her breathing evened out, but the frenetic terror didn't return.

"You weren't surprised when I told you I struggled with the cocoa for Taryn." It wasn't a question. He hadn't realized the error of what he'd said until that moment. He tried not to flinch, but couldn't keep the reaction from flowing through him.

"No."

"Why not?"

"Because one of your elves told me."

He waited for the eruption, but it never came.

"How long have you known?"

"A few days."

"Why didn't you say anything?"

"Because I didn't think it was a problem anymore."

A harsh sound scraped through her throat. "Yeah, right."

Shaking his head, Dash pulled her across the office to the chair positioned behind her desk. Dropping into it, he pulled her down into his lap. He had fond memories of this chair. Was this where those moments would end?

He hoped not.

"Elle, you've got to stop suppressing your Summer half. As long as you won't access all of your power, you're going to struggle."

"What are you talking about? I'm not suppressing anything."

Running his hand up and down her back, he enjoyed the feel of her against his palm. "You are. Do you remember that burst of energy and light when you cloaked the car? The one you thought I was responsible for?"

She tentatively nodded. "I'm still not sure you weren't."

"I promise I had nothing to do with it. Well, nothing aside from relaxing you enough that you couldn't hold it back anymore. I distracted you."

Her beautiful mouth twisted into a grimace. "You mean you blinded me with lust."

His own lips quirked up into a half smile. He couldn't stop himself from leaning forward to brush his mouth down the exposed column of her throat. "Yeah. That. It worked, though, didn't it?"

Her body went liquid in his arms. Her head dropped backward, arching her neck so he could access more of her. A sound of agreement vibrated against his lips.

"You can do whatever you want, Noelle. You just have to trust yourself. And your power." He pressed the words against her skin. "You might be part-Summer, but that's what makes you unique. I love your blue eyes and the way you smell like fresh-cut flowers. The inherent glow to your skin, a light that radiates from deep inside you."

He watched her struggle to accept the words he was saying. The fear and hope and remembered hurt.

"I don't..."

She looked at him helplessly. Noelle was a powerhouse. A whirlwind of competence and bravado. But he saw the insecurity beneath it all. And loved her more for it.

"You can do this, Noelle. I'll be there to help you. We all will."

She swallowed and reluctantly nodded her head. He expected her to jump up and get right to work. They had a lot to accomplish in a few short hours. Instead, she curled against him, tucking her head beneath his chin. Her fingers tangled into his messy hair and held on.

For the first time he could ever remember, she needed something from him. And was letting him give it to her. He'd watched her eyes darken with desire. Had lost himself deep inside her body as she'd surrendered her own to him. They'd been as close as two beings could possibly get.

And somehow, this moment felt more. More important. More profound. More terrifying.

He'd been upset when she'd left the first time. After this, he wasn't sure he'd survive if she disappeared again.

Whispering against her soft hair, he said, "You're the only one who ever thought you didn't belong here, Noelle."

***

Noelle had done it. It had been a rough start, but listening to Dash's soft voice, she'd managed to unlock the piece of herself she'd kept hidden for so long.

Until that moment, she hadn't completely believed what he was telling her. But now that she'd felt it again…he was right.

How could she not have known? How could she have been oblivious to the fact that she was closing off part of herself? Maybe she'd been doing it for so long it was subconscious.

But the feeling of euphoria and elation that rippled through her body along with the full heat of her power was addictive. She wasn't sure she'd be able to lock it away again, not now that she knew it was there.

But maybe that was a good thing.

She managed to keep her professional facade in place while they finished the cocoa and prepped it for transportation to the festival Ethan had thrown together at the last minute. Belle, who apparently knew the owner of A Cup of Cheer, had arranged to use their facilities.

Although the moment the details were all handled, Noelle couldn't hold back anymore. Launching herself at Dash, she trusted him to catch her even as her arms circled his neck. She rained kisses down across his cheeks, nose and chin.

"I did it," she said breathlessly.

"I never had any doubts."

"I know." She grinned at him like an idiot, finally beginning to understand just how much this man believed in her and supported her. And always had.

As much as she wanted to drag him back to her office and show him just how much she appreciated his help, neither of them had the luxury of time for that. She had to settle for a single, deep kiss.

Pulling away, she headed out to check on her elves. Dash followed behind her, his hands stuffed into the pockets of his dress slacks. She knew he'd be more comfortable in a pair of his ratty, worn jeans. But as Evergreen executives, they were all putting in face time at the event, so he was dressed accordingly.

Stopping to check with several of her team, she continued to the shipping bay, where the vat of cocoa was waiting to be loaded onto the delivery van.

She was beside the driver's door when two voices rumbled deeply from the other side.

"We can't load it yet. Zarla volunteered to test it. If it doesn't work on her, we'll just switch her batch with the one Gabriel made."

Noelle gasped. She thought it was under her breath, but the sound of it must have been louder because a scrambling clatter sounded from the other side. Two faces peeked around the edge of the van, shock, terror and apology written over every tiny, wrinkled inch.

"What do you mean the batch Gabriel made? When did my father make cocoa? I thought everything he'd made had been used or thrown out as unstable." After a few weeks, the magick had begun to weaken and become dangerously erratic, which was why they produced the concoction on an as-needed basis.

One of the elves cleared his throat nervously. The other's gaze flickered to the floor.

Pulling out her best "boss" voice, she demanded, "Tell me what you meant. Now."

Dash wrapped a hand around her arm and spun her to face him. But Noelle wasn't finished with the elves. She glared at him, but he wasn't even looking at her. His gaze was focused completely on the men behind her.

"Why don't you both go fetch Zarla?"

Before she could pull in enough breath to order them not to leave, they were scurrying away like roaches from the light.

The hurt blooming inside her chest was quickly being

overrun with anger, and Dash was making himself the perfect target.

Pushing into her personal space, he forced her backward. Her spine collided with the hard panel of the van. Lodged between her open legs, the hard press of his thigh rubbed against her. A thrill of need whipped through her, but she bit down on it and forced it away. Now was not the time.

She ground out, "What are you doing?"

"Talking some sense into you before you do something you'll regret." His hard voice softened. "Elle, he did it because he didn't want you to leave. He loves you and missed you and wanted you to stay."

Unexpected tears stung her eyes. She tried to blink them away, but it didn't help. "He didn't believe I could handle it, Dash. My own father thought I was going to fail."

His mouth turned down into a frown and his beautiful green eyes flooded with sympathy and softness. Part of her wanted it. She wanted to let him wash over her like a balm, soothing away the pinch of pain lodged in the center of her chest.

But that wasn't the kind of girl she was. At least not anymore.

"He didn't understand, Elle. How could he? You've locked everyone out, including him. He was trying to protect you. Help you."

"By lying to me? How in heaven's name is that supposed to help, Dash? 'Let's let the poor thing think she's good enough to handle this while we secretly clean up all her messes?' That's no way to live."

Letting go of his hold on her arms, he slid his finger over the ridge of her cheekbone and smoothed her hair away from her face. "I know, sweetheart. I'm not saying I agree with his methods, just that his actions came from a good place. You have every right to be angry with him, but just take a deep breath and think before you figure out what to do about it. Don't let your emotions force you into a decision you'll regret later."

Slowly, she nodded. His chest rose and fell on a deep sigh. He let his head drop, bringing them forehead to forehead. "I'm sorry, Elle."

Warmth slipped into her veins. Not the familiar blast of explosive need, but something gentler and more comforting.

Maybe if the churning heat had been there, her brain never would have started spinning, but it did. That lull left enough time for a single, irrevocable thought to slam into her.

Shoving his shoulders, she forced Dash backward.

Confusion, sadness and comfort all mixed together inside those damn mesmerizing eyes. Maybe they were enchanted, because they definitely had the ability to blind her.

"You knew what he was doing."

Dash started to shake his head, but stopped just shy of actually making the denial. Dismay and guilt swirled across his expression before he managed to slam a blank wall down.

"I knew he was hiding that he was well enough to return to work, but not what he planned to do with the cocoa."

"Oh, because that makes it better?" Her voice rang with accusation. "He lied to me. You lied to me."

He started to reach for her again, but Noelle flinched away from him. Dropping his hands to his sides, he let them curl into tight fists.

"What would you have done if he told you he was ready to return to work, Elle?" The hard edge in his voice cut across her skin.

"Gone back to my life and my job."

Something bright and painful flashed through his eyes before he gave one hard nod. "Exactly. Elle, you don't belong in D.C. or with the CIA. You belong here, with your clan. With your father." His voice dropped low, a shattering whisper that made her heart ache even as the rest of her body lit up with need. "With me."

She shook her head. Fear and hope and hurt tightened like a band across her chest, stealing her ability to breathe.

Jerking her gaze away from his, Noelle stared up the slope of the mountain she'd once called home. The sharp stab of longing surprised her, but it didn't change anything. Not really. "I don't belong here, Dash. I never have."

Strong hands wrapped around the curve of her shoulders. He moved in front of her, filling her gaze and forcing her to look at him. "You do, Elle. There are people here who love you. Accept you for who you are—everything you are."

Did he mean himself? Did he love her? And if he did, did it matter? Could she give up everything for him? Try again and risk getting her heart ripped into shreds again?

Fear made her entire body tremble. She wanted to. The urge was so strong she almost collapsed into his arms in a sobbing mess. But she couldn't. Noelle Frost was stronger than that. She'd worked hard to figure out who she was and where she belonged.

"Stay, Elle. I want you to stay. I *need* you to stay."

He didn't say he loved her. Or that he wanted to get married again and make this permanent. He'd lied to her. Manipulated her.

She couldn't think when he was this close. She needed logic and space.

Pushing him away again, she stared up into his deep green eyes and said, "Then you shouldn't have lied to me."

She walked away. And once again, he let her go.

Chapter 7

Almost the entire clan was in Gingerbread, making merry and serving mind-wiping cocoa to the entire population, Noelle thought as she looked around her room. Dark wood glowed with a warmth so inherent to the place that it seeped into every nook and cranny.

She was going to miss it. The realization startled her, although she wasn't entirely certain why. Whenever she'd thought back on her life at the lodge, it had been difficult to remember anything other than the painful memories.

Today all the good ones flooded in instead. The few memories she had of her mother, a soft, lilting voice that trickled over her like the melody of a babbling brook. Comforting arms and shocking blue eyes that matched her own.

Moments with her father, his gruff exterior hiding the heart of a teddy bear. She was still angry with him, but Dash had been right. What he'd done had been out of love, even if he'd gone about it the wrong way. But, now that her anger had burned off a little, she could admit some of it was her fault. She could count on one hand the number of times she'd seen him in the past eight years. Whatever had happened between her and Dash, her father hadn't deserved to be punished for it.

And whatever happened now, she made a vow it wouldn't continue that way.

Turning her back on the life she once had, Noelle wheeled her suitcase out into the empty hallway and headed downstairs.

Her chest ached with the force of holding back the tears

that wanted to slip free. There was a sense of déjà vu. The memory of leaving eight years ago melded with now. The difference was that today hurt more.

Why did it hurt more?

It was difficult to see through the sheen of unshed tears. And she was so lost in her own misery that she wasn't paying attention.

Her body slammed into something soft and solid. A high-pitched squeak blasted into the air. Noelle wasn't sure if she'd made the sound or if the person she'd nearly bowled over had.

Automatically, her body shifted to compensate for the change in her center of gravity. Reaching out, she steadied the woman, finally realizing she'd run into Merry.

The older woman blinked up at her with wide, unfocused eyes.

"Noelle, dear, what are you doing here? I thought everyone was in town."

Noelle shook her head, and for some reason the kindly eyes moving softly over her from head to toe were her undoing. Everything she'd been holding back spewed out in a choking sob. Huge, fat teardrops flowed down her face.

Without thought, the other woman reached for her, wrapping Noelle tight against her short, plump body.

"Oh, sweetie. Everything's going to be fine."

Noelle couldn't force words past the gurgling, shrill cacophony of her breakdown, so she just shook her head.

Merry's arms tightened around her. Her hands slipped comfortingly up and down Noelle's spine. She rocked them back and forth as if Noelle was a child and hummed a soothing melody beneath her breath.

Noelle had no idea how long they stood there, but eventually her sobs began to fade. The heavy weight of her grief and fear eased from her chest, leaving nothing but a hitching hiccup.

When the crying jag was finally over, Merry held her

at arm's length. She looked deep into Noelle's eyes and smiled. "Better?"

Noelle nodded, not sure what else to do or say. She'd known Merry her entire life and liked the woman immensely. Who wouldn't? She was sweet and kind and Mrs. Claus, for heaven's sake. But they'd never been overly close. Until today. For some strange reason, Noelle wanted to spill her guts to the woman who reminded her of the grandmother she'd always wanted and had never had.

Merry's gaze dropped to the suitcase at her feet. "Going somewhere?"

"I'm leaving," Noelle croaked out.

"That's a shame. Everyone's going to miss you, Noelle. Especially Dash and Gabriel."

She shook her head, an echo of her earlier anger slipping back. "My father lied to me. He's been well enough to resume his job for weeks. Dash knew and didn't say anything."

A sad smile flitted across Merry's lips. "Sometimes we do hurtful things to the ones we love, Noelle." Plump fingers slipped across her cheek. "Lying to you was wrong, but maybe they had good reason. And at the end of the day, you have to decide what's more important. Are you going to let one mistake destroy everything? Are you going to let your own fears and insecurities come between years of history and love?"

For some reason, Noelle thought maybe Merry was talking about more than her relationship with Dash and her father, but she didn't understand enough to untangle the undercurrents flowing beneath the words.

"Do you love Dash? Do you want a life with him?"

Noelle swallowed and nodded.

"Then what are you doing standing in the hallway with your suitcase? You're a strong woman, Noelle Frost. You've forged and fought. You stand toe-to-toe with anyone who gets in your way. Why are you walking away from what you want without a fight? Again?"

Goose bumps spread across Noelle's skin. Merry was right. She'd looked some of the most dangerous criminals in the eye—murderers, terrorists and spies—without flinching. Why did the thought of opening herself up to Dash make her want to run and hide?

Not anymore.

The smile hardened across Dash's face. He'd been wearing the expression for what felt like days, but was probably only a couple hours. The lie hurt. When would this torture end?

He desperately wanted to get to his hot shop. Not so he could bury his misery in something creative, but so he could smash anything he could get his hands on into tiny, irrevocable shards of glittering glass.

But he had a job to do first. Beside him, Cole and Taryn had their heads bent together as they whispered to each other. Ethan was laughing and Lark was giggling like a schoolgirl. Their happiness scraped across his last nerve.

And Belle...his little sister was nowhere to be seen. The little shit had disappeared barely fifteen minutes into this PR farce. Her untimely disappearances were really beginning to piss him off. He was stuck here, miserable, so why the hell wasn't she?

Dash stared at the gathered crowd. The street was filled. The air rife with happiness and good cheer. Apparently the cocoa had worked, because not a single citizen mentioned the flying car. Although, he'd never doubted. Noelle was one of the most powerful witches he'd ever met.

Just the thought of her had him fighting the urge to double over in pain. He'd lost her. Again.

Determination twisted through his gut. The difference now was that he wasn't willing to let her go. If he had to follow her to D.C., camp on her front porch and tail her on every single job, he'd do it. He'd give up everything for her. Because she was the one thing he couldn't live without.

He was about to tell Cole he was leaving, but before he could, a disturbance erupted at the edge of the crowd. The sea of humanity split. People leaped out of the way as a swirling dynamo forced her way through. A few people grumbled. A couple squeaked protests.

Noelle didn't seem to notice. She had a destination in mind and she was getting there. God, he loved when she was on a tear. His body reacted even as he worried all that seething energy was about to be pointed straight at his head... and not the one that was excited to see her.

As if she could sense his scrutiny, her head jerked up and her gaze slammed into him. Her eyes roiled with emotions, but she was too far away for him to decipher the mess. Her skin was flushed pink and her shoulders were tight and straight.

He held his breath as she approached the platform a couple feet off the ground. Cole and Ethan had both spoken, expressing their appreciation for Gingerbread's support of Evergreen Industries and offering a toast—and a sizable donation—to the entire town. The PA system was now turned off, and they were hobnobbing with the important people.

Without even bothering with the steps, Noelle pressed her hands to the floor and vaulted up onto the platform. God, she was gorgeous.

Every eye was trained squarely on the mesmerizing vision of her. Not that he blamed any of them. He couldn't force his gaze away from the petite dynamo that halted in front of him either.

Noelle glared up at him, her eyes flashing in a way that had dread settling thick and heavy in his belly.

At least she'd bothered to tell him she was leaving this time. Not that that offered him any comfort.

Dash braced. But while he waited for her to utter the words sure to slice straight through him, the anger slowly drained from her face. Placing a soft hand against his face, she went up on tiptoe and pressed a gentle kiss to his lips.

That was not what he'd expected at all. His heartbeat stuttered in his chest, hope blooming even as he tried to tamp it down.

Pulling back, Noelle stared up at him, attempting to fill her expression with a harsh sternness, but failing miserably. "If you ever lie to me again, Dash Evergreen, I'll hurt you. And we both know I can back up that threat."

Dash simply nodded, biting back a grin he knew would earn him some form of punishment.

Apparently satisfied, she wrapped her arms around his neck and pressed her body tight against his.

"I love you, Dash, and have ever since you found me curled up on the sleigh. Do you remember?"

How could he ever forget?

He'd gone into the barn, already in the process of learning the job he'd one day take over. The place had been quiet and, he'd thought, deserted. Until he'd looked inside Santa's sleigh and found Noelle curled up asleep on the seat. Her skin had glowed perfect and pale in the faint light. Her dark hair fanned out across the dark red velvet.

He'd had to touch. He'd only meant to wake her. At least that was what he told himself. But the moment her warmth trickled into his body he hadn't been able to stop himself. The curve of her shoulder, the slope of her collarbone, her cheeks and eyelids and lips. He'd wanted to touch all of her, even back then. The need had been an interminable ache.

And when she'd opened her eyes, so vivid and blue... he'd been a goner. Especially when she smiled at him, all drowsy and flushed and tempting.

He'd started falling for her in that single moment.

"I love you, too, Elle," he whispered, his voice gruff with choked emotion.

"You don't have to lie to me to get me to stay, Dash. All you have to do is ask."

"Please, Elle. Don't leave me. Not again. I don't think I can survive without you."

Brushing her lips against his ear, she whispered, "You don't have to," and then punctuated the words with a sharp nip of his lobe.

He groaned and tightened his arms to crush her harder against his body. Damn all the people.

Somewhere behind him someone giggled. Someone sighed, a kind of perfectly happy sound. Cole and Ethan clapped him on the back. Gabriel's voice boomed, "You better damn well marry the girl again, Evergreen."

Dash pulled back and grinned down into Noelle's perfectly blue eyes. "I don't have to. We're still married."

The shocked expression on Elle's face was priceless.

"Elle didn't rescind her vows before she left. And I sure as hell didn't. I knew there'd never be another woman for me. The year and a day is long gone, so she's stuck with me whether she likes it or not."

Her fingers tangled in the hair at his nape and tugged. "Oh, I like," she said, right before her lips found his. The kiss left them both breathless. A cheer went up around them, followed by a loud cough when it went a little too long for public consumption.

"We'll discuss you keeping that piece of information to yourself, Mr. Evergreen, as soon as we get home."

"Whatever you want, Mrs. Evergreen. I rather like it when you lose your temper."

Elle made a rude noise in the back of her throat, passion and the promise of retribution glittering in her gaze. Her mouth thinned, and he knew she was about to start the argument early, but he didn't give her the chance.

Sweeping her into his arms, Dash stalked to a dark corner and apparated them both home.

He took his time undressing his wife, cherishing the way she looked at him, lust and love, comfort and hope all twining together in her gorgeous blue eyes. Dash felt the echo of those emotions pumping erratically through his own bloodstream.

She reached for him, slipping her soft hands beneath his clothes, searching for skin. The feel of her sizzled through his system.

Slowly, deliberately, she popped each button free, her gaze devouring every inch of his skin she revealed. No one but his Elle had ever been able to make him feel this way, desperate and deliriously happy at the same time.

Bending down, Dash used his mouth to worship her, memorizing and discovering every inch of her body until they were both panting, need held barely in check.

They'd been hot and desperate for each other for days. But tonight, now, was different. Better. Deeper.

Entwining their fingers together, Dash pressed their joined hands into the bed beside Noelle's head. She arched up to him, opening herself and offering him everything.

With the easy, deliberate glide of hard flesh into soft, Dash reclaimed his wife. Noelle met the moment with a soul-deep sigh of acceptance and wonder that did everything to make him feel invincible.

This amazing woman was his.

They came together slowly, milking each stroke, caress and kiss until they were both drowning in sensation, their bodies quivering with release.

"I'll never get enough of you," Dash reverently murmured against her skin.

Hours later, weak sunlight was seeping around the dark curtains when they finally fell asleep, blissfully tangled together.

A loud pounding startled them both awake long before their exhausted bodies were ready. Dash groaned and rubbed at his scratchy eyes. Noelle vaulted out of bed. Her bare feet landed silently on the floor even as her hand groped uselessly at her side.

Recovering first, she threw on a robe and padded over.

The elf waiting on the other side shifted nervously from foot to foot as he wrung his hands. Horror and dread filled his eyes as he blurted out, "Kris and Merry are gone!"

* * * * *

SILVER BELLE

ANDREA LAURENCE

Andrea Laurence is an award-winning contemporary romance author who has been a lover of books and writing stories since she learned to read. A dedicated West Coast girl transplanted into the Deep South, she's working on her own happily-ever-after with her boyfriend and five fur babies. You can contact Andrea at her website, www.andrealaurence.com.

To Vicki, Rhonda and Kira, the ladies I shared this awesome experience with—Working on *Jingle Spells* with you guys was great. Probably the most fun I've ever had plotting and writing a story.
Thank you.

Seven Days until Christmas Eve

Belle hated cocoa. Even when it had fluffy homemade marshmallows or fresh whipped cream on top.

It was a dark secret she would take to her grave or else risk being ostracized by her family and friends. At Evergreen Industries, the witches, wizards and elves that made Christmas magick all drank cocoa. That's just how it had always been. There were no coffeepots in the building, at least none that anyone knew about. There was an emergency Keurig and a stash of pods hidden away in Belle's bottom file drawer. But that was it.

As far as Belle was concerned, their casual dismissal of coffee was a crime, and one that forced her out of the building every day to visit the local coffee shop, A Cup of Cheer. Her emergency brew couldn't hold up to the deep, rich flavors of the coffee she could get at the shop. It was only a few blocks away from the Evergreen corporate offices and worth it for her much-needed jolt of daily caffeine. This close to Christmas it was the only thing that helped her maintain her holiday cheer. Not even Ethan's sparkly, enchanted ornaments worked on her anymore.

Rolling over in bed, she spied the broad, bare shoulders of Nick lying beside her. But it wasn't all bad. She supposed she should really thank her cocoa-imbibing brethren for driving her out of the office each day. It was during those daily visits to the coffee shop that she met local contractor Nick St. John. The successful businessman was tall, dark and undeniably sexy. What had started as a casual flirtation each day turned into more, and before Belle knew it, they were getting their coffee to go and heading to Nick's place.

It wasn't easy being the youngest Evergreen and the only girl, to boot. Her older brothers were nosy, overprotective and could make her life miserable if they wanted to. Dating was impossible. She had her own apartment at the lodge, but it was on the same floor as her parents and her brothers. There would be no comings or goings from her place that someone in her family didn't observe and report.

Belle wasn't supposed to date a human, but they'd made it all but impossible to date a wizard. Besides, two of her three brothers were dating outside the Winter Clan, so she didn't want to hear a word about it.

It wasn't like she and Nick were dating, anyway. It was more of a mutually beneficial arrangement with no strings. Judging by the sore heat between her thighs, the dull throb of her belly and the raw scratchiness in her throat, today was one of their more adventurous mornings.

She watched Nick's shoulders move gently with his soft breathing. The poor guy had worn himself out working so hard to please her, and she appreciated his effort. He was by far the best lover she'd had, and that was saying a lot considering many wizards used magickal trickery in the bedroom. Nick didn't have a crutch like that to lean on, so he had to work hard for every gasp of pleasure that came from her lips.

Belle wanted to reach out and run her palm across his bare back. She wanted to weave her fingers through the dark curls of hair at his neck. With each passing day she was tempted to stay longer. To learn more about the man that ruled her mornings. But she couldn't do any of those things.

Instead, she flung back the sheets and swung her legs out of bed. She moved around his bedroom collecting her clothes from where they had been hastily discarded. Belle had only managed to slip on her red lace panties when Nick rolled over and frowned at her.

"Leaving already?"

"You know I have to go." She tugged her tweed slacks up over her hips and reached for the matching lace bra she'd worn today for Nick's sole benefit. He was very appreciative of her fine lingerie. "I'm already infamous around the office for taking the longest coffee breaks in history."

Nick sighed and sat up, letting the sheets pool low around his waist. *Good gumdrops*, he had a beautiful body. Every inch of Nick's physique was hard, wrought by building homes. Lifting wooden beams and sanding drywall did a body good.

Belle was so distracted by the sight, she buttoned her blouse crooked. She didn't notice until Nick arched a dark, amused eyebrow at her, and she looked down to see what he was looking at. "Oh, *snickerdoodle!*" she cursed, unbuttoning and re-buttoning her top.

"You're so sexy when you talk dirty." Nick slid out from under the covers and walked nude across the room to where she was standing. Judging by his proud, aroused state, he wasn't kidding when he told her that her second-grade swearing vocabulary turned him on.

Nick wrapped his arms around her waist and pulled her close. The press of his firm heat against her belly stirred new pangs of arousal in her. She wanted to strip off all her clothes and waste away the afternoon in his bed, but she couldn't. She had to get back to work. It was a week before Christmas, and things were about to get crazy at the office. Maybe in January she would have enough free time to take off a whole day and indulge in the pleasures Nick had to offer.

Belle lifted the loose strands of her hair between her fingertips and pulled them back into a ponytail. Nick took advantage of her movement, and his lips met with the sensitive skin of her exposed neck. The tingle traveled down her arm and along her spine, tightening her skin into goose bumps and making her tremble slightly in his arms. "Stay," he whispered into her ear.

His rough hands glided across her skin as he started to convince her to stay a little while longer. And then her phone rang.

"Damn it," Nick cursed and stepped away.

"I'm sorry." Belle picked up her phone from the nightstand and frowned. It was her brother, Dash. "Yeah," she said, bypassing any pleasantries.

"I don't know where you are or what kind of slow roast Sumatra coffee you're waiting on, but you need to get your jingle bells back to the office right now."

She planted her hand on her hip in irritation. "Since when did you become my boss, Dasher Evergreen?"

"Would you rather Cole be the one to call? He's in a foul mood, but I can ask him to relay the same message if you're going to be stubborn."

"No, thanks." Her oldest brother Cole was the CEO of Evergreen Industries, so in fact, her brother *was* the boss of her. But given a choice of being chewed out, she'd take Dash any day. "What's the big emergency?"

"I don't think we should talk about it on the phone."

"What? Why?"

"Because we've got a Code Red here, and this line may not be secure."

Dash's words were like a splash of icy water on her libido. A Code Red was the highest alert at the office, reserved only for Santa-related emergencies. Given everything that had happened the last few weeks with Kris and his midlife crisis, she wasn't surprised. But she was concerned. Christmas was only a week away.

"I'll be there in ten minutes."

"No. You need to *apparate*, now."

Belle glanced over her shoulder at Nick. He was tugging on his jeans and trying not to listen in on her discussion. "Now is not the best time for that."

"Then find an alley or go into the ladies' room or something because *Santa is gone!*"

The line went dead, leaving Belle to wonder if she'd heard him right. Santa was gone. That couldn't be right. She'd seen Kris just this morning. Or was that yesterday morning?

"Trouble at work?" Nick asked.

"Yes," she said with a weary smile. "There's a big emergency I need to get back for. Working with family is always special. And this time of year is so busy for us that everything is a crisis of one sort or another."

"I understand. We'd both better get back to work. I've got to install all the cabinets at my latest house today. Same time tomorrow?"

"That's my plan. I'll text you if it changes."

Nick leaned in to kiss her goodbye. The moment his lips met hers, she could feel her head start to swim. He had potent powers over her body. Every nerve lit up at his touch.

Belle pulled away reluctantly and picked her coffee cup up off the nightstand. "I'll see you tomorrow," she said.

Nick waved at her from the front door wearing nothing but his blue jeans. She had to take a deep breath to force her feet down the street toward her office building. Once he shut the door, she looked around for any humans. The street was pretty quiet, but she couldn't take any chances. She ducked between two houses and with one last look around, she flicked her wrist and disappeared.

Nick's truck rumbled over the icy gravel of his latest construction site. He pulled up alongside the van and car of two of his employees. Ben should be inside priming and painting the drywall, and Tom was working on plumbing fixtures. His task today, as he told Belle, was cabinets. He had to get those in so Tom could put in the sinks and faucets.

His heavy boots crunched through the yard until he stepped up over the threshold into the house. There was a large stack of cabinets on the floor, each wrapped with a protective outer layer. Nick had picked them up from the supplier early that morning and dropped them off before going to meet Belle. He pulled a pocket knife out of his belt and set to work unwrapping them all.

He had the base cabinets screwed into place when Ben came into the room behind him. "Hey, Nick. How are the cabinets going?"

"Good so far. Where are we with priming?"

"The downstairs is all done. I've got one bedroom left upstairs. Then I can start the base coat. I painted two coats on the kitchen and bathroom walls yesterday so you could get the cabinets in. I'm expecting to have everything painted with trim and crown molding by Christmas Eve. I thought that was a good stopping point before the holiday."

Nick frowned. Was Christmas really that close? He tried not to pay that much attention, despite the fact that Gingerbread was destination Christmastown, USA. Being surrounded by Christmas all year actually seemed to dull the impact of the real holiday. At least in Denver, he knew when the lights and decorations went up that it was getting to be that time. "How long until Christmas?" he asked.

"A week," Ben said. "Time just flies, man. I've still got to go get a gift for my wife at Baubles. She wants some fancy charm bracelet she saw on television. And of course my kid wants an impossible to get toy from Santa, so I've got to start haunting the internet for that. You got any fun plans this year?"

The answer to that was a resounding no, but Nick didn't tell people that. If folks thought he would spend Christmas alone eating a frozen dinner, they would feel bad and want to invite him to their family dinners and parties. He wasn't interested. He didn't dislike Christmas. Nick just didn't care for the commercial hype that went with it.

This, of course, as he custom-built Christmas-themed bungalows for wealthy snow bunnies. The irony was not lost on him. But that didn't mean he wanted to get all wrapped up in it, either. "Yeah," Nick said. "I'm going to drive up to see my folks in Denver."

"That's great." Ben smiled. "I'm going to haul in the last of my primer and get that bedroom knocked out."

Nick watched his employee disappear into the yard and focused his attention back on the cabinets. He snorted quietly to himself as he thought about the idea of actually spending Christmas with his parents. He couldn't imagine a more stressful, awkward holiday experience.

About six years ago, when he'd first started his business, he'd been too busy to go home for Christmas. The next year, it seemed like a good excuse to use again. Then he moved to Gingerbread, and the lie perpetuated itself year after year. No one seemed to miss him. They just sent a generic fruit basket like he was one of his father's clients. He was pretty sure they got the same cellophane-wrapped dome of apples and oranges he did.

Christmas had become just another day, and one where he couldn't even get food from a drive-thru at that.

Nick did wonder what Belle would be doing for Christmas. She hadn't mentioned anything, although he was certain the holiday was a big deal in the Evergreen household. Her family was famous for their Christmas ornaments, and her brother Ethan was a holiday fixture on television. They donated a small fortune to the community and other charities. But aside from that, no one really knew much about them or their company. You could sit outside the building for hours and not see a single soul go in or out. And aside from Belle and her brothers, Nick didn't know another person in town that actually worked there. It was a factory. There should be hundreds of community residents working for Evergreen Industries.

The Christmas cynic in him wondered if they secretly shipped in all their ornaments from a plant in India or Mexico and just claimed to make them here. Anything was possible when nothing was really known about them.

Despite the fact that he'd spent every morning with Belle for the last six months, he didn't have much more insight than anyone else.

At first, Belle's silence was refreshing. They were both very busy professionals. Their time together was fun and easy. She never lay in bed and bored him to tears with stories about the banalities of her day or how she broke a nail opening a pickle jar.

She also didn't demand quality time with him outside of their daily interludes. They hadn't been on a single date by his recollection. They'd never even shared a meal aside from the occasional scone with their coffee. Belle never called and rarely texted. It was the perfect relationship for him as he poured every ounce of energy into his company. Most women he'd dated hadn't understood how much time and effort it took to be successful, and they eventually gave up on him. Usually, that was just fine by Nick.

And yet...he'd found himself wondering about Belle. At first, he thought he'd hit the woman jackpot. She showed up daily for hot sex and was out the door before he could make up some excuse for her to leave. But over time, he found himself wishing she would stay even as she disappeared. She was the first woman he dated that left him wanting more, but he was too respectful of their arrangement to push for anything more substantial than what they had. He didn't want to be like the women that had always pressured him to give more than he could.

But it did make him curious about his elusive lover. Why didn't they ever go back to her place? He didn't even know where she lived. Hell, she could be married for all he knew. And what were all those calls and texts about that sent her scuttling off from his bedroom each day? Yesterday was a security problem and today, some emergency. What kind of emergency could she run into at an ornament manufacturing company? Nick couldn't come up with much. He knew one thing, though.

He couldn't wait for 10 a.m. tomorrow morning.

Belle reappeared in her office half a heartbeat after she vanished from Nick's neighborhood. She was dizzy for only a moment and didn't spill a precious drop of her double-shot latte with peppermint. As the details of her office came into focus around her, she took a deep breath. *Apparating* was not her favorite form of travel, even if it was the most efficient. She enjoyed the occasional brisk walk through the cold winter air. It helped clear her mind. But time was not on her side today.

Once she got her bearings, she slipped out of her coat and dumped it and her purse onto her desk. She picked up her tablet and walked over to the mirror on the back of her office door. Whenever she came back from Nick's, she had to make sure her appearance didn't give any signs of what she'd been up to. A quick glance confirmed that her golden-blond hair was still neatly slicked back into a low ponytail. Her makeup looked fine, although she could use more lipstick. Her clothes looked just as neat and professional as they had when she left the office. All was well.

Then she frowned. Leaning into the mirror she focused on a dark smudge just below her ear. She rubbed at it with her finger, but it didn't disappear. Then she realized what it was. Nick had given her a hickey. Of all the things... Belle groaned and dug in her purse for some concealer. She blotted the mark with the makeup, and then readjusted her scarf to cover it. Her brothers could not see that. Santa emergency or not, they'd be all in her business.

That done, she could finally go in search of Dash to find out what the *holly* was going on with Kris Kringle.

It wasn't hard to find them. She only had to follow the loud voices down the Hall of Santas to Cole's office. All three of her brothers were there, frowns lining their faces.

Sitting in the corner was Dash's ex-wife, Noelle. By some weird twist of fate, they were dating again, but she didn't look blissfully in love today. Not that she ever did. Noelle was an intense person. She'd left Evergreen to join the CIA, returning earlier this year to fill in for her ailing father as the head of security.

Today, Noelle appeared even more unapproachable. Her dark brown hair was slicked back into a severe bun. Her normally bright blue eyes were tired and bloodshot with gray circles beneath them. She looked as if she had been up all night. And not in a good way.

"Belle, you're here. Good. Sit down," Cole said, gesturing to the empty chair in the office.

The three brothers all turned to Noelle, mostly ignoring their sister. "Okay, now that Belle is here, start from the beginning."

Noelle took a deep breath. "Late last night, I ran into Merry in the hallway. She had luggage with her, but I was too distracted to think about what that meant. Dash and I had a fight, and I was considering leaving Gingerbread. Merry talked me out of it, and then she left. I ran back to apologize to Dash. It wasn't until this morning when we found the Corvette was missing that I realized I had caught her midflight and didn't know it."

"Merry is gone?"

The four other heads in the room turned to look at Belle. Apparently, she was behind the curve. "Dash only told me that Kris was gone," she explained.

"They're both gone," Noelle clarified. "They took off last night in the Corvette. We have no way of knowing if they're ever coming back."

Belle's jaw dropped open. This was a Code Red if she'd ever seen one. Santa was MIA. It was no wonder she was summoned back. The minute any employee issue arose, it fell into her territory to work on the problem, be it an elf strike or inappropriate wizardry in the workplace.

"We have to replace him immediately," Cole decreed.

"Wait a minute," Belle argued. "We don't know he's gone for certain. He might have just needed some air to clear his head. We know they've been having marital troubles. A couple days away together might be what they need to come back and rededicate themselves to the job."

"Yes, but all of their troubles have revolved around his role as Santa," Ethan argued. "He would sacrifice that for Merry and the sake of their marriage. He's not coming back. I can feel it. His Christmas spirit has fizzled out."

"But what if Kris does come back? Once the new Santa puts on his suit, the magick is severed, and Kris can never be Santa again. This is a huge step to take, and we can't go back. Did they leave a note? Anything to let us know what their plans are?"

"There was no note," Dash said. "But Kris left this behind." He held up the holly pin that Kris always wore on his lapel. The shiny brooch had three solid-gold holly leaves and a cluster of diamond-and-ruby berries in the center that were more than one carat each. It was handed down from Santa to Santa, an antique so priceless, any collector would kill to have it. *If* they knew it existed. "It was on his desk. That's a pretty clear sign to me that he's done."

"Belle, you need to find a new Santa. It's only a week until Christmas. Six days, if you consider Christmas begins in the Pacific twenty hours before Gingerbread. We can't waste any time."

Belle eyed her oldest brother as she twisted her lips in thought. Kris had been Santa for twenty years, almost her whole life. He was the only Santa she remembered. Choosing a new Santa was a monumental task, and one that only happened every other generation.

The role of Santa was always filled by a human, and he was selected by the Winter Clan's magickal means. Even if the person wanted to be Santa, and sometimes they didn't, it wasn't easy. She tapped at her tablet and pulled up the checklist that would need to be completed before a new Santa could drive off in the sleigh. The assimilation of a human into Gingerbread alone could take nearly a month if all went well.

"It's impossible," she said, shaking her head. "We'd do better to send out a team to look for Kris and bring him back. If we can convince him to do one more Christmas, we'll have a whole year to get his replacement ready."

"What if he won't come back? Or we can't find him? Are you willing to risk Christmas, Belle? Because if we don't get someone on that sleigh in less than a week, Christmas won't happen. If he comes back, great, but I'd rather have too many Santas than too few."

Six Days Until Christmas Eve

Belle had been dismissed from the meeting so she could immediately get to work. But she wasn't as convinced as Cole was that they needed to select a new Santa right away. If she could get a Santa ready in seven days, six wasn't much more of a hardship, and it bought her a day to try another tactic. Instead, she'd pegged two of her assistants, Ginger and Holly, for a special assignment.

Kris didn't know that Dash had put a GPS tracking system on the Corvette last week. It hadn't been intended to stalk Kris, but to track his Christmas flight and ensure they could recover the car if it was stolen. Kris had demanded that Dash enchant the convertible so he could fly it on Christmas instead of the sleigh. If by some chance Noelle's cloaking device failed and a human got into the car, they couldn't risk it accidentally flying through the air with them trapped inside.

None of the brothers had mentioned tracking Kris, but that was because they'd given up on him. Belle hadn't, at least not yet. She hoped that Kris and Merry were coming back. It wasn't like them to leave everyone in a lurch like this. But like Ethan, she knew in her heart that Kris had lost the joy of his work. She understood how he felt, but that said, if Ginger and Holly could find him, Belle wasn't above coercing him into one last trip around the world. Then she would happily replace him if that was what he really wanted.

Right now, the GPS was showing the Corvette was in Arizona and continuing south. She wouldn't be surprised if they were headed to Mexico or even South America and its warmer climate. Ginger and Holly were gone in search of them by midafternoon.

Belle had hoped to hear from them soon. Like that evening. But it was the following morning, and there was no word from her assistants yet. She needed to take a two-pronged approach and start the new Santa process, as well.

She made her way down the hallway to Santa's office. Belle rarely came into this room at Evergreen. If all went well, there wasn't any reason to. It was normally Santa's retreat, the place where he could work and think without constant interruption.

With a swipe of her security card, the heavy golden doors swung open, allowing her inside. The large space was filled with wondrous antiques and magickal artifacts from years of Christmases past. Large shelves along one wall housed a massive collection of leather-bound books. Some were first editions of beloved Christmas tales like *A Christmas Carol* and *A Visit from St. Nicholas*, but most were the naughty and nice archives from back before they went digital. Another wall was lined with all the gifts children had left him over the years. Milk and cookies were the American standard, but on the occasion that a child left Santa a drawing or a coffee mug, it was always brought back and kept here.

Santas, as a general rule, were very sentimental. They couldn't throw away anything a child gave them, be it a popsicle stick reindeer they made in school or a flashlight to help him see in the dark.

Belle continued through the office, stepping around several large burgundy velvet bags overflowing with mail. She frowned at the sight. Kris had not been reading his mail from the children like he was supposed to. He'd been too busy jogging and juicing lately to do his job. She would have to get Taryn to send down someone to log the gift requests in the system since she was the new head of the IT department.

At the back of the room was another door. Belle swiped

her card to open it, revealing the most secret and sacred of rooms at Evergreen Industries. In tall, lighted, glass cabinets were Santa's clothes from Christmases past. The uniform had changed over the years, and when an outfit was retired, it was displayed here as a revered museum piece. She stopped to admire one of her favorites. The old Father Christmas style included a long, dark green, velvet, hooded cloak lined in soft, white fur. It was hand-embroidered with a holly pattern; the gold thread and tiny gemstone berries made it sparkle in the light. It was beautiful. Much more festive and true to the spirit of Christmas in Belle's eyes.

Beside it was the original red-and-white suit from the early 1900s. It wasn't their decision to go with the style, but once popular culture set an expectation of what Santa wore, they had to follow along. A newer design was beyond it, modernized by the Coca-Cola styling of the thirties and forties.

A rack just beyond the cases held several replicas of the current Santa suit. It was still red and white, but the style was more modern, and they had made some technological advances to it over the years.

On the far wall was Belle's destination. The delicately carved curio cabinet was the home to the most sacred of the Winter clan's heirlooms. The side panels were inset with stained glass depicting falling snowflakes in blue, white and silver. The front was clear glass with a doorknob made of one gigantic sapphire.

Belle grasped the knob and opened the door. There were four shelves inside holding a variety of treasures. The wand of the Winter clan's founding mother was there. The heavy, leather-bound copy of the original naughty and nice list was there. As was the snow globe.

The large glass sphere was nestled in a sterling-silver base. All around the bottom were intricate Christmas scenes of the past. Silver reindeer antlers curled around the glass globe like talons keeping it in place. Inside was only snow. No snowman figurines, no quaint villages. Just snow.

This was what she had come for. She grasped the snow globe with two hands, surprised at how heavy it was. This was how the next Santa was chosen. An enchantment was placed on the snow globe hundreds of years earlier. It had the power to see into the hearts and minds of every person on the planet. It would choose, with over 99 percent accuracy, the perfect new Santa. With just a shake, the face of the chosen replacement would appear.

This was the first time Belle had needed to use it. Nervously, Belle gave the snow globe a good jostle, then held it steady to watch. The snow danced furiously inside, a mini blizzard swirling and sparkling with the faint blue magickal glow. When the flakes settled, a man's face slowly appeared. It was clear as day. The dark hair, the chocolate-brown eyes, the mischievous smile.

It was Nick.

No, Belle argued with herself. There had to be something wrong with this thing. Nick was about as far from Santa material as they came. He was too young, for one thing. Santas were usually in their forties at least, and Nick was barely thirty if she remembered correctly. Nick was sexy and hard-bodied, not cheerful and soft. He was career driven and health conscious. She'd never seen him so much as put a packet of sugar in his coffee, much less eat ten thousand sugar cookies in one night.

And frankly, she didn't get the touchy-feely vibe from him. She'd never seen Nick around kids, but she imagined he'd hold one at arm's length with suspicion in his eyes.

Belle frowned. Somehow, the snow globe had made a mistake. She gave it another shake, erasing Nick's image with a flurry of snow. She waited, her heart pounding in her chest as the next image slowly formed.

Nick's smiling face continued to stare back at her from inside the globe.

Her heart dropped into her stomach with a nauseating ache. This couldn't be right. At least, she didn't want it to be right. Maybe he was secretly soft-hearted and good with children. Maybe he secretly adored cookies, but stayed away to keep in shape. Belle didn't know as much about Nick as she thought. And that had been by design on both their parts. Their secret rendezvous were supposed to be easy, casual fun. A little stress relief in their crazy, busy lives.

And now she would lose him, like everything else, to the holiday machine.

Belle loved Christmas. And she loved her work and her life in Gingerbread. But sometimes...she needed to get away from all of it. She wanted to spend time with someone who didn't curse with Christmas slang and thought elves were make-believe.

Her mornings with Nick were her escape. The time she spent with him kept her sane. He was her daily dose of normal in a world of magick and merriment. And with one shake of a snow globe, she'd lost it all.

A chirp sounded at her hip. She placed the snow globe back in the cabinet and shut the door before looking at the screen of her phone. It was her fifteen-minute reminder of her standing coffee break appointment.

Belle sighed and put the phone back in her pocket. Nick was going to get a little more than a cup of coffee and some lovin' today.

Belle was late.

Nick sat at a corner table, nursing his grande black-drip coffee. He checked his cell phone again, but there were no texts saying she was running behind. Belle was punctual to a fault. It made him wonder if yesterday's emergency was just a rouse to leave. He'd never been with a woman so emotionally disconnected from sex. Was this her not-so-subtle way of brushing him off?

He got his answer when the front door opened and Belle

blew into the coffee shop. She turned to him and gave a short wave before ordering her coffee. Nick got up from the table and waited for her at the counter where the barista would leave her drink when it was ready.

There was something odd about Belle today. He picked up on it almost immediately. Her smile wasn't as bright, her green eyes were wary. Perhaps the emergency was real and more serious than he thought. She seemed to be carrying a heavy burden on her shoulders.

"Hey, Nick," she said with a weak smile as she approached.

"Decaf non-fat grande latte." Her cup was passed across the counter to her. She slid it into the cardboard sleeve and popped a lid on the top.

Decaf? Belle never ordered decaf. Something was definitely going on, but he didn't want to ask her with so many other people around. "Are you ready to go?" he asked. They usually didn't loiter long.

She nodded, and he held the door for her to step outside. They walked quietly down the block, sipping their coffee. She wanted to tell him something. He could tell. Perhaps she was about to break it off.

"Is something wrong?" he asked, once they were clear of the street traffic and on the quiet road to his subdivision.

"Wrong? No. But we do need to talk about something today. It's kind of important."

Nick's heart stopped. The breath was sucked from his chest in an instant as his brain pieced together the clues. Decaf coffee. Tired. Nervous mood. Important discussions. Belle never wanted to talk about anything.

"Are you pregnant?" he choked.

Belle's eyes grew wide at his question. "Pregnant?" she repeated, her voice sharp with surprise. "Of course not. Why would you think something like that?"

Nick closed his eyes and took a deep breath. It was as though he'd been jerked back from a cliff, and his whole life was about to change if he fell. She wasn't pregnant. Great. He wasn't opposed to children, but he wasn't exactly in that place right now. Especially if it meant having them with a woman he really knew nothing about. "I'm sorry," he said. "You were acting nervous, drinking decaf, wanting to talk… you never want to talk, Belle."

She smiled and shook her head. "I'm sorry I scared you. I am definitely not pregnant. I was up early, and I've already had one cup too much caffeine to deal with everything going on. My nerves are on edge. But I do have a uh…*business proposition* to discuss with you."

Business proposition? "Do you need a house built?"

"Not exactly." Belle paused at his doorstep, and he unlocked the door to go inside. "Let's sit down."

For the first time, they didn't head down the hallway to his bedroom, but turned right to the living room and kitchen. Belle sat down on his brown leather sofa and tucked one leg beneath her. Nick followed suit, sitting on the other end of the couch and turning to face her while he sipped his coffee.

"So what's going on, Belle?"

"That emergency yesterday was kind of a big deal where I work," she began.

"How bad of an emergency can you have at an ornament factory? Someone lose a hand or something?"

"No, but still very bad. We lost a very important member of our staff unexpectedly." Belle reached into her coat and pulled out a small silver flask. She sat it on the coffee table.

"Are we drinking? It's a little early."

"No. That's just my back-up plan."

Nick frowned. "Back-up plan?"

"Nick, I need to tell you a secret. It's a big secret that only a few people in the whole world know about. I have deliberately kept it from you for your own good, but I've been given no choice. I have to tell you the truth."

"You're a spy?" he joked.

"No, I'm a witch. And you are going to be the next Santa Claus."

Nick was glad he didn't have a mouthful of coffee or he would've made a mess of Belle's cream-colored blouse. He was on the verge of laughing at her joke when he realized her expression was deadly serious. "So, will the Easter Bunny be joining us later?"

"No. Spring isn't my territory," she retorted without missing a beat. "We're from the Winter clan. My family is responsible for Christmas. We use our magickal powers to make Santa and his reindeer fly, deliver toys around the world in a single night and spread holiday cheer."

Nick was beginning to think he liked Belle better when she didn't say much. Now that she was talking, he was sad to realize she was batshit crazy. "Did you skip some important medication today?"

Belle's lips tightened into a firm line. "I have to show you, don't I? You're not going to believe it until you see it."

"See what, Belle? Are you going to use your magic wand to make me into Santa Claus?"

"Something like that." Belle stood up. Reaching inside her purse, she pulled out a long, thin piece of wood, like a conductor's baton. She tapped it a few times against the palm of her hand, sending a few tiny, sparkling snowflakes out of the tip.

"What the hell?" Nick stood up and took a step back.

Belle flicked her wrist and pointed the wand to the bare corner of his living room. A surge of white, glittering light shot from it, and in an instant, there was a seven-foot Christmas tree in the corner. With another swipe, a silvery swirl wrapped around the pine branches, leaving lights and ornaments behind it until the tree was completely decorated.

"Are you more of a star or angel kind of guy?"

"What?" His heart was pounding too hard in his chest to grasp what she was asking him.

"A star, I think." A quick jab of her wand conjured a shining silver star on the top of the tree. When she was done, she slipped her wand back into her purse and calmly sat down on the couch.

Nick swallowed hard and stepped backward from the tree and its conjurer until his back met with the brick of his fireplace. "What is going on?"

Belle sighed and patted the couch beside her. "I'm sorry for the theatrics, but I need you to listen and believe what I'm telling you. We don't have much time. Christmas is less than a week away."

Christmas. Witches. Santa. Magick. The words swirled in his mind as he tried to make sense of it.

"Nick, please sit down. I'm not going to hurt you. I'm the same person you've seen every day of the last six months."

"Not exactly," he sputtered.

"Yes, exactly. We just didn't talk much about ourselves."

"If we had, would you being a witch have come up?"

"No. We can't tell humans our secret. It's for our protection as much as yours."

"But you're telling me now."

"Only because I have no choice. You are the chosen. The next Pere Noel, Sinter Klaas or Babbo Natale. If you choose to accept this honor, you *will* be Father Christmas."

"And if I don't accept your crazy offer?"

The light faded from Belle's green eyes. "If you decline, you need only take a sip from this flask. You will remember nothing about this offer or anything that you saw. It will be as though it never happened. It will also be as though *we* never happened. The next time you see me on the street, I will be just another stranger."

There was a sudden, restrictive tightness in Nick's chest. He didn't think he wanted to be Santa Claus, but he didn't want to lose Belle, either. "Wait—can't we just go back to yesterday like this conversation didn't happen?"

A small smile curled Belle's lips. "No, I'm sorry. I assure you that I am as disappointed as you are by this development. There are only two choices. You come with me now to Evergreen Industries and become the next Santa Claus, or you drink from the flask, and you and I are done."

Nick eyed the flask and slowly eased back down onto the couch. "What's in that thing?"

"Cocoa."

He arched a dark brow at her. "Just cocoa?"

"It's a special batch."

Nick sank back into the cushions. "If I turn down the job, what happens on Christmas Eve?" Part of him couldn't believe the words coming from his own mouth. Santa wasn't real. Flying reindeer didn't exist. His parents bought all his presents. He remembered the crushing disappointment when his father told him the truth. The magick of Christmas had died for him in that moment, leaving only a hollow, commercial shell behind. And yet there was enough of a spark in his mind to wonder what would happen if what Belle said was true.

"I'm not sure. We've never had this happen before. I'll go back and see if a new Santa can be chosen in time. If not..." A shimmer of tears formed in her emerald eyes. "...I failed. And for the first time in hundreds of years, there will be no Christmas."

Nick wanted to reach out to her and comfort her. Belle had always been so even-keeled. She came off as a no-nonsense businesswoman with her sharp suits and slicked-back hair. This was the first time he'd noticed a crack in her emotional veneer. "What happened to the previous Santa Claus? Is he...uh..." He hesitated to ask a teary woman if Santa was dead.

"He's fine," she said with an irritated tone lacing her words. "Kris disappeared in the night, leaving us high and dry with days left until Christmas. We've looked everywhere for him, but we haven't had any luck yet."

Santa went AWOL? This job might not be as merry as it seemed. "Will you excuse me a moment?"

Belle turned to him with concern, but nodded. She probably thought he was about to sneak out the back door but was polite enough not to follow him, anyway. "Of course."

Nick brushed past her and slipped into the guest bathroom. Hovering over the sink, he splashed cold water on his face. He braced his arms on the porcelain edge and looked at himself in the mirror.

Was it possible that Santa Claus was real? Disappointment and disillusionment had hardened him to the season. It was supposed to be about love and family, giving and sharing. Instead, it had become about Black Friday sales and the latest, impossible-to-find toy. People would spend the whole month gorging on cookies and candy and turkey, while tossing a token can of expired peas into the food drive bins at work.

That's why Nick had mentally checked out. If he just pretended Christmas never happened, he wouldn't have to face the reality of what it had become.

But maybe he was wrong. Maybe there still was some magick left in the season. If there was any chance that he could have back the holiday of his childhood, he would take it. But even with wands and elves, was it even a possibility? Was his own heart too hardened to embrace Christmas again?

His own dark eyes reflected to him, a faint shimmer of tears blurring his vision. Perhaps it wasn't too late for him or for others like him.

He snatched the towel from the nearby rod and dried his face before going back into the living room. Belle was still sitting patiently on the couch when he returned.

She stood up and turned to face him when she saw him walk back into the room. Belle had such a fragile beauty about her. There was something about the golden waves of her hair, large jewel-tone eyes and creamy, blush cheeks that reminded him of a china doll. He'd thought at first he might break her, especially considering he was a foot taller and at least eighty pounds heavier. But Belle had a spine of steel and enough ambition for two or three people. He loved the contradiction of her.

For the last six months, she had been the highlight of his day. Even before he laid a hand on her, he'd timed his breaks so he would see her at the coffee shop. She was always so businesslike and proper. He had wanted to see her wild and free. And he had, many times. She was never as beautiful as when she came undone in his arms. But Belle had never let him see all of her. She held so much back.

He never expected her secrets to be so earth-shattering. And yet, once the panic subsided, the truth had suited her so perfectly. This was the puzzle piece he was missing. The mysterious details of Belle's life that he'd craved all this time. And he'd only gotten a tiny taste of the true woman. He wasn't ready to drink the cocoa and let her go just yet.

"Do I have to decide right now?"

She shook her head. "We still have some time. I can take you to the Evergreen offices first. I'll introduce you to the clan and show you around. It will give you a better idea of what you're signing up for. It isn't all like the children's books, but it's still quite magnificent. Then you can decide."

Nick could deal with that. If things got too weird, he could always drink the cocoa, walk out and go back to being his old, cynical self. "Let's go, then." He grabbed his coat and keys off the kitchen counter. "Do you want me to drive? I don't even know if you have a car."

Belle smiled brightly for the first time today, and it made his heart feel lighter to see her happy again. "We don't need a car."

Nick frowned. "It's a long walk. What are we going to take? A broom?"

Belle chuckled. "Only the Autumn Clan rides brooms. We're going to *apparate*. It's faster and one of the only ways to get inside the building with our extensive security system." She reached out and took his hand.

Nick wasn't sure he even knew what *apparate* meant.
"You don't get motion sickness, do you?" she asked.
"What?" Nick said, turning to her with concern.
And then they were gone.

Sixty-Three Hours until Take-off

Belle looked at her cell phone and frowned. She'd just received a text from Holly. Apparently, she and Ginger had a bit of an issue at the Mexican border and had missed their chance to intercept the Corvette. Since neither of the girls had ever set foot out of Colorado, they were unable to envision the location in their mind. And witches and wizards could only *apparate* to locations they had been before.

Awesome. The longer they waited, the farther Kris and Merry traveled without them.

Things weren't much better at Evergreen Industries.

Cole stuck his head into Belle's office, the stress of the last few days visibly lining his face. "Has he signed yet?"

"No, he hasn't signed yet," she snapped. He'd asked her this question at least ten times since Nick came. "We've started the orientation process to get ahead of the game, but Nick hasn't signed the contract or tried on the suit."

Cole rolled his eyes and bashed his forehead forcefully against the door frame. "Remind me why I was chosen to be the CEO?"

"Because you're the oldest Evergreen and the most responsible of the four of us."

"And you're the baby," he noted, "and everyone does what you want. So get out of this office, find Nick and do whatever it takes to convince him to take this job. Today."

Belle watched Cole disappear down the hallway in a huff. Usually, Cole was a lot more easygoing. If any of the Evergreens were going to send wizards and witches fleeing from the sight of them, it was usually Belle. She was tiny, at five-foot and an angel's hair tall, but feisty enough that her size didn't matter. She could intimidate the smallest elves and tallest wizards alike.

She didn't like to think of herself as intimidating. That's not what she wanted to be. She kept the employees of Evergreen Industries happy, but productive. Christmas was no small undertaking. There were procedures to be followed, checklists to tick off and policies to uphold. If that made her come off as strict, she'd live with that for the sake of the children. She didn't have time to waste on silliness.

And she didn't have time to waste on Nick, either. When she said he didn't have to decide right away, she thought a tour and a couple of hours would do the trick. It had been two days and so far, nothing. It was a big decision, but it was now or never.

Belle grabbed her tablet and headed out in search of Nick. He'd spent the morning touring the underground toy and ornament production floors with Ethan. The security system showed his last badge swipe was the cafeteria. They'd gotten him a temporary card to move around the facility and get comfortable. It had proven to be a useful tool in keeping track of him, as well.

She summoned an elevator and headed to the cafeteria to find him. As she entered the large dining hall, she stopped short. It was lunchtime, and the room was quite full, but it took only a moment to locate Nick. The six-foot-two construction manager was seated in a green plastic chair more suited to an elf. His knees protruded over the top of the table, so he had to lean in between them to reach his tray of food. It looked miserably uncomfortable. Belle could hardly stand to sit in those chairs, and she was one of the tiniest witches in the building. Despite all of that, he was smiling and chatting animatedly with the crowded table of elves around him.

Belle couldn't help but smile. Despite her reservations, the snow globe knew better. Perhaps Nick would fit in here just fine. Now it was only her selfishness motivating her reluctance for him to become Santa.

Honestly, she didn't know why she cared. Whether he became Santa or not, Belle had lost her morning coffee breaks. If he left, he wouldn't remember her. And if he stayed, things between them would be…complicated to say the least. She certainly couldn't continue her affair with him as Santa. That was just wrong on so many levels. And she had no intention of being the next Mrs. Claus, either. She couldn't bake or knit, and the idea of doing either bored her to tears.

Her only real choice would be to sit back and watch as another woman took her place. Maybe a human, maybe a witch. Their Santas usually came married, so it wasn't an issue they had dealt with in her memory. It was miserably selfish, but Belle knew she would rather Nick leave and Christmas be ruined than to watch him with another woman for the next forty years. She didn't realize she had such a jealous streak, but it seemed to run deep where Nick was concerned.

Either way, in the end, Belle was left with nothing. Well, not *nothing*. She still had a job to do. They needed a Santa, and Nick needed to make a choice.

Nick turned in her direction and noticed her watching him. He waved, and all the elves at the table turned and waved, too. Despite the pain of losing Nick, Belle knew she had to smile and wave back. She didn't want her feelings on the situation to influence Nick's decision. This was his life on the line, not hers, even if it felt that way at the moment.

Nick said a few things to the elves, and then stood up from the table with his lunch tray. He weaved through the tiny tables to where she was standing. "Afternoon, Belle."

"Hi, Nick."

"I was thinking about you when the glockenspiel chimed ten this morning."

Belle couldn't help the blush that instantly colored her

cheeks. "Shh…" she whispered. "No one knows about all that."

"We're in a crowded, loud room. Who's going to hear us?"

"Elves, Nick. Those big ears aren't just for show. If you're done eating, dump your tray, and we can go somewhere more private to talk."

They went out into the hallway, and Belle gestured for him to follow her to the nearby Cranberry conference room. She shut and locked the door behind them. Nick immediately rounded the large meeting table and walked to the wall of windows that looked out over Gingerbread. "It's hard to look at this town and see things the same way I did three days ago. I drove by this building every day and never imagined there was a toy production facility run by elves fifty feet below my tires. And do you know how many times I've gone hiking or mountain biking on Mistletoe Mountain? And to think there's an entire wizard village up there, and I never knew it."

Belle sat at the edge of the table and crossed her arms over her chest. "You weren't supposed to know. Not everyone is allowed to see."

"That's a shame," he said, turning from the window to face her. "Most people could use a little more wonder and magick in their lives. Adults, especially. They lose the childhood wonder too soon."

"We do what we can," Belle explained, "but most adults have lost their ability to believe."

Nick nodded and took a few steps closer to her. "Despite all the wonderful things I've seen and learned, I've still missed you these last few days."

Belle straightened up a bit, stiffening at his approach. She had wanted to keep this discussion professional. "I've been here the whole time."

He leaned into her, pressing his palms into the hardwood table. Nick loomed over her with his large frame, forcing her to lean backward or find herself in a compromising position on the conference table. If she caught one of her employees like this, they'd find themselves in her office getting a reprimand.

"It's not the same," he said, his dark eyes focused on her lips while he spoke. "I've been able to touch you, taste you, nearly every day for months. Then all of a sudden, everything changed."

His voice was low, his words like a verbal caress. Belle was too close to Nick not to respond to him. The warm scent of his cologne teased at her senses and took her back to his house. To the smell of him on the pillowcases. It made her want to inhale deeply and keep that part of him with her when she lost the rest. An ache of need gnawed at her center, forcing her to clamp her thighs tightly together. A lot of things may have changed in the last few days, but her body hadn't gotten the memo.

Nick frowned at her silent rebuff of his advances. "What's the matter, Belle? Have I lost my appeal now that I'm not the unsuitable boy from the wrong family? Is the thrill gone if I'm a part of your world permanently?"

She had thought that once. The thrill of seeing Nick had to be because of the secret, forbidden nature of it. Belle swallowed hard, and his eyes focused on the movement of her throat. Her breath was rapid and quick, moving in time with the desperate beating of her heart.

She was wrong. Nick knew all her secrets, had nearly become an integral part of Evergreen operations, and she wanted him more than ever.

Nick leaned in closer, his lips a whisper away from her own. Any movement would bring them together, and Belle knew that if she kissed him, she wouldn't be able to stop.

"I'm sorry, Nick."

"For wha—?"

Before he could finish his question, Belle vanished and reappeared on the other side of the room. Nick stared at the empty table in front of him for a moment, not quite sure what to think.

"For that," she said.

Nick jerked to face her direction. She expected him to be angry, but his lips twisted with amusement. His dark eyes watched her with appreciation, although he didn't approach her again. "You know, our affair could be that much more interesting for all the new tricks you could bring to the bedroom."

"Nick..." Belle began, not quite sure what to say to him. *I can't date you if you're Santa* seemed silly.

He didn't wait for the words. Instead, he crossed his arms over his chest and widened his stance. "So if you didn't come to see me for a jolt of caffeine, what do you want, Belle?"

"I need you to make your choice."

"You said I had time."

"I said that two days ago, Nick. It's December 21. You have to choose. The suit or the cocoa."

"That depends," he said. "You said the cocoa would make me forget you."

Belle was afraid he would focus on that. "And everything else you've seen and heard while you were here," she reminded him.

"So if I go home, I won't remember anything I've seen, and you and I are done."

She nodded.

"And if I stay?"

"You and I are still done," she said, as much as the words pained her.

"Why? Is there some sort of conflict of interest? Are we forbidden to be together if I'm Santa Claus?"

"No."

"Okay. I know it's not a human-witch thing. I've seen two of your brothers roaming around the building with human women. So what is the problem? Will my hair turn white and my belly get flabby the instant I put on the suit?"

"You'll age normally. Your appearance will be a direct result of your lifestyle like anyone else."

He ran his fingers through his dark hair in irritation and considered her words before he spoke again. "So I was right before. You were just using me as an escape from your world. Now that I'm a part of it, you don't want me."

"That's not true."

His dark gaze pinned her in place, his voice low. "Then you *do* want me."

A shiver of desire ran down her spine at the deep rumble of his words. She did want him. But that didn't matter. "It's complicated, Nick. Once you become Santa, things will change. I would be the village outcast if people found out that we were having an affair."

"What if we were dating?"

Belle narrowed her gaze at him. "You're splitting hairs."

"No, I'm not. Meeting up for sex once a day in secret isn't dating. Dating involves dinner. Talking to one another and getting to know each other."

"To what end?"

Frustrated, Nick threw up his hands and turned his back to her. "What, Belle?" He spun back and took a few large steps toward her. "Do you think that if we really date and people know about us that we'll end up married? Is the idea of being Mrs. Claus so terrifying that you won't even consider it?"

"Being Mrs. Claus is different than just being Mrs. Nick St. John. It's not what I've pictured for my life."

"And you think being Santa Claus is what I pictured for *my life?* Come on, Belle. My whole world changed with a flick of your wand. Don't you think I'm having a hard time adjusting to this new reality, too?"

Belle dipped her head and gazed at the berry-hued carpet. He was right. She wasn't taking his feelings about this into consideration like she should. "You're right. I'm sorry. But I don't want your choice to be a reflection of whether or not we're going to be together. Being Santa is a huge commitment. You can't just change your mind and return to your normal life. What if we break up a year down the road? Then what? If you choose to be Santa, you need to want to be Santa in your heart, with or without me."

Nick's brown eyes looked her from top to bottom as he processed her words. The heavy inspection brought heat to her cheeks and her belly. How would she survive life with Nick here, unable to touch him the way she craved?

"Okay. I've made my decision. I will accept the job offer on one condition."

Belle's breath caught in her throat. This was the moment. Yes or no, Christmas depended on his answer. "Yes?" she managed in a hoarse whisper.

"You have to agree to go out to dinner with me tonight."

Dash offered to drive Nick back to his place that afternoon to pick up some of his things. After Christmas, they would worry about selling his house, moving all of his belongings up to the lodge, and dealing with his company.

Nick called the members of his crew, gave them paid vacation through the New Year and had Ben close up the house they were working on. They were thrilled. It didn't cross their minds that he wouldn't be back. He was hoping to sell his company to one of the guys. That way everyone could keep working. "Are you going to miss construction?" Dash asked from the living room.

"Not really. I was getting tired of it, but I'd worked too hard to quit." Nick tossed handful after handful of clothes into the large duffel bag Dash gave him. No matter how much he put in there, the bag still had room for more. "What's with this bag you gave me? It won't fill up."

"Yeah," Dash chuckled, coming down the hallway to peek into the bedroom. "It won't. It's the same kind of thing you'll use at Christmas. How do you think we get toys for every child into one little bag?"

It would take Nick a while to get used to having magick as a part of his daily life, but it certainly was handy. He moved faster, not being as discriminating about what he put in now. For his own amusement, he grabbed a lamp off the dresser and watched it disappear into the bag. "Amazing."

"What are you going to tell your family?"

Honestly, he hadn't given a lot of thought to it. "I'm not very close with my family. We don't get together much. I think the snow globe knew what it was doing when it chose me. No one is going to miss me."

"No one? Were you dating anyone?"

Nick eyed Dash to see if he was fishing for information about Belle, but he seemed genuinely curious. "No."

"Okay. That sucks for you, but it's fewer loose ends for us to deal with. I'm sure you'll find some attractive and willing witches interested in you before too long."

Nick tossed the last of his shoes into the bag and lifted it up. It was ten pounds at the most, and it had nearly all of his clothes, shoes, suits, belts and toiletries in it. And the lamp. "Speaking of willing witches, can I ask you something just between the two of us?"

"Sure," Dash said. "Shoot."

"It's about your sister."

At that, a grin spread across Dash's face. "Good luck with that, man. Belle is probably the least willing of them all."

"What do you mean?"

"My sister doesn't date. She says it's because Cole, Ethan and I chase all her suitors off. I think we just have high standards for our little sister. I haven't seen her so much as flirt with anyone for months."

If nothing else, that made Nick feel good. They made no promises of exclusivity, but in that moment, the thought of her being with someone else while they were involved made him want to punch his fist through the drywall. "I asked her to dinner tonight. She said yes, but I feel a hesitation. Do you know why she's so—" he searched his mind for the term at least one woman had flung at him in anger "—emotionally unavailable?"

Dash reached out to pick up the duffel bag and gave Nick a pat on the back. "My sister is like a tiny drill sergeant. She's a lot like our mother that way. She could probably run Evergreen single-handedly if she tried. But don't let the suits and tight ponytails fool you. I think if you get to know her, you'll find she's a marshmallow on the inside. For a while, Ethan and I thought she might actually be in love and keeping the relationship a secret. We could never figure out who the lucky guy might be, but we might be wrong. You might stand a chance with her."

Dash's words haunted Nick all the way to the lodge. There was a nervous excitement in his stomach as they made their way up the mountain. He couldn't tell if it was because he was getting to see their home at the top of Mistletoe Mountain for the first time, or realizing that Belle might be harboring secret feelings for him.

Both thoughts vanished from his head as they approached a dead end. The road ended at a sheer rock face that stretched up a hundred feet in front of them. Hikers typically pulled over and parked around here. But instead of slowing down, Dash turned to him with a wicked grin and slammed his foot on the gas. Nick clutched the armrest of the SUV and braced himself for the impact, but it never came.

When he opened his eyes, they were in a dark tunnel that ran through the mountain itself. "You scared the crap out of me, man."

"I know," Dash said with an evil laugh. "I love doing that to people."

Reaching the end of the tunnel, the road curved to the right and revealed a small cabin, similar in size to the bungalows he built in town. He expected Dash to drive past it to the lodge, but instead, he parked at the house.

"Home sweet home," Dash said, getting out of his SUV to unload Nick's bag.

"This is the lodge? Where all the Winter clan live? Are there more than three of you?" Nick had expected something massive and grand like a resort in Aspen.

"The thing about magick is that you can't always trust what you see."

Nick eyed the house with suspicion. It looked just as real as that wall of rock they drove through earlier. He followed Dash through the front door and froze dead in his tracks. He'd stepped into a small cabin, yet he found himself in a massive five-story open atrium. Dark wood beams arched across the ceiling, framing a stone fireplace that roared on the far wall. It was large enough that he could stand inside it without hitting his head. There were people everywhere, sitting at leather couches talking, having drinks in what looked like a lounge. It was incredible.

"Now this is more like I was expecting. Although in my mind, it was made of gingerbread with candy cane beams and gumdrop roof tiles. How does all of this fit into a tiny little cabin?"

Dash smiled. "Magick. Your room is on the third floor now, but that's temporary. Santa's suite is on the sixth floor with the other Evergreen suites. We've got to track down Kris and ship the rest of his things to him before we can move you there."

Nick followed him to the elevators and down the hallway to his room. His badge from Evergreen opened the door, and Dash sat his bag just inside the doorway.

"There's a red button on the phone. If you need anything, press it, and the front desk will help you out. I'm sure Belle will be by shortly to continue your orientation."

Nick noticed a thick notebook sitting on the kitchen counter with a yellow note that said "Read this" stuck to it. "I think she's already left me my homework."

"Good. Read up. Tomorrow we're going to do some work with the reindeer and check out your skills driving a sleigh."

What skills? Until that moment, Nick hadn't really, truly, considered that he would be flying the sleigh. Being Santa was still a nebulous concept to him, but reality got clearer with every day. Flying. He hated airplanes, but wouldn't admit that to Dash. Hopefully, there wouldn't be turbulence. "Thanks, Dash. I'll see you later."

"Good luck with dinner tonight," Dash added, his voice heavy with doubt, before slipping out the door.

Left alone, Nick roamed through the two-bedroom apartment. It was nice. Well furnished. It had a massive plasma television mounted on the wall, so he couldn't complain about that. He walked to the sliding glass door that opened to a small balcony. From there, he had a view of the entire Winter clan settlement. In the distance, he could see the chimney smoke and rooftops of the elf village. Several small buildings and businesses lined the tiny streets with wizard-owned shops and specialty stores. Elves and witches mingled in the streets below. In a clearing to the right, there were reindeer grazing on fresh hay. They were a lot bigger than he imagined, even from a distance.

It was amazing. He wanted to blink his eyes and make sure it was real. But it was. And now it was home. He had signed on the dotted line and was officially *Saint* Nick now.

But his agreement came with a price, and he intended to hold Belle to her end of the bargain. Tonight they were going to the Crystal Snowflake for dinner. It was the nicest restaurant in Gingerbread and *the* place to go for a romantic evening. He hoped it would be just the thing to melt Belle's resolve. If Dash was right, and she was hiding her feelings for Nick, she might warm up to the idea of seeing him again. He'd never taken a woman there before, but if he was only going to get one date with Belle, it was going to be a good one.

Fifty-Four Hours until Takeoff

Belle was falling fast and hard.

She'd agreed to this dinner because it was a small price to pay to have a Santa for Christmas this year. But she would be lying to herself if she didn't admit that at least a small part of her wanted to go on the date with Nick. Belle just hoped she would be strong enough to resist him while she did what had to be done.

That wasn't happening. It was impossible in a restaurant like the Crystal Snowflake. It was dark and romantic with candles and a roaring fireplace. Tiny LED lights in the ceiling glittered overhead like twinkling snowflakes falling over them. The booths were small and intimate, the dinner designed to be shared by two. Once the wine started flowing, Belle was lost.

Dessert was done, the check was paid, and she found herself watching Nick intently as he told her a story about college. He had been right when he'd said dating was different. There were so many things she didn't know about him because they didn't share much more than idle pillow talk. Nick was smart, funny, ambitious, passionate and lonely.

Belle hadn't anticipated the last. She knew he was a workaholic like she was. It was easy for family and friends to fall to the wayside when every moment went to being successful. That had become painfully evident to Belle the last few weeks as she watched each of her brothers find love. Maybe that was why she'd been so resistant to losing Nick to the red suit. When Christmas was over and the family gathered together to celebrate another successful year, she didn't want to be the only one that was alone.

Nick seemed to be growing weary of his breakneck pace, as well. As he spoke about his family and his time alone in Gingerbread, she sensed a sadness. Their coffee breaks had become more important to both of them than they had planned. *Nick* had become more important than she had planned.

"What?"

Belle refocused on Nick with raised brows. He finished his story, and she'd missed something by getting lost in her own thoughts. "I'm sorry?"

"You were staring at me with an odd look on your face. Do I have chocolate soufflé on my face?"

"No, I think this wine has finally hit me." She smiled, hoping he wouldn't question it.

"So, after a great meal, decadent sweets and plenty of wine, are you feeling relaxed and content?"

Not exactly. She was well fed, but her mind was swirling with thoughts, desires and doubts. After tonight, Nick would put on the suit and become Santa. What happened between them after that was uncertain. But for now, he was just her Nick. He was a bit more educated about her life, but still just Nick St. John, the guy that captured her attention at a Cup of Cheer by holding the door for her and flashing his charming smile.

There were a lot of reasons why she should thank him for a lovely night and return to her room alone. But she wouldn't. This was her last night with Nick, and she wanted to make the most of it, even if it would just make it hurt more to lose him later.

Belle eased closer to him in the curved booth for two. "If I didn't know better, I'd think you were trying to ply me with wine and chocolate to soften me up."

Nick scooted over and wrapped his arm around her shoulder. "Absolutely not," he whispered in her ear. "It's a blatant attempt at seduction."

Belle scooped her clutch up and looked at Nick through her lashes. "It worked. Take me home."

"Absolutely. Wait inside where it's warm while I have the valet bring the car around."

"No," Belle said. "We can come get it later. I want you right now."

"In the restaurant?" Nick laughed.

"Not even a witch could disguise that. But…" Belle took Nick's hand in hers and looked around the restaurant. Everyone was wrapped up in their own romance, the servers well trained to be scarce. Taking the opportunity, in an instant, they were gone.

Nick tightened his hand around Belle's as he adjusted to the unexpected trip. It took a moment for him to stop swaying on his feet and realize they were in Belle's suite at the lodge. They'd always gone back to his place, so there was a sudden, unexpected thrill at finally being in Belle's home.

They were in her bedroom. The large master suite had a king-size, four-poster bed in the center of the room. It was made from a dark wood with intricate etchings in the headboard and the posts. Dark green velvet curtains draped around it, held back with twisted ropes of gold thread.

"You really need to warn me when you're going to do that."

"I'm sorry," Belle said, unbuttoning his shirt and slipping her hands inside to roam over his bare chest. "But I couldn't wait any longer."

Nick let his blazer and dress shirt slip off his shoulders to the floor. He bent down to caress Belle's face in his hands and capture her lips with his own. It had only been a few days, but he was desperate to taste her again. Usually, there was peppermint mocha on her lips, but tonight she tasted of crisp chardonnay and her own, natural sweetness.

Belle wrapped her arms around his neck, reaching to pull him closer. She had worn some fairly high heels to dinner, but it wasn't enough to close the gap between their heights. He slid to his knees at her feet, parting from her lips only when he had to. For once, he was looking up at her. She had worn her hair down tonight, and the lights from overhead backlit the loose golden waves making her almost glow like an angel.

Nick's eyes didn't leave hers as he untied the belt of her wool trench coat. Beneath it, his hands made contact with the sapphire-blue lace of her dress. The short sheath dress was completely layered with lace. The floral design of it was nice, but it covered too much of her. It barely exposed the skin beneath, only hinting at the swell of her breasts and shapely legs. He sought out the hem, pushing the fabric higher and exposing inch by inch of her smooth thighs.

He dipped his head to press his lips to her skin. Belle quivered as the dress moved up, and his mouth followed the trail. When he reached the sheer fabric of her panties, his fingertips hooked beneath them and drew them down her legs. She stepped out of them and shrugged her coat off.

Nick slid off each of her heels before his hands roamed over the smooth skin of her legs as they traveled back up her body. He placed a searing kiss at her hip, then the soft skin just above the cropped golden curls of her sex. Belle gripped Nick's shoulders for support as his fingers slid over the delicate skin between her thighs. She gasped softly as he probed her, stroking the wet heat that beckoned him. She was ready for him, but wasn't going to rush. If this was the last time he made love to Belle, he was going to make certain neither of them ever forgot tonight.

Nick used his thumbs to gently open her up to him. His tongue immediately sought out her swollen, sensitive flesh, wrenching a desperate cry from Belle's throat. He moved quickly to brace her hips with his hands as her knees threatened to give out beneath her.

"Nick," she gasped, her cries growing more desperate as his mouth devoured her flesh.

She was on the edge, and he intended to push her over. Holding her steady with one hand, he used the other to dip inside her. The combination was her undoing. Belle threw her head back and cried out, her body thrashing against him with the power of her orgasm.

When it was over, Belle slid to her knees in front of him. She lay her head on his shoulder, gasping and clinging to his biceps with both hands. Nick took the moment to reach for the nape of her neck and unfastened the button at the top of her dress. She eased back and lifted her arms over her head so he could pull the lace dress off.

Belle hadn't worn a bra beneath it. Her creamy breasts were instantly exposed to him. The back of her dress was open, so he should've anticipated it, but the realization sent a surge of white-hot desire to his already aching groin. He covered one with his hand and sucked the hard pink tip of the other into his mouth.

"Yes-s-s," Belle hissed. She buried her fingers into his hair, massaging his scalp and pulling him close. "Oh, Nick," she panted in his ear.

He couldn't wait much longer to have her. It already felt like it had been weeks instead of days since he'd found oblivion in Belle's enticing body. "Hang on," he instructed, wrapping his arms around her waist.

Belle clutched his neck, wrapping her legs around his waist as he rose from the floor. He carried her to the massive bed and eased her back onto the soft coverlet. She watched him with flushed cheeks as he unbuckled his belt and slid out of the last of his clothes. He pulled a condom from his pocket before he dropped his pants to the ground and quickly sheathed himself.

She slid back toward the headboard, her green eyes dark and inviting. Nick followed suit, climbing onto the bed and covering her body with his own. Belle opened herself to him, and he slowly pressed into her welcoming heat. A surge of pleasure rushed through his body. Being with Belle was the most divine experience he'd ever had. He eased back and thrust into her again. He was tempted to close his eyes, but he couldn't. Not this time. Not if it were the last.

Nick tried to memorize every expression on Belle's face, every gasp, every sensation. No woman had ever affected him like this. She drove him to distraction, starred in his every fantasy. How could he possibly walk away from her, even if it meant leaving his whole life behind? He couldn't. Wouldn't. And he would do everything in his power to convince her not to give up on them.

Belle bent her legs and pulled them back toward her chest. The movement shifted him deeper inside her, wrenching his focus from anything but the throbbing ache of mounting desire. Nick buried his face in Belle's neck and wrapped his arms behind her back to pull her tight against him. Her cries rang out in his ears as he drove into her body with desperation.

"Yes, Nick!" Belle gasped as she found her release again.

The tightening flutter of her body wrapped around him as it climaxed, coaxing away the last of his restraint. He buried himself hard and deep one last time and he was lost. A burst of sublime pleasure surged through him, racking his body with the violence of his long-awaited orgasm.

Nick closed his eyes, hovering over Belle and savoring the moment. He didn't open them again until he felt a cold prickle along his back and legs. He turned his head to look around them and saw snow. It was snowing in Belle's bedroom.

"Are you doing that?" he asked.

"Not intentionally," Belle admitted. "That's what tends to happen when I completely let go."

He propped onto his elbows and arched a brow at her. "You were holding back the other times?"

"It was a struggle, believe me. More than once a few

flakes fell and I had to focus so hard to make them stop before you rolled onto your back."

"Well, let it snow," Nick said with a laugh, shifting his weight to lie beside her on the bed. He pulled a blanket up over them and rolled onto his back. Belle curled up beside him and rested her head on his chest. They sat silently for a few minutes, watching the sparkling flakes until they finally dwindled away to nothing. "This is nice," Nick said at last.

"What's nice?" she asked.

"You don't have to leave. You've always run out the door. And tonight I get to keep you right here." He protectively wrapped his arm around Belle's shoulders. In his mind, he was still expecting her to run off, even though this was her place.

Belle snapped her fingers, and the lights in her bedroom went out. Now there was only the moonlight from the window, sending a silvery cast to everything in the room.

The darkness and warmth worked quickly to lure them both toward sleep. "I'm glad you chose to stay here, Nick," Belle mumbled into his chest.

Nick held her close and lay quietly, waiting for her breathing to become soft and even. "I chose to stay here to be with you." He whispered the words into the strands of her golden hair before finally drifting off to sleep.

Belle couldn't sleep, and for once in her life, it wasn't because of too much caffeine. It was guilt.

For a while, she thought she'd imagined what Nick said. She'd been teetering on the edge of sleep until the low rumble of his voice made his chest hairs tickle at her nose. Suddenly wide awake, she wasn't certain if he'd really said the words or it had been a fleeting dream.

The longer she lay there thinking, the more convinced she was that it was true. It rang true to her ears. Nick would make a great Santa, she had no doubt of that now, but if he only did it to be with her...

Nick had given up everything for her. His successful business, his home, his friends and family...all gone because some snow globe told her he was *the one*.

Her stomach ached with dread almost as badly as her chest ached with longing for him. She was torn.

A quick glance at the clock confirmed it was the early hours of December 22 now. In about forty-eight hours, they would be loading the sleigh and taking off for the kickoff of Christmas in the South Pacific. Last she heard, Kris and Merry were somewhere in Belize, and it didn't seem likely they were coming back in time. Nick was their only hope of pulling Christmas off. She knew that.

But that didn't make her feel better about it. Later, all of this would be her fault. When Nick became restless and unhappy in his role as Santa, Belle would be the recipient of his blame. Just look at Kris—he willingly signed up to be Santa, and yet he'd walked off the job a week before Christmas.

How long until Nick's white fur collar started to chafe?

Belle slipped silently out of bed, pulled on her warm, flannel robe and went down the hallway. She flipped on the kitchen light and made herself a cup of decaf with her Keurig. The warm drink helped her think, but she didn't need any help staying awake. When she opened the refrigerator door for cream, she spied the silver flask of cocoa sitting beside the carton.

She had intended to dump it out after Nick took the job. There was no reason to keep it. And yet, there it was.

Drinking the cocoa wouldn't do much good since he signed the contract. He might forget, but come Christmas Eve, he would technically still be Santa, just the amnesiac version. That would just make dealing with him harder.

But how could she get him out of the contract? It was signed, notarized and sealed with magick. The only way to terminate the contract was if Nick quit, which he wouldn't do. Or...if he was fired.

The idea was like a bolt of lightning straight down Belle's

spine. *She could fire him.* As the head of Elf Relations and Evergreen staffing, she was one of the only people that could. That would release him from the contract, and the cocoa could wipe his memories clean. It could work, but the timing would have to be just right. If she fired him first, he would never drink the cocoa. And if she waited too long to fire him after he drank it, he might remember her and the lodge.

But if she moved all his things back to his house while he was asleep, she might be able to give him the cocoa, fire him and transport him back to his own bedroom fast enough that all of this might be like some fuzzy dream he couldn't piece together.

Belle's chest ached as she looked at the cocoa, but she knew what had to be done. This wasn't fair to Nick, and she needed to put things right. He wouldn't suffer. He wouldn't know the difference. She would be the one left with the memories and the fallout of her actions.

After she finished her coffee, Belle changed into a pair of jeans and a sweater. She slipped Nick's access card from his wallet and went to his suite. He hadn't unpacked much, so it didn't take long to load his things back into the bag and return them to his house. She tried not to loiter in his home. They had too many memories together there. Instead, she put away his things as quickly as she could and returned to her suite before sunrise.

Belle waited, tense, until she heard a stirring in the bedroom. She quickly heated the cocoa and poured it into a mug.

"Good morning," he said as she came into the room. Nick pushed himself up in bed. His hair was charmingly messy, and his eyes more closed than open with the sunlight streaming in the window.

Belle sat on the edge of the bed and pasted a smile on her face. "Good morning, sleepyhead. Here, I made you something." She held out the mug to him, filled high with warmed memory cocoa.

"What is this?" Nick asked, frowning at the cup.

"It's cocoa. It's all folks drink around here, remember? That's why I go to Cup of Cheer every day. Maybe after you finish training with Dash today, we can go into town for some real coffee."

"This won't mess with my head, will it?"

"No," Belle lied. "Only Noelle's special brew does that. This is just plain cocoa. Try it. You might like it. Everyone else around here seems to."

Either she was too good a liar or Nick had placed too much trust in her. His concern immediately faded away. Belle held her breath as Nick brought the cup to his lips and took a tentative sip.

"This is pretty good," he said, taking another large sip. He then lowered the mug into his lap, his expression confused for a moment, and then the tension in his face melted away as his mind stopped fighting the magick. His dark gaze was blank, his memories of Mistletoe Mountain, Evergreen Industries and Belle, fading away.

Moisture welled in Belle's eyes, but she didn't dare to hesitate. "Nick, you're fired. As staffing manager of Evergreen Industries, I do hereby nullify your employment contract."

And then, with the flick of her wand, he was gone, and Belle burst into tears.

Seventeen Hours until Takeoff

Nothing felt right to Nick. It must be the holidays throwing off his routine. He'd given the guys the week off, so there was no work to be done on the house. His family had accepted his excuses not to drive up to Denver. He had free time, and Nick never had free time. He couldn't come up with anything that he needed to do, and yet he had this nagging anxiety in the back of his mind that insisted he was missing something important.

A beep chimed in his back pocket. It was his cell phone alert for his daily break. It was almost ten when he walked down to Cup of Cheer for some coffee. Maybe that was what he thought he should be doing. He went nearly every day, so it was a fairly ingrained routine. But for some reason, he didn't want to go there today. And they were closed on Christmas Eve and Christmas day. He'd just have to make his own coffee at home for a while.

And yet something still felt wrong. His house seemed unfamiliar. He recognized it and all his things, but nothing seemed to be quite where it should be. He opened his sock drawer and found underwear. His shoes were lined up neatly in the closet when they were usually in a jumble on the floor. His toothbrush was in the wrong hole of his toothbrush holder. It was as though someone had scrambled all his things while he slept.

Nick had woken up yesterday with one hell of a headache, and he'd been in a fog ever since then. He didn't remember what he'd done the night before, but it must've involved tequila if he felt like he did. He'd rolled out of bed around noon, taken an aspirin and tried to distract himself with television, but every channel he turned to had a Christmas program on it.

While he didn't care for the holiday, the shows seemed to make him more irritable than usual. Almost angry. He couldn't figure out why he was in such a bad mood. It must've been the dreams he had the last two nights. He couldn't remember them, but every now and then he had a flash of one thing or another. The first night, he recalled a sexy blonde, a rustic mountain hotel…and Christmas elves. There definitely had to have been some tequila involved if he was dreaming of elves.

Last night he was certain he'd dreamt of the blonde again, but had a feeling the dream had taken a decidedly naughty turn. When he woke up, thinking of the blonde made him crave coffee so badly, his throat ached for it like a man in the desert without water.

"I'm going stir-crazy," he said aloud to his empty house. "I need to get out of here."

Maybe he should go get that coffee, anyway. Nick tugged on his coat and decided to walk into town. It didn't take him long to reach Main Street. It was a Sunday, and the day before the Christmas holiday, so things were pretty quiet. He popped into A Cup of Cheer for coffee, then carried it out with him to drink while he walked.

Nick wasn't sure where he was headed, but he pressed on. The crunch of the fresh snow and the bite of cold air against his cheeks were soothing somehow. He didn't stop until he found himself standing across the street from the high-rise building of one of the local businesses—Evergreen Industries. He wasn't sure why the building had drawn his attention. He knew they made nice ornaments. He'd mailed one to his parents once as a gift. But that was it. They looked closed today, too. Nick supposed they had several months before the rush of production started for Christmas again. By now it was all over.

Nick turned to continue down the street, but he stopped again. He fought the urge to cross the street and this time, his eye went to the top floor of the building. For a second, he thought he saw a silhouette of someone watching him from one of the windows. But again, he was imagining things. There was no one there.

Cold and frustrated, Nick spun on his heel and headed back to his house to get his tools. He may have given his guys the time off, but he needed to occupy his hands and his mind if he was going to get through this holiday.

"You fired him?" Cole yelled at Belle. And he never yelled at anyone.

She deserved it, though. Belle had let her guilt ruin Christmas for every child on the planet. She would get coal in her stocking this year, if anything at all. As it was, she'd put off this moment as long as she could by telling Dash that Nick got food poisoning at dinner and couldn't go out yesterday. She'd hoped her stalling tactic would help her think of a plan. When she woke up this morning, she had no ideas and still, no Santa.

"I had to," she insisted. "But I'll get out the snow globe and we'll pick a new Santa."

"Today? We'll pick one today? It's December twenty-third, Belle. Santa is scheduled to take off around 3 a.m. tonight. Pulling off a new Santa in a week was a miracle." Cole looked down at his watch. "Fourteen hours is damn near impossible."

Belle was already teetering on the verge of tears. She'd given up the man she loved for his own good, ruined Christmas and made everyone hate her in one swift move. She couldn't take much more. One wrong word and she was going to start bawling again. "Make Dash do it."

"Dash can't be Santa," Cole argued with her.

"He knows how to fly the sleigh. He works with the reindeer. I'm sure he can figure out the rest. If anyone could fill in as a last-minute replacement, it's Dash."

Cole sighed and leaned back in his leather executive chair. "You go to Santa's office and try to conjure a new replacement. I'll have Dash ready on standby. If nothing else, maybe he can go along and drive the sleigh for the new Santa."

For the first time since Nick vanished from her bed, Belle started to feel a lift of encouragement. Maybe they could really pull Christmas off without Nick.

Today when she went into the back room, a freshly cleaned Santa suit was hanging on a hook by the door. Two shiny black boots were on the floor beside it. The outfit was ready to go for Christmas Eve, even if Santa wasn't.

Belle brushed past the costume to the magickal cabinet and pulled out the snow globe. Once again, her heart raced as she shook it and waited for the snow to fall again. A face appeared.

It was still Nick's image.

This couldn't be right. In the past, when a Santa quit, the globe showed a replacement immediately. It should be the same with firing Santa. "What is wrong with this thing?" she yelled, shaking it again, harder.

When Nick's face showed up again, Belle clutched it to her chest. She backed against the wall and let herself slide to the floor. The tears flowed in earnest now with nothing to stop them.

Christmas was ruined. Dash could fill in if he had to, but that would only solve the trouble this Christmas. If she shook the globe tomorrow, would Nick's face still be there?

"Belle?" Ethan stepped into the room.

She couldn't move fast enough to hide the fact that she was on the floor, crying and clutching a snow globe. So she didn't bother. Instead, she set the globe aside, sniffed and wiped her eyes with the sleeve of her suit coat. "What?"

"Are you okay?"

"Do I look okay, Ethan?" Belle said the words and immediately felt bad for it. Ethan was in charge of Christmas spirit, not to mention her brother. Of course he'd be concerned to find her crying at Christmas. "I'm sorry."

"Don't be sorry," he said, sitting down on the floor beside her. "Tell me what's going on. Is this about Nick?"

Just the mention of his name sent the tears flowing again. She nodded, silently crying. Ethan put his arm around her and hugged her to his chest.

"He's the one you were in love with, wasn't he?"

Belle was too exhausted and emotionally spent to deny it. If her brothers knew it, she might as well come to terms with it herself. "Yes," she sniffed. "He did it because he didn't want to lose me. But I couldn't let him give up everything for me."

"How do you know that he was? Nick seemed like a great guy. He might have made the perfect Santa and been happy to do it. Especially with you by his side."

"Me, Ethan? Mrs. Claus?"

Ethan shrugged. "Did you imagine I would end up with the most outspoken Christmas cynic on the planet? Or that Cole would find the woman he had to leave behind all those years ago? And Dash and Noelle? I never saw that reconciliation coming. But love is a funny thing. And just like it helped turn Lark from a cynic to a believer, it could turn you into the perfect Mrs. Claus. You don't need to knit and bake like Merry if you don't want to. You could give it your own spin."

Belle appreciated her brother's encouragement, but this talk was a few days too late. "He's forgotten all about me now, so this is a pointless conversation."

"Well, just don't give up on love yet. That's all I'm saying."

Belle nodded and sat up. "What are we going to do about Christmas? Nick's face is the only one that will come up."

Ethan climbed to his feet and held out a hand to help Belle up. "We go out there and make Christmas happen. We're Evergreens. That's what we do."

One Hour until Takeoff

"Put on the suit."

"I don't want to put on the suit," Dash snapped. "I will drive the sleigh, I will handle the reindeer, but someone else is putting on the red suit."

It was 2 a.m. Christmas Eve morning, and Belle had had a very long day with virtually no sleep since Nick left. She had a headache that wrapped around her skull like a vise. With every hour closer to Christmas, it seemed to grow tighter. The toys were nearly loaded in the sleigh. The reindeer were hitched up and ready to go. The naughty-and-nice list was downloaded into the control panel on the dashboard display. Everything was set. Except for a Santa.

"Please, Dash."

"You know what? You fired Nick. You wear the suit."

"How about *I* wear the suit?"

Belle was about to yell at her brother when another man's voice came from behind her. She turned and froze in place, her eyes disbelieving what they saw.

It was Nick. He was standing by Blitzen, casually feeding the reindeer a handful of oats and patting his neck. It was like he was meant to be there. Like the cocoa and the last forty-eight hours never happened.

"Nick!" Dash exclaimed. "Thank goodness you're here. Are you ready to fly, man?"

Nick nodded, but his dark eyes didn't leave Belle's. There was an intensity in his gaze. She couldn't tell if he was angry with her or ready to devour her. Either way, he shouldn't even know her. Or this place. Or anything about Santa Claus and Mistletoe Mountain.

"I'll get everything ready to go," Dash said, making a quick exit.

Belle finally found her voice as Nick slowly made his way through the snow to where she was standing. "The cocoa worked," she said, shaking her head. "You forgot."

"I did forget. I walked around for two days trying to figure out what was bothering me. Something felt wrong. I was at the job site yesterday, installing closet shelves. One of my guys left a radio there, so I turned it on to drown out the doubts nagging my brain. The station was doing a live reading of *A Visit from Saint Nicholas*. Normally, I would've changed it, but I couldn't. As I listened, the pieces started coming back, one by one."

"How is that possible? The cocoa has never failed. Maybe it was a faulty batch."

"Absolutely not!" Noelle interjected from the other side of the sleigh, where she'd been testing the cloaking device and other security systems. Belle hadn't even realized she was there, or listening. Years in the CIA had paid off. "There wasn't a thing wrong with that cocoa. Nick just stumbled into the loophole."

"There's a loophole?" Belle said, her eyes wide. How did she not know this?

"It's a minor thing." Noelle shrugged. "The only way someone can remember us after drinking the cocoa is if they really, truly believe in their heart in the magick of Christmas. Most people, adults especially, don't believe. But even without remembering what he saw, Nick believed."

Nick turned to Belle and nodded. "I had this feeling deep in my gut that told me it was all true. Then I remembered that I was Santa Claus. And that I lived here on the mountain. I remembered you. And what you did."

Belle felt her heart sink. She was hoping her betrayal

would be the one thing he wouldn't recall. "I didn't want you to do this for me."

"I know. And I want to thank you for caring enough about me to make the hard choice. But—"

A loud honking noise interrupted them. Everyone looked around before finally peering into the night sky and seeing what looked like a falling star headed straight toward them.

"What is that?" Nick asked.

The light glowed brighter and more yellow in hue as it came closer. The honking noise continued until she could spy the shape of…a Corvette convertible. "You have got to be kidding me!" Belle shouted at the sky. "It's Kris and Merry."

"He doesn't look like Santa Claus," Nick noted.

"Neither do you."

The canary-yellow Corvette made a dramatic landing, skidding in the snow and coming to a stop a few feet away. Kris and Merry climbed out, suntanned and dressed more for a beach holiday than a Colorado winter.

"Hey, everyone!" Kris shouted. "We're back." He turned to Dash, who'd just stepped outside carrying the Santa suit. "The flight mods to the car worked great. We made great time coming back from Belize. Just in time, by the looks of it. Say…" Kris frowned. "What's with the suit?"

Dash turned to Belle. "Tell him, sis."

Belle shot Dash eye daggers before turning to Kris. "Kris, we didn't know where you were or if you were coming back. You left your holly pin behind, so we thought you'd quit."

"Quit?" Kris said. "I left the pin in my office so I didn't lose it on the trip. It's too valuable. We left a note." He turned to Merry. "You left a note, didn't you?"

Merry frowned. "I thought *you* were leaving the note, Kris."

"Aww, fudge. We're sorry, guys. We just needed to get

away for a little time just the two of us. We always intended to be home in time for Christmas."

Belle glanced back and forth between her two Santas, not quite sure what to do. She'd gone from no Santas, to too many in just a few minutes' time.

Cole pushed through to the front of the crowd of elves and witches with Taryn by his side. He surveyed the scene with an expression nearly as bewildered as Belle's. "Nick is back. *And* Kris is back."

"That's what it looks like," Belle agreed.

Cole nodded. "Kris, I'm sorry to say we replaced you. Or we did until Belle fired your replacement." He turned to Nick. "I don't know why you're back here or why you're not at home in a cocoa coma. I know this has been a whirlwind of a week for you, Nick. Since you haven't tried on the suit, you're under no obligation to stay. Kris is still technically Santa. With him back, Christmas can go on without you."

"And what if I want the job?"

Cole seemed mildly surprised by the declaration. He turned to Kris. "Are you ready to retire, Kris?"

Kris hesitated for a moment too long before Merry sent an elbow into his ribs. "Ooof," he gasped as he bowed over and nodded. "Let the kid have the job. You all can hire me back as a part-time consultant until he gets up to speed. I'll even ride with him tonight and show him the ropes."

"If you want the job, Nick, you've got it."

"I want it."

"Excellent. We'll deal with the paperwork later. Right now, you need to go with Dash and put on that suit to make it official. The elves are about finished loading, and we've got to get you to the South Pacific before it strikes midnight there."

Belle watched Nick disappear inside with Dash. Things were happening so fast, she wasn't quite sure what was going on. Their conversation got interrupted. She didn't know if Nick was angry with her or where they stood. He'd thanked her and followed it with an ominous "but" before Kris showed up. Now she could only mill around the launch site and wait.

Nick returned a few minutes later, dressed for the first time in his official Santa Claus attire. The suit adjusted to fit the Santa, but somehow the red velvet and white fur looked so much sexier on him than she ever imagined it would.

"Departure in ten minutes," someone announced.

Belle frowned and clutched her tablet to her chest. Christmas was the first priority. Her talk with Nick would have to wait.

"I need to say something before I go."

Belle turned to see Nick standing behind her. "Yes?"

"I wanted to tell you that I truly want to be Santa Claus. And not just to be near you. This is my chance to reconnect with the magick of Christmas. I lost it so young, and I've mourned that loss my whole life. Now I not only have the joy and excitement of the season back, but I get to spread it around the world. How could I possibly turn that down?"

"You're going to be a great Santa, Nick." And Belle meant it. No matter what happened between them, he had been born to wear the red suit.

"Thanks. And I think you're going to make an excellent Mrs. Claus."

Belle started to argue the point with him, but shut her mouth when Nick dropped to one knee in the snow.

"Belle, you have turned my life upside down. And despite your attempts to put things back the way they were, I wouldn't change a thing because I wouldn't love you the way I do. This job and this place are all the more special because you're here. I want to spend the rest of my life spreading Christmas cheer, and I want you to do it with me. Will you marry me and be my Mrs. Claus?"

Tears stung Belle's eyes. She had always thought that she didn't want that for her life, but Ethan had been right. She could make it whatever she wanted it to be. And the moment

Nick asked, she couldn't think of a single thing she wanted more. "Yes," she said. "I will marry you."

Nick stood up and covered her hands with his own. "I wanted to get you a ring, but all the jewelers were closed. The day after Christmas, I'm going to get you the most beautiful ring you've ever seen."

Belle didn't care about a ring. She threw her arms around his neck and pulled his lips to hers. Falling into the arms of the man she loved and almost lost was more precious than any metal or stone. The days of anxiety and sadness faded away, and she let her body melt into his. Christmas wasn't ruined, and Nick wanted to marry her. The only thing that would feel better than this moment was when he got back and she could make love to him again.

Nick pulled away. "Belle? Is it snowing or is that you?"

She looked around them at the shower of sparkling flakes coming down only in their immediate surrounding area. "It's me. I've just never been so happy."

"Nick!" Kris called from the sleigh. "Let's get a move on!"

"I've gotta go," he groaned, reluctant to let her go.

"I know. Have fun tonight," Belle said with a smile. "They say you never forget your first Christmas as Santa Claus."

"I know I won't. But what I'll remember most is the moment you said yes." Nick kissed her again, this time pulling away to jog off toward the sleigh. He climbed inside beside Kris and spent a few minutes with him going over the controls.

Nick turned one last time to give her a wave before calling out the reindeers' names and taking flight. He looked... as excited as a kid on Christmas morning.

The reindeer started moving through the snow and a few seconds later, they were gone. Left behind, as always, were the workers that had made Christmas possible. Now was time to clean up, to go to bed and start resting up for another year.

Belle was the last to stay outside. She watched the sleigh's streak shoot across the sky and disappear into the darkness. Her work here was done for now. With nothing else she had to do, she was overwhelmed with the sudden urge to bake snickerdoodles. Unfortunately, she hadn't the slightest clue where to even start.

"Congratulations," Merry said, joining her outside.

"Oh, thanks, Merry. Congratulations on your retirement."

Merry laughed softly and shook her head. "It was a long time in coming, and it got a little rocky toward the end, but things worked out for the best. Now I can pass on my book of cookie recipes to you and work on perfecting the perfect piña colada, instead."

"Do you have a recipe for snickerdoodles?" Belle asked.

"Absolutely." She put her arm around Belle and led her back toward the lodge. "What do you say we go make some right now?"

Belle smiled and eagerly followed Merry inside. "That sounds wonderful."

Christmas Eve, One Year Later

"This is the first Christmas in over twenty years that you haven't had to work," Merry noted. She buried her toes in the sand that was still warm despite the darkness that had swallowed up the tropical heat several hours earlier.

"Retirement is awesome," he said, taking a sip from his frothy, tropical drink. "And Christmas in the southern hemisphere is even better."

"I'll drink to that," Merry agreed. Belize was amazing. Their beach bungalow was perfect for two retirees looking to spend some quality time together. "After so many years in Gingerbread, I almost can't believe I'm spending Christmas in shorts and flip-flops. No sweaters, no turtlenecks…"

"I'm glad we decided to come back here. Christmas cut the trip short last time."

Merry had jumped at the chance to move to Belize after Nick's training was completed. She had enjoyed their road trip, but Belize was where they had really reconnected. They had spent their honeymoon here, and it was where they had started their marriage over again. After twenty-five years of marriage, most of which was dedicated to Christmas, it was nice to just be a couple again. There were no sexy, Italian ski instructors to distract them. Kris had let the artificial color fade from his hair and grew out his beard, returning both to the silky silver waves she remembered and loved. There were no more tricks, no more games. Just an appreciation for one another that they had lost along the way.

"It's almost time," Kris said, eyeing his watch.

They both looked up at the sky, waiting to catch a glimpse

of Nick on his first solo flight. Dash had sent them a Christmas card and told them to watch. He'd added an exciting new feature to the sleigh that they were sure to love.

"There it is," Merry said, pointing toward the silver streak that stretched across the sky over their heads. To their amazement, the twinkling stardust it left behind started falling toward them. A moment later, they found themselves in a tiny blizzard with magickal snowflakes falling around them. It was an amazing sight considering the humid tropical climate of Belize. Each flake danced through the air, disappearing the moment it touched the smooth sand.

They had found a way to give everyone a white Christmas, even if just for a brief moment. It was beautiful. Mesmerizing. Enchanting. Just as Christmas should be.

"Dash has outdone himself this time," Merry said.

"Indeed he has." Kris took her hand and lifted it to his lips. "Merry Christmas, my darling."

"Merry Christmas, Kris."

*****

MILLS & BOON®

Sparkling Christmas sensations!

This fantastic Christmas collection is fit to burst with billionaire businessmen, Regency rakes, festive families and smouldering encounters.

Set your pulse racing with this festive bundle of 24 stories, plus get a fantastic 40% OFF!

Visit the Mills & Boon website today to take advantage of this spectacular offer!

www.millsandboon.co.uk/Xmasbundle

MILLS & BOON®

'Tis the season to be daring...

The perfect books for all your glamorous Christmas needs come complete with gorgeous billionaire bad-boy heroes and are overflowing with champagne!

These fantastic 3-in-1s are must-have reads for all Modern™, Desire™ and Modern Tempted™ fans.

Get your copies today at
www.millsandboon.co.uk/Xmasmod